STREETS OF NEW YORK

VOLUME

I I

FOREWORD BY
K'WAN

WRITTEN BY
ERICK S GRAY

WRITTEN BY
ANTHONY WHYTE

WRITTEN BY
MARK ANTHONY

WHERE
HIP HOP
LITERATURE
BEGINS...

© 2009 Augustus Publishing, Inc.
ISBN: 978-0-9792816-8-6

Novel by Anthony Whyte, Erick S Gray and Mark Anthony
Foreword by K'wan
Edited by Lisette Matos and Joy Leftow
Creative Direction & Design by Jason Claiborne

Augustus Publishing paperback May 2009
www.augustuspublishing.com

"It is only when we forget all our learning that we begin to know."

– Henry David Thoreau

The Augustus Manuscript Team is fundamentally the best editorial staff in Hip Hop Literature. The team is headed by Jason Claiborne, and has Tamiko Maldonado AKA Hawk-eyes, Joy Leftow the poet, Lisette Matos, Erick S. Gray and Anthony Whyte. Augustus Publishing and Hip Hop Literature is grateful for the services provided by this team of talented individuals.

fore word

K'wan

When you see pictures of New York City on television, they make it out to be this big glowing metropolis, with glass towers that stretch to the heavens, and neon streets. But that depends on what angle you're looking at it from.

The New York City I know is full of run down buildings and niggaz posted on the corners chasing that. Dope fiends, crack heads and niggaz on the road to nowhere bubble through the city like they actually got a clue. The New York I know is 125th street before the mayor chased the vendors away. High rollers posted up in front of Willie Burgers, showing off the latest whips or trunk jewels, way before snitching became cool. Yeah, I've seen those glass towers and neon-lit sidewalks, but I don't know them. I know the streets of New York.

The New York I know is the one where Pooh was taken in the prime of his life. Where best friends become bitter rivals and Spanish speaking niggaz with heavy artillery wanna pop your fucking head off because you stepped on the wrong niggaz toes. I know the New York where Promise found himself a wanted man and abandoned by his crew because he was just trying to feed his daughter.

This is the New York I know. See it's cool to fool yourself into thinking that the city of broken dreams is all glitz and glamour... that keeps the tourism market fat. Do you, kid. Snap your pictures and take your kids to the museums. But do yourself a favor and stay the fuck outta the slums. Though you might be ready for the dreams, you sure as hell ain't ready for the harsh reality. This is New York, where a vacation can become a charge.

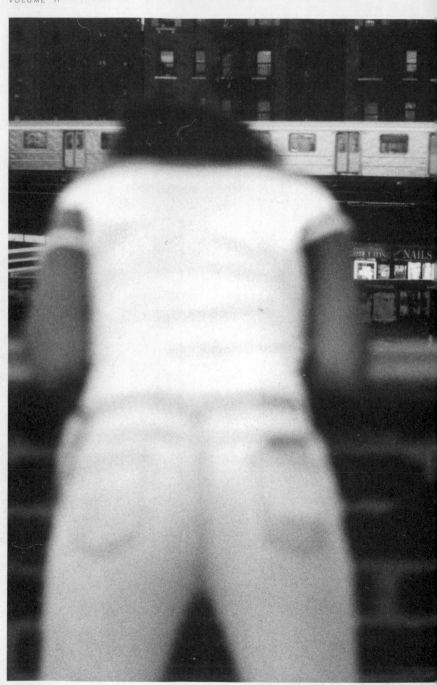

down -ass bitch

MARK ANTHONY

A Year after Volume One…

Brooklyn, NY, 2:00 a.m.

When my girl and I crossed the Brooklyn Bridge and maneuvered towards the club, the scene that we saw as we drove closer was absolutely bananas! There were people and cars everywhere. The line to get inside stretched a block and a half long. There was this buzz of excitement that filled the air and it let you know that other than where we were at, there was no other place to be than New York City.

I had been on the run for more than a year now. More specifically, I had been hiding out in Philly with my new girl for the past six months. Although Philly was about a two hour drive from Brooklyn, word about a club called *The Brooklyn Cafe* had spread all over the east coast. Word on the street was that this nightspot had it going on! It was part strip club on one level and a hip-hop/reggae club on the other level.

But what made me risk my freedom and travel to New York to see first hand what *The Brooklyn Cafe* was all about was the fact that I had heard that my mans and 'em, Squeeze and Show, actually owned the place. I desperately wanted to get back to New York and link up with 'em. At the same time I knew that I had the feds and the NYPD looking for me so I had to be careful.

My girl that I had met in Philly was a Puerto Rican chick who had a body like a J-Lo and an attitude like Eve. Her name was Marissa, and she wanted to come with me to New York to see what all the hype was about concerning *The Brooklyn Cafe*.

We let the valet park Marissa's white 745 BMW and the two of us headed straight to the front of the line and searched for the VIP entrance. There was no way in hell that we was gonna wait on that long ass line!

"Who y'all wit'?" the bouncer asked as he put his forearm against my chest and grabbed Marissa by the arm to prevent us from walking inside the club.

"My man! Are you fucking crazy or what? Don't be putting your hands on my girl like that!"

"Calm down money. I just wanna know who y'all wit'! I just can't let y'all walk up in here like that. Y'all on the guest list?"

As I purposely tried to disrespect the bouncer and walk by him, I replied, "Come on man! We ain't on no list! I own this muthafuckin' club!"

The gigantic, round bouncer was not going for it. He wasn't gonna be easily intimidated.

"Money, you about to get knocked on your ass right in front of your girl so I suggest you shuddafuckup right now!" the bouncer said as he came right up on my chest.

Coming from inside the club, I could hear Fat Joe's smash hit song playing in the background, *Lean Back*. I lifted my shirt and exposed the handgun that I had in my waistband and replied,

"And your big ass is about to get leaned back if you don't let me up inside this club!"

I immediately got the bouncer's respect. It was more than just the steel that I had flashed. I got his respect. Looking at my face, he knew that the person holding the steel had the balls to use it and wouldn't hesitate to lay his big ass out on the concrete.

Just as the bouncer stepped away from me and as I was about to pull out my gun and blast him, from the corner of my eyes, I saw another man about six foot five, looking about 300lbs and wearing a tight, black wife beater. He was showing off a cross tattooed on one of his huge biceps. Another bouncer was coming to the aid of the first bouncer, this was crazy I was thinking. A small crowd was standing around waiting to get inside the club. They could tell that something ugly was about to go down.

"Promise?" a familiar voice sounded off.

I saw Show with a questioning look on his face. A smile crossed my face when I realized the man I had mistaken for another bouncer was in fact my man, Show. I took my hand off the steel and greeted Show.

"What up, my nigga!" I yelled.

The bouncers were quickly forgotten as I gave Show one of the biggest ghetto hugs that I had ever given anyone in my life. We embraced each other in a most loud and rowdy way, nearly losing our balance and almost falling to the ground. He adjusted the gun in his waistband, almost doesn't count. We raucously kept shaking hands like kids in a gang.

"I ain't know if you was dead or what! Where you been at?"

At that point, the bouncer stepped up and asked, "Yo, Show, is dude cool wit' you?"

"Yeah, no doubt! This is my muthafuckin' man right here!"

The bouncer came up to me and attempted to give me a pound, "Pardon me, I was just doing my job."

I didn't even acknowledge the bouncer. I simply took Marissa by the hand and followed Show into the packed club.

Fat Joe's *Lean Back* was still blasting in the background and people were literally losing their minds on the dance floor doing the Rockaway dance.

I shouted over the song, "Marissa this is my man Show! He's the one that I had been telling you about! Show, this is my girl, Marissa. I'm staying with her out in Philly!"

"Word! That's what I'm talkin' bout. Nice to meet you, sweetheart!" Show shouted back as he also scoped out Marissa's body.

Marissa was wearing some open toe high heel shoes, a mini skirt and a backless top. She had tattoos on her lower back, thighs and lower abs. She started grabbing on me trying to get me to dance but I wasn't in the mood for dancing. How could I wanna dance after just being reunited with my peoples who I hadn't seen in over a year? And now here I was finally chillin' with them. Right on cue with the song, I recited the lyrics to Marissa.

"*Niggas don't dance, we just pull up our pants and do the Rockaway. Now lean back... lean back...*"

Show put his shirt on and lead us to the bar. He got us

drinks and then he took us to the crowded VIP area. I immediately saw Squeeze posted up with two honeys. I used to sport braids and never have any facial hair, but since I had been on the run I decided to keep my hair bald and to grow out my mustache and goatee. I wasn't sure if Squeeze immediately recognized me when he saw me. I certainly recognized him.

"What up, baby pa?" I said as I looked at Squeeze and attempted to get a pound and hug from him. All the while interrupting the conversation he had going on with the two honeys.

Squeeze paused and looked at me. I couldn't tell what was going on in his mind but I knew that he had to know who I was. After all, I had been his man for years.

"It's Promise!" I replied to Squeeze's puzzled look.

"Oh shit! 'cuse me, ladies... My muthafuckin' nigga, Promise! Where the fuck you been at?" Squeeze said, finally snapping out of whatever zone he was in.

"Been hidin' out, nigga. Jake's looking for me kid!"

While lifting his drink to his mouth, Squeeze purposely showed off his iced out watch, then sipped.

"I kinda figured you was on the run... you on the news like every night for a couple of weeks..." he smiled showing his platinum grillz.

Squeeze then took me to the side so that we were out of earshot of everyone else and asked, "I been wantin' to ask you, what da' fuck was you thinkin' when you popped that cop? And then on top of that you tossed the gun in the sewer while somebody was watching your every move?"

Actually, I had never known that someone had seen me toss the gun in the sewer. I had just figured that it was good police work that had led them to the murder weapon so quickly.

"Squeeze, on the real, I don't even wanna talk about that right now. I just gotta get my hands on some paper and get my situation correct. The muthafuckin' state got my daughter and the whole nine! Remember that chick, Audrey, that I was fuckin' wit?"

"The schoolteacher?"

"Yeah her... Well she got bagged!" I paused tugging my goatee and stared at him. He looked kind a shook up. "She doing federal time because of a nigga." I continued. He stared at me as if I was making a joke. Then he slowly smiled.

"Get da' fuck outta here!" Squeeze replied.

"Word is bond! We was robbing banks down in Virginia, *Bonnie and Clyde* style, and the feds rolled on us. She got caught out there but I bounced on them cats and made it to Baltimore. I was hiding out there and hustling out there for a minute. Then I met my girl Marissa, and I been chillin' wit' her for the past six months... She's been holding me down. Her man is locked up but he stashed some paper before he went up and we been eating off that."

Squeeze shook his head. He took another drink from his glass and he looked at me with the cockiest look imaginable. He stuck a toothpick in his mouth and twirled it around. He shook his head, smiled and said, "Dog, see, you in the predicament that you in cuz you started to lose that hunger! You kna'imean."

The music was blasting inside the club and I could barely hear what Squeeze was saying. Marissa spoke in my ear. She told me she was gonna head down to the dance floor. I instructed her to meet me in the strip club area in about fifteen or twenty minutes.

I replied to Squeeze because I didn't know where he was coming from. "Whatchu talkin' about, kid?"

"Come on man! You know exactly what I'm talking about. You started getting soft on niggas! You started losing that thirst for the streets. That's why right after Pooh got killed, when me and Show started coming up and we got this club and we took over the Tompkins houses, it didn't even faze me that you wasn't around to trick off on all the cake that we been getting."

I looked at Squeeze but before I could comment he continued, "Dude, I'm just keepin' it real. I mean, a lotta cats, if they ain't see you in a year and y'all had been running together back in the days. They would look at you and tell you it's all love and invite you right back into the mix to get this cake together. But I'm sayin'. You know me, dude. And you know how I gets down. We boyz and all but I'm just sayin'."

As I stood there listening to Squeeze, spitting arrogantly like he was the man, I couldn't help but get tight like a mu'fucka. I knew I had to cut to the chase and get right to the heart of what Squeeze was getting at. Although I was heated, I managed to drum up a fake smile. I began to speak but Squeeze cut me off and continued feeling on himself.

"I mean look at tonight, for example. You come up in *my* spot wit' a fly-ass Puerto Rican chick talkin' about how she's been holding you down wit' her man's money! I mean, come on! Even if you are on the run, nigga, you gotta get out there and get yours."

I looked at Squeeze and the only thing that I could reply was, "What da' fuck?"

"Promise, you my man, but I'm just sayin', I gotta tell you what you need to hear. And straight up on the real, you gotta decide what you want! Is it leeching off these hoes? Is it your daughter? Or is it this paper?" Squeeze asked pulling out a knot of $100 bills.

I was heated but I had to remain on the humble because I wasn't in no position to come at Squeeze in any other way but humble. See one thing about niggas is that if you let them talk long enough, eventually whatever is in their heart will come out of their mouth. From what Squeeze was spittin', he was basically saying that the fact that we had been boyz for years didn't mean shit! And the fact that we had did countless stick ups together, that too didn't mean shit!

Squeeze was making it clear to me that money will definitely change a nigga. He didn't give a damn about my situation. The only thing that he cared about was his money. Back in the days if a cat had to go up north and do a bid, he could always count on his homeboys for holding down his spot for him until he did his time. And in my case it definitely should have been the same way. I was on the run for a year and not because I wanted to be on the run. It was the cards that I had been dealt.

Matter of fact, it was Squeeze who had called me and told me that Pooh had been shot and that him and Show were ready to ride on Nine and his crew. I guess that my only mistake was trying to be a real nigga and be there for my crew... And where did that get my ass? It left me assed out! If I had stayed my ass home wit' Audrey that night then I never would have been in the position to shoot at the cop. And I never would have robbed banks either! It was ahight though because Squeeze was helping me to see niggas for their true colors... I knew just how to play the game.

"Squeeze, I feel you man!" I said as I gave him a pound. "You right. I gotta decide what it is that I want and just go after it. I had been thinking that and that's the main reason that I came back to Brooklyn tonight. I mean, I was like fuck it! Fuck the feds and fuck the police! I knew that I had to link back up wit' y'all and just get busy and I'm ready for whatever."

I was just attempting to tell Squeeze what he wanted to hear but I could sense he wasn't buying it.

"So what exactly are you sayin'?" Squeeze asked.

"What I'm sayin' is I need to get this paper! My niggas' holding figgaz. I been laying low and outta the game and now I'm ready to do what I gotta do."

Squeeze attempted to play me as he responded sarcastically, "So in other words you need some money and instead of just asking me to hit you off wit' some dough, you gonna stand here and front like you still gangsta?" Squeeze began to laugh as he shouted, "Oh my gawd! Niggas' funny. Word is bond!"

Again, I held my position and I remained humble as Squeeze continued to play me. Trying to switch gears, I replied, "Yo, take me to see the strippers in the strip club. Introduce your boy to some pussy!"

Squeeze smiled as he put his drink down and led me to the strip club. As we walked, I shouted, "Gimme your cell number so I can program it into my phone!"

I know that Squeeze heard me but he ignored me and kept walking.

I pulled out my cellphone and proceeded to program Squeeze's info into it.

"Squeeze, what's your number?"

"My celly?"

"Yeah."

"Lemme give it to you in a few days cuz too many people got this number and I'm about to switch it up."

"Oh, aight," I replied.

As we made it to the strip club area, I could see Marissa chillin' wit' Show. Before we reached the area where they were standing, I attempted to get some more info from Squeeze.

"So Squeeze, how much are y'all niggas holding? What exactly are y'all sittin' on?"

"What da' fuck? You working with da feds or what?"

Squeeze played me as he patted me down acting as if he was checking for a wire. He pretended like he was joking but I knew what time it was.

"Son, it ain't like last year, kid. We holding some major paper but I'll bring you up to speed. Just chill and have a good time tonight. Da fuck wid' all da fucking questions!"

Marissa was mad cool and she didn't trip about all of the guys losing their minds over the thick strippers that were in the joint. In fact, she even paid for a lap dance for me.

Show was definitely feeling Marissa's style and just from the vibe that he had been giving off, I could tell that he was still my man. Or at least it seemed that way. He had given me his home number and his cell number and he told me that he had bought a crib out in the Canarsie section of Brooklyn.

From the looks of everything, I could clearly see how he could afford the cribs in that area. The club had to be making money hand over fist and I knew that Show and Squeeze were getting other kinds of money but I just didn't know all of the ins and outs yet.

From the cocky way that Squeeze had been acting all night long, it wasn't long before I was ready to bounce. I just couldn't take the way he was feeling himself. I also had the uneasy feeling that there were plainclothes cops all over the place inside the club. All of my instincts were telling me to get the hell out of the club so that is exactly what I did.

Marissa wanted to stay and enjoy herself but I explained to her why we had to bounce and she clearly understood. Before we left, Show handed me $500 dollars and he hugged me and said, "Bring yo ass back to New York and let's get this money nigga!"

"No question kid! I'm a holla at you tomorrow."

Squeeze pretended to be wishing me the best as I prepared to leave but I could see right through his phony ass.

"Show, da nigga Promise is working wid' da feds. Tell him not to bring his ass 'round here no more!" Squeeze laughingly said and stretched out his hand to me for a pound. "My nigga!" Squeeze grabbed my hand and pulled me close to him. In my ear, he whispered, "You still my dog for life. Just let me know what you wanna do."

"No doubt," I replied as I walked out of the club with Marissa. Squeeze walked out with us and waited for the valet to bring us Marissa's car.

As we left the club and waited for our car, I still had that paranoid feeling that undercover cops were everywhere and that people knew my face and knew what I was wanted for, and constantly looking over your shoulder, a feeling hard to describe. Only cats on the run, can relate to that feeling. Not to mention that only a month ago, the TV show, *America's Most Wanted* had done a segment on me so beads of paranoia followed me everywhere I went.

Fortunately, Marissa and I made it on to the New Jersey Turnpike headed south. I was able to breathe a little, as I felt somewhat safe.

As we drove, Marissa asked, "What's up wit' your boy, Squeeze?"

"What?" I asked.

"Homeboy is on some other shit! I don't know what it is but he ain't really real."

"You peeped that too, right?"

"Yeah, the nigga just come across like he the man. Like his shit don't stink. I don't know about that dude. You should just chill out in Philly wit' me and try to get something going wit' these Philly cats cuz Squeeze come across like a snake type nigga."

Marissa was right on the money and she had only been around Squeeze for a short time. But see, the thing that was motivating me to get back to NY to try and make some dough out there was the fact that my daughter, Ashley, was in New York. I couldn't confirm anything but I had this sick feeling that she was being bounced around foster homes and that was driving me insane.

My plan was to get to New York, get my hands on some real long money, find out where Ashley was staying so that I could straight up kidnap her and bounce out of New York for good and never return. So if putting up with Squeeze and his phony ass was gonna get me the things I wanted plus get me in touch with my daughter in the shortest amount of time possible, then I was willing to put up with whatever it was that I had to put up with. But at the same time, if that nigga tried to snake me or play me I wouldn't hesitate to go to war wit' his ass...

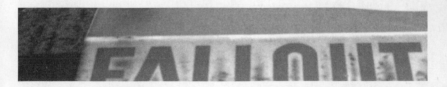

The next day when I was back in Philly, I made numerous attempts to contact Show. I called his crib and his cellphone. Each time his phone would just ring through to his voicemail. I left the nigga like seven messages and he never called me back, not once.

My head was really spinning trying to figure out what was up with Show. Maybe Squeeze had started filling his head with some garbage about not messin' wit' me. I didn't know. As Marissa walked around her house in a red thong and a matching red bra, she reminded me so much of Audrey in terms of the advice she would give me.

"You see this tattoo?" Marissa asked me as she was referring to the tattoo of a pair of yellow and black snake eyes that was on her lower back.

"Yeah," I replied. I couldn't help but also stare at Marissa's big Puerto Rican booty.

"I put that tattoo there because cats always wanna get at me because of my body. And they always wanna hit it from the back and they are always happy as long as they're getting what they want. It's all good when they getting what they want but I know that even the niggas that I let hit this, as soon as they feel they don't need it anymore, those are the exact niggas that will snake my ass the fastest. They'll snake me faster than my biggest enemy simply because they'll feel like they know me better than any of my enemies."

"I still don't get the whole reason behind you tattooing the snake eyes on you," I replied.

"Well it's basically like this, nobody knows how to get back at a snake better than a snake. So niggas might get close to me and then later try to get over on me and snake me but it's like my snake eyes tattoo is letting niggas know that I can be a snake too. If they try to snake me, I'll come right back at them and snake they ass right back!"

After that long drawn out explanation of her tattoo, I sarcastically asked Marissa, "So is there a point to why the hell you brought that up?"

Marissa playfully punched me as she said, "Yeah there's a point to what I'm getting at... What I'm trying to say is that your boy, Squeeze, is gonna try to snake you so you better be prepared to strike back."

"Yeah, I know that. You right. I don't trust that nigga no more. Especially the way his ass was coming across all sheisty."

Later that night after Marissa and I had had sex, she fell asleep but I stayed up and watched music videos. It had to be about four o'clock in the morning when I heard some noise outside that sounded like an army of footsteps.

The only light that was on inside the house was the light coming from the television in Marissa's room. I immediately turned off the TV, went downstairs, ducked and crawled to the living room window. I peeked from behind the burgundy vertical blinds.

"Oh shit!" I said to myself. "Muthafucka!"

Marissa's front yard was crawling with cops who were more than likely about to raid her house in an attempt to capture my ass! I darted back upstairs to Marissa's second floor bedroom and violently shook her awake.

"Get the fuck up, Marissa! Five-O is rolling on me right now!"

Thank God Marissa immediately woke up. She was somewhat in a daze but she came to her senses very quickly. As I grabbed the handgun, my heart was pounding a thousand beats a minute. "Hurry up and run downstairs to the door. Try to stall them for like a minute!" I instructed Marissa.

She quickly grabbed her robe and did exactly as I'd instructed. I paced back and forth as I quickly weighed my options. Fortunately for me, I had prepared for this situation many times. I had my escape route planned well in advance just in case the cops ever tried exactly what they were doing.

My escape route was out the second floor window of the bedroom, which was right next to Marissa's bedroom. The reason was that right underneath the bedroom window was a two-foot ledge that I'd be able to stand on and launch myself into the neighbor's yard. That was assuming that I'd be able to clear the neighbor's ten-foot fence in the process.

My belief was that the cops might have Marissa's yard filled with cops but not the neighbor's yard. If I was able to make it into the neighbor's yard with the big fence, then I would be able to buy myself about thirty seconds to a minute of lead time to get away on foot from the pigs.

I stood at the top of Marissa's steps gripping my gun and listened. I didn't wanna just open up the window and jump out until I absolutely had to. Marissa opened the front door but she kept the metal screen door locked and that separated her from the police. Based on what the police were shouting, Marissa must have surprised the cops while simultaneously taking away their element of surprise.

"Can I help you?" Marissa asked.

"Philadelphia Police! Open the door right now!"

"Is there a problem?"

I could hear the sound of metal clanging that sounded like the cops were trying to pry open the front door.

"You know why we're here! This is your last warning! Step away from the door!"

When Marissa asked the cops if they had a search warrant, I knew that the cops were not there simply to question people. They were coming in the house and there was no two ways about it!

With the vertical blinds closed and all of the lights off in the house, I darted to the escape window and I made sure not to create too much movement at the window. I attempted to open the escape window. I realized that I had fucked up big time. Not once had I ever practiced opening the window. The unlocked window was stuck and it was not budging! I began panicking as I heard all kinds of noise and commotion coming from downstairs.

"Get the fuck outta my house!" I heard Marissa yell.

"Goddamn!" I thought to myself. I was beyond shook and didn't know what to do or where to go.

"Go!" I heard the cops yell. Seconds later, I heard them yell, "Clear!"

I knew that they were checking room by room and I ran and hid in the closet. I could hear mad footsteps and mad noise. I felt like I was in a horror movie running from a nightmare. My heart was beating so fast that I thought the cops could hear it. I gripped the gun with both hands and hid behind the clothes hanging up in the closet. My legs and feet were fully exposed. If the cops were to open the closet, I would immediately be busted.

"Clear!" the cops shouted from another room. They were definitely on the second floor of the house by now.

I looked down and I could see light from a flashlight creeping underneath the closet door. I knew that the cops were now in the same room as me.

"What the fuck, what the fuck, what the fuck?" I cursed to myself.

I didn't know if I should just let them open the door and hope that they wouldn't see me but I knew that that was a long shot. The odds would be against me. I also wanted to bust out of the closet and run but that would have been an even longer shot.

For some strange reason, I began thinking about my daughter Ashley. At that point something told me to grab the doorknob. And that is exactly what I did. I took my left hand from off of the gun and with it. I reached and grabbed hold of the door knob. As soon as I grabbed the knob I could feel the knob slowly being twisted.

I knew that playtime was over and there was no time left to figure out what to do. I immediately put both of my hands back on the gun and stood off to an angle so that I was not right in front of the door. Although I was nervous as hell, I made sure not to make any noise. My heart felt like it was going to jump out of my chest. Before I knew what was what, the door violently swung open.

"Mu'fucka!" I screamed, rapidly firing three shots.

"Gun!" one of the cops yelled.

I knew that one of the cops had got hit. I couldn't tell if the other cops were shooting back or what. Maybe my shots were ricocheting off of the protective shields that some of the cops were carrying.

My shots had caught the cops off guard and I had a split second to capitalize on that. As I yelled, I continued firing and bolted from the closet. When I was about three feet from the escape window, I closed my eyes and dove head first out the window, breaking the glass and everything.

"Aw shit!" I yelled as glass shattered and shots rang out from what sounded like every direction.

The advantage I had was that the cops didn't want to get hit by their own friendly fire so they had to hold back somewhat as they fired at me. The craziness and boldness of me jumping out of the window was my other advantage.

It was pitch black outside and I hoped and prayed that I would clear the neighbor's ten-foot fence before I hit the ground. The move was mad risky on my part because I couldn't see where I was going and I could have literally killed myself but I had no other options. I had to do what I had to do.

In a matter of seconds, I came crashing down, face first into the neighbor's garbage cans. The crash sound was tremendous! Glass rained down on top of me. The wind had been completely knocked out of me and pain shot through my body. I was going purely on adrenaline as I quickly made it to my feet. I stumbled a bit and tried to gather myself.

Shots were being bust at me from what sounded like shotguns as well as handguns. I didn't waste any time shooting back. The truth was it wouldn't have mattered because I had dropped my gun when I jumped out of the window and it was too dark to look for it, not to mention that I didn't have the time.

I got my wits together and I immediately hauled-ass, jumping over neighboring fences. I could tell that the cops would soon be right on my tail as I heard all kinds of commotion, yelling, tire screeching and numerous police sirens. Somehow I'd made it into an alley area. I came across an abandoned car that looked as if it had been stripped of its parts. The tires and everything were missing as the car sat only on its four axles. The abandoned car was extremely close to the ground and it didn't look as if a human being could fit underneath the car.

That was my only hiding spot and chance of escape. I knew I had to act quickly. I dropped to my stomach and forced myself underneath the car. I scraped my flesh in the process but that was my least worry. I squirmed to make certain that all of my body was fully underneath the abandoned car. I could barely breathe due to the weight of the car pressing down on me, which barely left room for my lungs to contract and expand and I began hyperventilating due to nervousness.

It was a hot and humid summer night and I was sweating my balls off! Suddenly I heard and saw footsteps... I could only look one way because there was absolutely no room for my head to fully turn. I tried to force myself not to breathe but I was so out of breath from running and the pressure of the car on top of me forced me to breathe real heavy. I was afraid that the cops might hear.

"I know that black bastard is out here somewhere," one said.

My heart continued to pound into the pavement. I saw at least six sets of feet and I knew that there had to be more cops but I just couldn't see them all. Then things just got real quiet. And I saw the six sets of feet briskly walking off.

"Just chill right here Promise," I told myself as I wondered if the cops seen me and were they just frontin' like they were walking away in order to bait me out of my hiding spot? I didn't know but I did know that it didn't make any sense to take a chance of coming out, so I just laid face down on the ground and tried to calm down. Then I saw more feet.

"Hot-damn!" I hissed to myself.

"Who got hit?" one cop asked another.

"Schwartz got hit and so did the bitch! She took one in the neck and Schwartz got hit on the wrist."

"Anybody else?"

"That's all we got so far but it could be more. I bet you even money that bitch fucked up the raid! This job ain't meant for no woman!"

From what I could make out, the cops had to be talking about their co-workers.

"No way! We can't just blame it on her because she's a woman... It's that fuckin' criminal bastard! Can you believe the balls on that cocksucker? If I see his ass out here I'm blasting him! I don't give a shit if he's armed or not. Shit, call Al Sharpton, call Jesse, I don't care. I'll shoot that bastard in the back of his head if I see him!"

"I'm with you on that... And I didn't see anything when the DA questions me."

That was exactly why I didn't care about bustin' a cop. It's like they got their own little gang or something. I couldn't believe how they were talking.

As I continued to lay on the ground the entire area around me became bright as daylight. The sound of a helicopter hovered above and it must have been shining its searchlight down on the ground.

"Just relax, they don't know where you at," I told myself.

I lay on that ground for hours. The sun had come up and I was still on the ground underneath the abandoned car. It had to have been at least five hours since I'd made it underneath the car and cops were still mulling around checking for me and checking for clues. I had been smoking weed and drinking Hennessy all night long up until the cops had showed up. I had never made it to the goddamn bathroom and I had to shit and piss like a muthafucka!

There was no way that I was gonna take a chance and come out, but I literally couldn't hold it no more. So right there on the ground, I straight pissed in my pants. All that Hennessy was coming out of me by the gallon!

My stomach and my legs and my crotch got warm as hell from the hot piss, but I had to do what I had to do. I just was hoping that the piss wouldn't start to roll from underneath the car. But I felt confident that my clothes would absorb it all. Pissing solved one problem, but I still had to take a shit. I was ready to shit in my pants just to get some relief, but couldn't take the chance on the smell possibly giving me away. So I clenched up my butt cheeks and held on for as long as I could.

As I lay there scraped up, marinating in my own piss and in pain, I got more vexed. "That nigga Squeeze, had to have tipped off the cops!" I convinced myself. I was coming to that conclusion because I just found it too much of a coincidence that right after I had visited *The Brooklyn Cafe* and Squeeze was acting all shady, that's when the cops show up? Come on! Any nigga wit' common sense could put that together and know what was up. But the thing I couldn't figure out was why would the nigga do me so dirty? I had been his man for life! And I always had the nigga's back, no matter what.

Maybe him and Show was seeing some major figures and he didn't wanna split none of it wit' me? If that was the case, cool... I would have been like whateva. If the nigga ratted me out, then he is beyond foul! Niggas don't do they mans like that! Word!

More hours passed by and I was still face down on the ground smelling like piss. I had endured an entire day underneath the car, a day of intense summer heat and humidity. And on a number of times I felt like I was gonna pass out or have a stroke from the heat. Nighttime had rolled back around.

The shit that I had to take from earlier in the day managed to creep back up on me. Soon it would be a total of twenty four hours since I'd been underneath the car but my freedom was at stake so I still wasn't confident that I could come out from underneath the car. Yet, I couldn't hold it anymore. So right there I shat on myself and since I don't know how to shit without pissing so I pissed again too. This was the absolute lowest point in my life bar none!

As I lay there in my own shit, I completely convinced myself that Squeeze had ratted me out. What pissed me off even more was that I wouldn't have been on the run and dealing with all this if the mu'fuckin' rat bastard, Squeeze, hadn't called me and begged my ass to ride with them when they were rolling on Nine and his crew that night! I vowed that if I made it up out of this present situation without getting bagged, that I was gonna go all out and get back at Squeeze and his punk ass! Even if I had to murk that fool, I was willing!

I was certain that he had gotten Marissa's license plate or something when he walked us out of the club that night. That had to be how the cops rolled on me. How else would they have known where I was resting?

About two more hours passed and I just couldn't take it anymore. If the cops were still staking out the area that I was in, then I would just have to take the loss. I was ready to come out. There was no easy way for me to get from underneath the car. In fact it seemed like it was harder for me to get from underneath than it had been for me to originally get under it. I finally managed to free myself.

As I stood up and brushed myself off, I felt very lightheaded and mad nervous. My wrists, arms, and chin were scraped up from the concrete and I smelled worst than a street bum in Times Square. Dogs were barking and I wanted to get out of that location as soon as possible so that I could take off my pants and get out of my underwear, which had been violated with feces.

I wouldn't leave any evidence lying around. I knew I had to keep on my underwear and just troop it. My pants were sagging real low and it wasn't because I was trying to be stylish, it was because of the crap that was in my underwear! I couldn't walk fast as I had to walk real gingerly.

I had no money and I knew that I definitely couldn't take a chance on calling or going back to Marissa's house. I figured every cop in the city was working overtime looking for my black ass so I had to be real careful about who I reached out to and where I went.

Marissa lived in an area known as Mt. Airy. Other than her, I didn't know anyone who would be cool enough to let me hideout at their crib. Plus, I knew that the cops would have some type of financial reward for anyone that would rat me out and turn my black ass in so I wasn't trying to hide out with anybody. The only person that I could think of who was gutter and cool enough to not rat on me was this cat named Grams.

I had met Grams when I first came to Philly. I would buy weed from him and we would kick it with each other. He had lived in Philly all of his life and he knew a whole lot of people from New York, so maybe that was why the two of us was cool wit' each other from the jump. I had hung out at his crib a few times and I knew that he lived not too far from Mt. Airy in a section called Glennside.

Glennside was about a mile or so away from Mt. Airy and since I didn't know the Philly streets like I knew the New York streets, I had to take the only route to Glennside that I knew, which meant that I had to walk down Wadsworth Ave. Although it was real late, I knew in my heart that somebody on Wadsworth Ave was gonna recognize me, or that some cop on patrol was gonna spot me and bag my ass.

The funny thing about being wanted by the police is that you really get paranoid and think that the whole world knows you and is concerned with you. But as I walked I had to remind myself that most people wouldn't be able to recognize me that easily.

My heart pounded as I walked towards Grams' crib. I tried to walk as calm and as cool as I possibly could with a sack-load of shit in my pants and I hoped like hell that Grams was home. Finally after about forty-five minutes of walking, I reached Grams' crib. All of the lights were out inside his house and I wondered what I should do. I didn't exactly know his living situation that good and I didn't wanna be interrupting anything. Since I didn't have many options, I rang his doorbell.

After ringing for about five minutes I got no answer so I began knocking real loud. I didn't wanna knock too loud because I didn't want any of the neighbors to look out their window and get suspicious. Finally after about two more minutes, Grams came to the door.

"Who da' fuck is at my door at this time of night?" Grams growled with an obvious attitude.

"Grams, what up, baby pa'? It's me, Promise."

"Who?"

"Promise from New York! I'm in some shit. Open up the door."

Grams opened the door. He was real groggy and I could tell that I had woken him up. He had on some slippers, boxer shorts and a wife beater.

"Oh! What da' fuck? What up, nigga?" Grams asked as he

reached to give me a pound.

As I stuck out my hand, Grams let out a yell of disgust.

"Oh shit! What the hell is that smell? Nigga, where you been at? You smell like muthafuckin' shit! You drunk, nigga?"

"Nah, nah, I ain't drunk. Yo, it's a long story. I'll fill you in but on the real, I need somewhere to stay tonight. I ain't got no cake on me or nothing."

"Where your girl at?" Grams asked, sounding like he didn't wanna take my smelly ass in.

"Honestly, I don't even know. Ahight look, you like one of the only niggas that I vibe wit' out here in Philly so I can be straight up wit' you and don't have to worry about you opening your mouth. You kna'imean? You a real nigga and real recognize real!"

"Fo'sho!" Grams replied.

"Ahight, check it. I ain't never told nobody in Philly this. Nobody except for Marissa but before I came to Philly, I stayed in B-More for a minute. That was because I was on the run and I'm still on the run but shit just got a whole lot thicker."

"What's up?"

"About a year ago when I was in New York doing my thing, I got into a situation and I bussed down a cop."

"Get da' fuck outta here? Did he die?"

"Hell yeah, he died."

"Yeah! My muthafuckin' nigga, Promise! Killing cops! My nigga!" Grams said as he reached out his hand to congratulate me. Then he spoke up as if a revelation had hit him. "Somebody just shot like nine fuckin' cops in Mt. Airy! It was all over the news."

"Nine cops?" I asked.

"Yeah, and the nigga was on some ol' Larry Davis type shit. He jumped out the window and everything and the cops didn't catch his ass."

"Goddamn!" I said out loud.

I became more frustrated because I knew that I hadn't shot no nine cops. Even when I had overheard the cops talking while I was under the car, they had said that only two cops had been hit. If it had been nine, they would have known it was that many.

Some of those cops had to have been hit by friendly fire. I wasn't sure how many rounds I had let off but I was sure it wasn't me. Truth be told, it didn't matter because if the cops were to catch me, they were gonna get me on all nine counts.

"So what's up, my nigga?"

"Them cops that you talking about that got shot over in Mt. Airy. That was me who shot they ass."

"Get da' fuck outta here! Say word?"

"Word is bond! I was chillin' at Marissa's crib and the cops raided the joint. Luckily, I got hip to what was about to go down so I hid in a closet. When them pigs opened the closet door, I was like bla-dow, bla-dow, bla-dow! I shot at them niggas and bolted from the closet and jumped out the window like fuckin' I was fuckin' Rambo and shit!"

"For real, nigga?"

"I'm for real! And then I hid out for damn near 24 hours underneath this abandoned car in some alley and they couldn't find my ass. That's how I ended up like this! I was under that goddamn car for so long and the car was so low to the ground, it was pushing me down. I just pissed and shit right there while I was hiding out."

"Damn, Promise! You one grimy-ass nigga! So that's how y'all New York cats get down?"

"Yeah," I said shaking my head. "I had to do what I had to do... Fuckin' feds is after me for these banks I robbed while I was in Virginia. The shit is bananas!"

"Stay right there. I'm a be right back," Grams said.

I stood there in front of his crib desperately hoping that he would lookout for a nigga. A smile lit up my face as Grams returned with a plastic garbage bag and some clothes in his hand.

"Go on the side of the house, strip outta them clothes and throw those clothes away in that garbage can right there. Put them in this bag first. Here, this is some gear that you can rock. You can chill here and figure things out... But after you throw those clothes away, come inside and take a shower, nigga! Yo ass stinkin' like you dead, nigga!"

I was so relieved to here those words come out of Grams' mouth. I did exactly as he had instructed. A shower had never felt as good as that shower that night at Grams' house. As I washed the dried up shit and piss from off my body, I thought about my daughter. I wondered how she was living. Was she with some family that she didn't want to be with? Was she scared? Did she miss me? Did she think that I had abandoned her?

I got so vexed with frustration over not being in control of my life and especially for having lost control of my daughter. Ashley was the most important person in the world to me and I knew that I had to figure out a way to get her back and then just bounce from all of this drama and nonsense. Maybe I could kidnap her and go to Mexico or something? I didn't know.

As I ended my shower, I knew that someday I would be reunited with my daughter again. In fact, I felt so strong about it, that in my mind, seeing my daughter again was a reality not just a possibility. It was definitely going to happen! The other thing was I was definitely gonna see Squeeze and Show, them two clown ass niggas!

Grams had a cool one-bedroom apartment that he rented. He let me sleep on the sofa bed that he had in his living room. The first night I was there I continued to fill him in on all of the details and criminal dealings that I had been involved in. I told him about my daughter and about Audrey, Pooh, Squeeze, and Show. Grams couldn't believe that Squeeze wouldn't have welcomed me back with open arms considering that we had a real history together. But at the same time he knew exactly how sheisty some dudes are.

"See, one thing I learned about the street is that you learn real fast how to separate the real from the fake. On the street, it's like the majority of niggas ain't really real," Grams said.

"I know."

Grams added, "So yo, this is what I'm sayin'. If you telling me that they own this *Brooklyn Café* spot then them niggas gotta be holding some paper and they got some other hustles going on? Yo, them niggas don't know me so I ain't got no problem running up on them niggas and making them come up off they shit."

I smiled as I listened to Grams talk. Although he wasn't from New York, he had the spirit of real street dude and I liked and respected that. Listening to him talk reminded me of a whole lot of the days I'd spent in the basement in Brooklyn when we used to sit around to plot and scheme on how we were gonna get money.

I had really no choice but to trust Grams. But I knew that even trusting him was risky because of the fact that he could talk a good game and then turn around and rat me out to collect the hundred grand reward the police were offering for someone to turn my criminal-black-ass in.

If it turned out that Grams could be trusted then I would respect him for as long as I lived because he didn't even know me that well and yet he was willing to take me in, give me some of his gear to rock, feed me, plus he was willing to risk robbing Squeeze and Show rather than going after the easy reward money that the police were offering.

As Grams and I talked, he could sense and tell how badly I wanted to get back at that nigga Squeeze for ratting me out to the police. But he had some real good advice that I heeded to.

"Promise, listen to me. You and I both know that Squeeze and Show are holding some real long money right now... You definitely need some dough, and hell, I need some money, who da' fuck doesn't need money! But you gotta be smart and move real slow."

"Fuck dat! I'm ready to move on them niggas right now! They

had me under a car laying in my own crap like a fucking animal!"

"Promise, I know that. But trust me. I know how the streets work and how to operate in the game... And what you gotta do is just chill here at my crib, lay low for a about three weeks and let some of the heat die down. Don't even come outside or nothing. And then what you do is you call Show just before you're ready to come out of hiding. But you don't get at him or Squeeze for dissin' you and rattin' on you. You don't even bring it up. You just play things cool, like everything is aight wit' you. You gotta do that just to feel them out and not let them suspect that you're about to hit they asses!"

"Grams, I feel you and I know where you coming from, but dog I can't just sit here on this anger for three weeks!"

"Promise, trust me. You see how them terrorist cats did the United States on 9/11? Bin Laden and 'em was patient for years! But when they hit us, everyone felt it! And that's how you gotta hit Squeeze and Show! Hit them niggas when they least expect it and make them muthafuckas respect yo ass!"

Grams was right. There was no sense in me striking too soon or reacting too emotional cuz all that would do is got my ass locked up. I knew that Grams was hot on this scheme for me to get back at Squeeze and Show simply because he was seeing a whole lot of dollar signs. But whatever his motivation was, I was just glad that I had him in my corner.

The three weeks in Grams crib felt more like three years. I couldn't remember the last time that I had been in one spot for so long. For the most part I was alone in Grams' crib by myself. He would be out on the street hustlin' for most of the day and only came back to his crib late to crash. Staying at his crib confirmed that I definitely didn't want any parts of the prison system. Not that his crib felt locked up.

It was just the isolation that I couldn't take. I knew I would go absolutely crazy if my ass was caged up in some goddamn cell. I was tired of eating chicken wings and French fries from the Chinese restaurant. I was tired of all of the trash television shows and tired of the news reports that focused on the nationwide manhunt for me. And I was tired of wearing Grams gear.

On the twenty-first day of hiding out, I decided to call Show and feel the nigga out. I called from Grams' phone and I made sure to block the number before I dialed but each time I called Show's numbers, both his cell and his home number would ring out to voicemail. I decided to take a chance and unblock Grams' number before dialing Show. The same thing happened each time, goddamn voicemail!

This went on for literally two days. For two straight days, I got nothing but the nigga's voicemail. I decided to try something else to see if it would work. I called this chick that lived in a section of Queens called Rochdale Village. Her name was Candy and she had been on my dick since high school.

Candy was the type of chick that if she was feeling you, she would let you have uncommitted sex and wouldn't trip about a nigga having a girl or not spending enough time with her. She even spent money on a nigga and didn't expect nothing in return. Candy wasn't exactly a jump-off or anything like that. She was mad cool. She looked ahight and her body was tight. She had it going on! She had a good job with the Transit Authority, and she had her own apartment. But the bottom line was that she was feeling a nigga.

I didn't have Candy's cellphone number but I had her home number memorized so I immediately dialed her to see what was up. The phone rang like six times and then her answering machine came on.

"Damn!" I said to myself. I knew that I had to leave a message but I just didn't feel too comfortable leaving her Grams' number as a call back.

I began speaking to the answering machine, "Yo Candy! What's up, mama? This is Promise. I know that..."

"Hello?" a voice on the other end said, while stopping the old school answering machine.

"Candy?"

"Promise, hey, what's up, boo?" Candy asked. She was obviously glad to be speaking to me.

"Candy, I know that I ain't speak to you in a minute. I ain't gonna even sit on this phone and front but I'm calling you because I need a favor from you."

"Okay, what's up?"

"I know you probably saw all of the shit on the news about how the cops is looking for me, right?"

"Yeah, I know..."

"Well, I've been laying low and I can't really tell you what's up just yet but I promise I'll let you know..."

"Promise, listen, you ain't got to explain nothing. How long have we known each other? Come on now," Candy replied.

I laughed a little bit into the phone's receiver.

"So, what's up? You need some place to stay for a few days?"

I hadn't actually considered staying with Candy but since she'd brought it up, I decided to capitalize on her offer.

"Well, actually, if I could stay wit' you for a few days, I'd be grateful."

Candy cut me off as she said, "Promise, you know I got your back. You remember where I live, right?"

"Yeah, I do but I might not come through right this minute. I'm not sure when."

"Well, I gotta work the next few days but I'll be home every night this week. If you come through just make sure that it's after 8 at night."

"That's what's up!" I replied then added, "Candy, you remember Show, right?"

"Of course."

"Ahight, listen, get a pen and take down his cellphone number. I want you to call him for me but I need you to three-way him. And check it, I don't want you to let him know that I'm on the other end of the phone. Okay?"

"Okay," Candy replied, "What's the number?"

I proceeded to give Candy the number and then I instructed her that if Show asked her how she got his number, that she was to say that she had bumped into me on Flatbush Avenue a couple of weeks ago when I was leaving *The Brooklyn Cafe* and that I had given her his number and told her that I would be staying at Show's crib. The reason that she was calling was because she hadn't heard from me since that night."

"'Kay," Candy replied.

"Candy, are you sure you got what I said?" I asked.

"Yeah, Promise."

"Okay, call him now and make sure that your phone number ain't blocked when you call him. Just get into some small talk if you have to but make sure you don't tell him that I'm on the phone."

"Okay,'kay,'kay, be quiet now, it's ringing."

I put my phone on mute so that my breathing wouldn't be heard. Show's phone rang two times and the nigga picked right up.

"Ain't that a bitch?" I hissed to myself.

"Hello? Who this?" Show asked.

"What's up, Show? This is Candy."

"Candy who?"

"Come on now, Show! You know which Candy this is!"

"Candy from Rochdale?"

"Yes."

"Oh, what's up, ma? I ain't speak to you in a minute. Where you been at? How did you get my number?"

"I got your number from Promise. He gave it to me the other night when he was leaving *The Brooklyn Cafe*. He said he was gonna be staying with you and if I needed to reach him I should call you."

"Oh word? I don't know why da' fuck he told you that! That nigga ain't staying wit' me. That nigga got too much heat surrounding his ass."

"Do you have a number where I can reach him or anything, cuz I gave him my number and he ain't even call me or nothing."

"Nah, I ain't got no numbers for him. But, yo, fuck dat nigga. If you wanna hang out, you need to come to the spot, to *The Brooklyn Cafe*. You know me and Squeeze own this spot now, right?"

"I know. My girls and me gonna come through and check it out. We might come through in a few weeks. It's still free for City workers to get in, right?"

"Yeah but you ain't gotta worry about that. Just call me when you wanna come and I'll put you on the guest list."

"Ahight, no doubt. Well, I gotta go. If you here from Promise, tell him that I called for him."

"I doubt I'll speak to him but if I hear from him, I'll let him know."

With that, I hung up the phone and so did Show and Candy. I called Candy right back.

"Hello."

"Yeah, Candy, it's Promise."

"I didn't know ya'll wasn't cool no more. What happened?"

"It's a long story. I'll explain it when I see you and if Show or anybody else calls or comes by make sure you tell them you haven't heard from me or seen me, okay?"

"Okay."

Before hanging up, I made sure that I took down Candy's cellphone number. After hanging up the phone with her, I thought to myself. That three-way phone call confirmed that Show and Squeeze both were acting in tandem and both were purposely dissin' my ass.

Show had picked up the phone right away when he saw a New York area code on his caller ID but when I had been calling him from a Philly area code or from a blocked number and even after leaving him messages telling him that I was gonna be calling him, he was no where to be found.

"Fuck that nigga!" I said to myself.

Later that night when Grams came home, he relayed a message to me from Marissa. She had wanted me to know she was okay and that in case she and I didn't speak for a while. Under the circumstances she completely understood and also asked him to make certain he told me that the cops had questioned her for hours. And she hadn't given them any information.

Considering how a year ago I had wrecked Audrey's life, I was glad to hear that Marissa was doing ok but it made me nervous that Grams had even discussed me with Marissa. I wanted to press him on why he'd said anything at all or how to Marissa and how did she know to ask him about me, but then decided not to mention it all. I still needed Grams' help and I didn't wanna piss the nigga off in any way.

It was a Thursday night and instinctively I knew that within twenty-four hours I had to get out of Grams' crib for good. I was already pressing my luck and rolling the dice on my freedom. Instead of questioning Grams on this I decided to switch subjects and bring up what had transpired over the phone with Show.

"Grams, tomorrow night we gotta get to New York and see them niggas. Check this shit out... I tried to get in touch with Show, right. I call the nigga's cell his crib and both phones kept going to voicemail. So check it, I call this chick from Queens that I'm cool wit' and I have her call Show from her home phone while I was on three way..."

Grams, who was rolling some weed, smiled and looked up at me and finished off my words, "And the nigga picked up, right?"

"Yeah, the nigga picked up cuz he saw a New York area code

on his caller ID but I never said nothing. I stayed quiet and just let him and the chick kick it and when the chick asked him about me, that bitch ass nigga starts talking all kinds of underhanded shit! Talkin' bout 'fuck dat nigga, Promise!'"

Grams took a break from rolling the weed and added, "It's ahight. You did the right thing. Just let any nigga talk long enough and you'll know what he's about."

Grams got up and walked to his closet and retrieved a brown paper bag. He reached inside the bag and pulled out a chrome 38 revolver.

"I know you ain't got no heat so I got this for you from my man. I got my joint in the other room so we'll both be strapped. We straight now."

I got up and gave Grams a pound.

"You said Squeeze was rocking an iced out Rolex, right?"

"Yeah."

"So, if worse come to worse, we at least leaving with that watch!"

"Grams, trust me, them niggas is holding cash! The club is a goldmine! Whatever cash up in that club, we leaving wit' it and with the watch and whatever else we want!"

Grams finished rolling the blunt. He sparked it and the two of us got high as we plotted for an hour straight how we were gonna get at Squeeze and Show. Our I's were dotted and our T's were crossed. All we had to do now was wait for Friday night to roll around.

Grams' crib had begun to feel like house arrest. Thank God Friday night finally came. I was excited about getting back out into civilization and was even more excited about getting back to Brooklyn. Grams let me borrow another of his outfits, gray Sean John sweats that went with my all-white Nike Airs. I was hoping this would be the last outfit of his that I would have to borrow.

It was a little after midnight when Grams and me piled into his black Yukon Denali and headed towards Brooklyn. We made a stop for gas and a stop at the McDonalds drive thru window. From then on, there wasn't too much talking as we listened to the G-Unit CD and continued to maneuver closer to our destination.

After an hour on the New Jersey Turnpike when we were about at exit 7, I got the scare of my life! A New Jersey State Trooper had begun following us. Grams was driving and I had the front passenger seat reclined back as far as it would go.

"Muthafucka!" Grams shouted as he turned down the volume on the CD player.

"What's up?" I asked.

"A State Trooper is tailing us."

My heart pounded as I contemplated my options. I began to wonder if someone had spotted me like the girl in the drive thru window at McDonalds?

"You think he's gonna pull us over?" I nervously asked Grams.

"Hell yeah! He wouldn't have followed us for this long if he wasn't gonna pull us over."

I became more nervous and contemplated having Grams slow down so that I could bolt from the car. I also thought about having Grams cause a realistic looking accident just to create a real and major distraction.

"All your paperwork is straight, right?" I asked Grams.

"Yeah, I'm good."

We drove for about two minutes more and then the State Trooper signaled for us to pull over.

Grams complied.

"Just lay back in the seat and act like you sleeping," Grams instructed.

I did exactly as he told me. Thirty seconds later, the State Trooper came to the window. From the sound of the voice it sounded as if it was a female officer. A female officer was the last thing we needed. I say that because them women cops always seem like they got something to prove, like they gotta act extra tough and all that.

"How's it going?" the officer asked.

"Everything's good," Grams replied. He didn't sound nervous.

Even with my eyes closed, I could tell that the officer was shining her flashlight into the car. I tried my best to breathe very evenly but I was scared like a bitch! The cars whizzing by in the background created noise and I could barely hear the officer's voice as she asked, "What's with your friend over there?"

"Just chill," I whispered to myself, "and keep your eyes closed."

Grams responded perfectly, "Oh, he's sleeping. We ate some McDonalds and it messed his stomach up so he's sleeping it off."

There were McDonalds bags in the front of the truck so I knew that the officer might buy that line.

"Do you know why I pulled you over?"

"No, I don't," Grams replied with no attitude at all.

"Your windows... The tint is too dark."

"Oh, yeah? I'm sorry about that, officer."

"Let me see your license, registration, and insurance please," the cop asked.

Grams complied with her wishes.

"You guys weren't drinking, were you?"

"We wasn't."

"Where are y'all headed this evening?" the officer asked.

"Brooklyn."

"Okay, I'm just gonna check your information and write a summons for the windows then you can be on your way..."

"Okay, officer."

"There's no drugs or guns in the car, is there?"

"We not into any of that," Grams replied, sounding like a skilled actor. The officer walked away.

"Promise she's gone. But yo, you should sit up and act like you up. I think it would look more real when she comes back to the car."

I did exactly like Grams suggested. I desperately wanted everything to go good because aside from me being a wanted fugitive, we also had two guns in the car, duct tape, and a small amount of weed.

"Ah, shit!" Grams yelled.

"What happened?"

"Another trooper is pulling over. Why the fuck do they need two cars?"

"That bitch made me! I think I should bounce into them woods over there."

"Just chill," Grams said, "They both coming to the car right now. The other cop is on your side of the car."

As the female officer approached the driver's side window, she ordered Grams to step out of the car.

"Is everything ok?" Grams asked, he now was sounding nervous.

"Oh, I see your friend is awake now. Just put your hands on the hood."

The other officer opened my door and told me to step out of the car and motioned for me to assume the position. I put both hands on the hood.

"I'm gonna ask you both this time. Are there any guns or drugs in the vehicle?"

"Nah," I said as Grams remained quiet and shook his head no.

Both officers patted us down and then the male officer looked under the front seats and inside the dashboard. Thank God he didn't look anywhere else.

"It looks good," the male officer told the female cop.

At that point, the cop handed Grams his license and other paperwork and in an attempt to smooth things over, she explained that she would let him slide this time on the tinted windows but that he had to get it taken care of quickly.

"I'll make sure it's taken care of tomorrow officer," Grams replied, sounding like a straight up house nigger. With that, the cops went back to their cars and pulled off.

"Holy shit!" I yelled then whistled a sigh of relief, "Whew!"

"Word is bond, Promise! Nigga, you have an angel watching

over your ass or sump'n! I ain't never seen a nigga as lucky," Grams said smiling and pulling back on to the Turnpike.

That traffic stop had thrown us off schedule. We had wanted to get to the club at about 3 AM and scope things out but now we probably wouldn't get there until around 3:30. Under the circumstances, we couldn't complain at all.

Soon we were crossing the Brooklyn Bridge and rolling past *The Brooklyn Cafe*. Even at this time, there were people and cars everywhere.

"This spot's jumpin'!" Grams exclaimed.

"I told you."

Grams and I cruised back and forth. There was no place to park and we wanted to be in close proximity to the club so that we could quickly bounce to the car when we were done. It was four in the morning and although there was a lot going on, people were also starting to leave the club.

"Park right here at this hydrant! We might get a ticket but we gotta hurry."

Grams did as I said then climbed to the back of the truck to retrieve the guns and the duct tape. He handed me the chrome 38 and stuffed his gun into his waistband. He managed to bend the roll of duct tape so that it fit into his back pocket then he pulled his shirt over it in order to hide the bulges.

"You think that same bouncer's gonna be at the door tonight?" Grams asked.

"Yeah, he should be but if he ain't, I'll get one of them to get Show to let us in so we don't get frisked."

I knew now it was a good thing I had never tipped my hand to Show or Squeeze and let them know I was pissed off at them. Marissa told me about snake eyes. It was my turn to behave like a snake. Out of nowhere I'd strike!

As Grams and I walked across Flatbush with guns in our waists, he said "Promise, trust me, with a spot like this, there has to be a safe and some kind of cash! We leaving with some cash tonight, buddy."

When we made it to the front, I immediately recognized the bouncer and I took it upon myself to remove the rope and head towards the VIP entrance.

"My man, what up? Show inside?" I asked the bouncer, showing him respect.

The bouncer looked at me and immediately recognized me. He gave me a pound and was like, "Yeah, he's there. He's up in there somewhere."

"Ahight cool. He's wit' me," I said, referring to Grams.

The bouncer nodded his head. I was hoping that neither he nor anyone else would put two and two together and realize that I was the wanted cop killer. I was also desperately hoping that there were no undercover cops staking the place looking for my ass.

Once inside we headed to the strip club section of the club. Even though we had a mission to accomplish, I hadn't had any ass in three weeks so I at least wanted to look at and rub up next to something thick, just for a minute.

"Son, this is what's up!" Grams said as we walked around looking at the sexy strippers in their thongs.

We were there for five minutes before we bounced. I asked the different bartenders had they seen Squeeze but none of them had. I asked one of the bouncers had he seen Show and he said he thought Show was in his office.

"Ahight, thanks," I shouted over the loud music.

I didn't want to seem suspicious by asking the bouncer where the office was so I went back to the bar and I asked a different bartender where Show's office was. Lloyd Banks' hit song *On Fire* was blasting throughout the club as I shouted over the music.

"Miss, excuse me, Show told me to meet him at his office tonight but I don't know where it is?"

The shapely and sexy bartender yelled into my ear and she directed me to go upstairs. I signaled to Grams that the steps that led to the office were back at the VIP entrance on the ground level where we had come in. Grams and I headed in that direction. He reminded me to just play everything cool.

"Yeah, when we get inside just introduce me and act like everything is normal. We'll chill for a minute and I'll give you a nod, or you give me a cue and that's when we'll make our move. I'm a follow your lead but don't worry about nothing cuz I gotchu on this!"

We made it to the black metal spiral staircase that lead to the office.

"This will lead us right there," I said.

Grams nodded, signaling me to proceed. When we reached the top, we knew we had reached the jackpot. There was a door with a 'private' sign. It was locked. The music from the club could still be heard so we couldn't tell if someone was inside or not. With such loud music, it would have been useless to knock. There was a buzzer and I didn't hesitate to ring. I rang twice. There was no answer.

"You think they in there?" Grams asked.

"I don't know."

I rang the bell two more times and this time, I laid on the bell for about thirty seconds. Finally the door was opened by a nice looking, dark skin chick. Tall and looking like Naomi Campbell, she appeared to be about twenty.

"Can I help y'all?" she asked, her perfect full titties fully exposed.

"Yeah, we looking for Show. He around?" I asked.

"Who are you?" the chick asked with neck twisting attitude.

"Tell Show it's Promise."

The girl stared me down with unnecessary drama then I heard Show yelling asking who was at the door. The dark skinned chick told him who was there and then with Show's approval she let us in.

"Goddamn nigga! It's like Fort Knox trying to get up in here!" I jokingly said to Show as I gave him a pound and a ghetto hug.

"What's the deal, kid?" Show asked. He came across like he was genuinely happy to see me. "What's really good?"

Squeeze was sitting behind a small desk on the other side of the office. He didn't greet us. His first question was, "Promise how da' fuck you bringing muthafuckas up in my office that I don't even know?"

I could tell that Squeeze was probably already pissed off about something.

"My bad. This is my nigga from Baltimore. He's good people. Squeeze, this is Kendu. Kendu this is my mans and 'em, Show and Squeeze."

Everybody said what's up to each other while the sexy chocolate chick went over and sat on Squeeze's lap. There was an awkward silence before Squeeze spoke. He spoke with a toothpick sticking out from the side of his mouth.

"On da' real, I ain't tryin' to disrespect you but Promise, you can't really stay up in here but a minute."

I looked at Squeeze and couldn't believe he was still feelin' his self that way. I looked at him without responding. My silence made him uncomfortable and he spoke up again real quick.

"I'm just saying, wit' yo ass on *America's Most Wanted* and on CNN, I don't need heat from the feds, you kna'imean?"

I still didn't respond. There was more awkward silence in the soundproof office. The only thing we could hear was each other. We couldn't even hear the club music now.

"Yeah nigga, what's up wit' that shit in Philly? I heard you bussed down nine cops and killed two?" Show asked.

I remained quiet not saying a word. The room went back to being awkwardly silent. I simply looked around the office and quickly scoped the whole layout. I nodded to Grams.

Breaking the silence, I reached into my waistband and pulled out my gun. All the anger that had built up when I was underneath the abandoned car shitting and pissing on myself suddenly returned. Liked he'd promised, Grams followed my lead and pulled out his burner. I pointed my gun at Show while Grams had his joint pointed at Squeeze and his girl.

"You wanna know what was up wit' that shit? I'll tell you what's up! You know exactly what the shit was about cuz you and this punk ass set me da' fuck up! Y'all ratted my ass out! Payback's a bitch!" I said moving in on Show.

"Money, don't even think about reaching for your joint!" Grams barked at Squeeze. "Me and my man got this..."

Show stood up and demanded to know what was going on, while denying emphatically that he and Show had not set me up.

"Show, sit yo ass back down in that chair!" I ordered. "Y'all niggas knew that I was on the run for a whole year. When I show back up and find out that y'all are living, I thought it would be all love, like y'all would lookout for your boy! But then y'all try to front on me and shit on me! Come on, man! Can I live?" I shouted. I continued ranting as Grams held everybody at bay.

"And why was I on the run? Huh, Squeeze? I was on the run cuz your ass called me and told me we was rolling on Nine and his crew. I was laid up wit' my girl and I come up out of some warm pussy to help y'all niggas and then y'all front on me and try to play me? All I'm sayin' is can I live? Can I eat?"

Squeeze attempted to interrupt me.

"Shut da fuck up, Squeeze! I'm talking now and I'm running this muthafuckin' club now!" I boasted.

Squeeze didn't care what I had ordered him to do. He proceeded to swear and warn, "Promise, word is bond! You better kill me up in this piece tonight cuz I swear to God I'm a buss yo ass when you stop buggin' 'em drugs you's smokin'!"

"Promise, you want me to handle this cat?" Grams asked with attitude.

I was silent then I spoke up, "Nah, I see how this is gonna go down... Niggas still wanna play me for a sucker and disrespect my ass. You know what? Squeeze, and Show, both of y'all stand da' fuck up and strip butt ass naked, right now!"

"Promise you trippin' for sure!" Show stated.

"What?" I walked up to Show and slapped him upside the head with the butt of my gun. He spun around and fell to the ground. Blood spilled out of his mouth.

"You thinking I'm bugging now! Huh nigga? Take off your goddamn clothes right now or I'll murk yo punk ass right here up in this club!"

Show and Squeeze still didn't budge. The sexy dark skin chick looked shook like crazy. She had amazingly lost that neck-twisting attitude and was acting completely humble.

"Grams, kill this nigga right here!" I ordered dead serious.

"Which one?" Grams asked. "This one?" He questioned as he sought confirmation and pointed his gun towards Show.

"Ahight! Ahight!" Show screamed as he began unbuckling his pants and removing his shoes. Before long he was standing butt ass naked.

"Squeeze, what you waiting on?" I asked.

Squeeze shook his head as he began to unbutton his shirt and remove his clothes. "Word is bond!" Squeeze added as he continued to shake his head.

"What about her?" Grams asked.

"Don't worry about her! Get them jewels and the money first," I stated. "Show, where the cash at? And don't play me. You got thirty seconds or I'll blast your ass."

"Look in my pants pocket," Show quickly responded. "Promise, if you needed some dough all you had to do is ask me."

I walked over to Show and kicked him in the ribs, "So why da' hell you ain't pick up your goddamn phone or return my phone calls?"

"Cuz, nigga, how da' hell did I know if you was working with the feds or not? You disappear for a year and then you show back up and wanna get money? Shit don't work like that."

"Yeah, I know, I know. That's why I'm getting my money the ski-mask way!" I responded.

Grams had collected Show and Squeeze's Rolex watches and their diamond encrusted dog tags. While he was relieving the girl of her diamond earrings and diamond ring, I shouted to Show, "You got fifteen more seconds. Where the hell is the money at!"

"I told you it's in my pocket!"

Grams reached up in their pockets and pulled out a knot of money from both Show and Squeeze. Combined it looked like it was about $5000.

"Show, you got five more seconds to show me all of the money!" I threatened.

"Where da' safe at!?" Grams growled, sounding like DMX.

"Two seconds..." I warned, as I cocked the gun.

"One..."

"Just show it to 'em," Squeeze reluctantly stated from his face down position.

"It's over there under the desk," Show gritted through his teeth.

Grams immediately scurried to Show's desk and located the safe on the floor underneath a mat.

"What's the combination?" Grams asked and Show yelled it out.

Grams quickly opened the safe and let out a joyous scream. "Promise, this is better than raw sex over here!"

"Ahight, just load it wit' the jewels so we can be outta here."

Grams scooped the loot along with some weed. He handed me the bag of cash, jewels, and weed and proceeded to duct tape the hands, feet and mouths of Show and Squeeze.

"You wanna hit that?" I asked Grams, referring to the sexy chocolate chick.

Squeeze stared at me and he tried his best to yell through the duct tape that was around his mouth. Although I was in the middle of a robbery, I was horny as hell and the icing on the cake in getting back at Squeeze would have been to *hit* his girl right there in front of his punk ass!

"Nah, Promise that's whack. We got the dough, we ain't raping nobody! That's some punk shit," Grams said.

"Ahight just tape her hands, mouth and feet and we're outta here."

With that order, Grams bound the chick to a chair and the two of us calmly walked out the door heading for Grams' truck.

As we walked out, I gave the unsuspecting bouncer a pound and he told me to be careful cuz five-o was lurking everywhere. I appreciated the tip. Me and Grams jumped in the truck and were out. I directed Grams towards Atlantic Avenue and looked inside the bag of goods. I couldn't believe how much cash was in the bag.

"There gotta be close to fifty thousand in that bag," Grams predicted.

"That's what's up!"

I directed Grams to Rochdale Village in Queens. As we got closer, I used Grams' cell to call Candy. I knew I'd be waking her up but also knew she'd be cool with it.

"Yeah, I'm in Queens now. I'll be there in twenty minutes," I said.

We pulled into the parking lot of a 24-hour Burger King and divided up the spoils. We took a little less than twenty-six thousand each. Plus we each took a Rolex and a dog tag. I decided to swap the handgun that Grams had loaned me in exchange for letting him keep the weed that we had unexpectedly stumbled on during the robbery.

"This was the biggest stickup I ever did in my life!" Grams cheerfully exclaimed.

"Kid, this was what I did every day a few years back," I boasted. "This is what I was born to do."

Rochdale was right down the block from the Burger King so Grams drove down 137th Avenue and dropped me off at Candy's building. Before we parted, I thanked Grams for looking out. He was more than thankful to me for having given him the opportunity to make so much loot.

"If you need me, dog, just holla at me and I got you," he assured me as he wrote down his home number and cell number on a piece of paper so that I would be sure to have it and wouldn't just be relying on my memory as I usually did.

"No doubt," I said as I gave him a pound.

Handing Grams one thousand dollars, I said to him, "Do me a favor, make sure that Marissa gets this and tell her it's from me."

Grams nodded and took the money. I instructed him on how to get to the Belt Parkway so that he could make his way to the Verrazano Bridge and back onto the New Jersey Turnpike. As Grams pulled off he appropriately blasted Ja Rule's song *Clap Back.*

I rang Candy's intercom and she immediately buzzed me into her lobby. I rode the elevator up to her apartment and she stood at her apartment door waiting for me. Although she looked as if she had just woken up, she was extremely excited to see me. She gave me the warmest hug and told me that I looked like I had gained some weight.

"You still look good, Promise."

"Candy, you telling me I gained weight? Look at you, where the hell did you get that butt? You ain't have that phatty a few years ago," I jokingly said as the two of us laughed.

Candy escorted me into her immaculate apartment which had some bangin' shiny hardwood floors. She grabbed me by the hand and escorted me over to the couch. Wearing her pajama pants, slippers and a T-shirt, Candy sat on her fluffy leather couch, crossed her legs and looked at me.

"So, how have you been, Promise?" she asked.

"How have I been?" I rhetorically asked. "How much time do you have and where do you want me to begin?"

The sun was up and it was still early so Candy began making breakfast.

"I got all day. Just talk," she encouraged.

I didn't mind talking to Candy and it turned out to be somewhat therapeutic. I told her about Squeeze and Show and what was really up between them and me. She had already heard Pooh had been killed and I told her about the circumstances leading to his death. To my surprise, she related a different story that had been circulating on the street about Pooh's killer. I had always thought it was Nine and his crew who had killed Pooh but she said that everyone had heard that it was some Spanish kids.

Candy had no reason to lie to me. If it was true, that should have been the first thing that Show and his punk ass should have told me when I saw him that first night with Marissa. If Candy knew what the streets said about who Pooh's killer really was then he and Squeeze should know what the deal was. Whateva... I didn't even wanna think about it and I continued talking.

I filled her in on the horrible way in which Ashley's mother had been killed. Then spilled that shit about all the drama with the cops and the feds and why they were after me. I even told her about Marissa. I gave her a full run down of what I had been through for the past year or so.

As I began to talk to her about Ashley and how much I missed her and worried about her, tears welled up in my eyes. I was too hood to just start bawling or to straight up cry in front of Candy but she could see how all this talking had made me feel real emotional about my daughter. Candy got closer trying to comfort me. She told me that everything would be alright.

"I hope so," I said. "I just wish I knew where she was."

That probably was eating at me more than anything. And the thing, I can't just pick up the phone and start calling around searching for my daughter because I'll get locked up.

I didn't want any breakfast, so Candy came to the kitchen table sat in front of me and began eating the food that she had prepared. She asked about my family and if there was anybody that I was close to that would be willing to help me out in terms of locating my daughter.

"Yeah there's relatives and close friends I could reach out to but those are the exact same people that I can't have contact with because the cops and the feds are watching. You kna'imean? With me on the run, it's not like I can just pick up the phone and call whoever I want to or just go by and visit whoever I want to."

"I'll see what I can do for you. I mean, I know some people

that work with me who might be able to help. There's this cool Italian dude at my job and I think his wife is a social worker so maybe she might be able to get some info on your daughter."

"Candy, whatever you can do, I would really appreciate it... Matter of fact, if you can help me find out where Ashley is at, I'll hit you off with like two g's. It'll be like a finder's fee," I said with a smile.

"Two thousand dollars? Promise, you ain't gotta do that!"

"I know I don't but I want to..."

Our conversation continued for hours. When we were through talking, Candy showed me around and explained where the towels and soap were so I could take a shower. Being that I couldn't just leave her apartment and freely walk the streets, I couldn't take Candy up on her offer later in the morning but I gave her $1500 and told her to buy some food with that money. I also gave her my clothing measurements and instructed her to pick up some much needed clothing outfits for herself and for me.

Eventually I got tired and as Candy went about her business for the day, I crashed in her bedroom. She had a nice king size waterbed. It was so much better than the hard lumpy sofa bed that Grams had me sleeping on. Chillin' at Candy's crib was real cool and seeing her was even better. I really liked her vibe.

Later on that night after Candy had come home and was preparing to go to sleep, she started talking church and bible talk. She told me that I needed to pray and ask God to help me figure things out.

I laughed as I said to Candy, "Yeah right! God don't wanna hear from me. I already know I'm going to hell so it don't matter. I can't remember the last time that I prayed to God and I ain't never read the bible in my life!"

Even after saying what I had said, Candy didn't trip and didn't get all pushy with the religious nonsense. She did say that she was gonna show me something in the bible that would shed some light on what I had been going through.

"When did you get all religious?" I asked.

"I'm not religious. I'm spiritual!" Candy replied. "And there is a big difference."

Trying to bring the conversation in another direction, I moved closer to Candy and said, "So why don't you and me let our spirits connect right now?"

"What you talkin' about?" she asked.

"I'm sayin'."

"You sayin' what?" Candy asked with a smile.

"Why don't you let a nigga hit that?"

Candy fell out laughing.

"What?" I asked.

"Is that what it's gotten to now? That's how niggas ask for pussy?" Then in a playful attempt to mock my voice, Candy stated, "Why don't you let a nigga hit that?"

The two of us both started laughing at the situation because it really was funny. I moved closer to her and I started kissing on her neck and I told her, "Come on, you know how I do..."

Candy was getting turned on and I could tell that she was gonna comply with my request to let me hit it but out of nowhere she stopped and told me to hold up.

"I'm a give you some but I just want you to see this first." Candy left the room and I couldn't believe that the bitch came back with a bible and flipped it open and started reading from Proverbs. "Promise, this is from Proverbs 1:10 -16"

My son, if sinners entice you, do not give in to them.
If they say, "Come along with us;
let's lie in wait for someone's blood,
let's waylay some harmless soul;
let's swallow them alive, like the grave,
and whole, like those who go down to the pit;
we will get all sorts of valuable things
and fill our houses with plunder;
throw in your lot with us,
and we will share a common purse" —

my son, do not go along with them,
do not set foot on their paths;
for their feet rush into sin,
they are swift to shed blood.

"Do you understand that?" Candy asked.

"Yeah, actually I do... That's deep right there," I responded with full sincerity.

"Promise, I am definitely not preaching to you and I know I have my own issues but your problem is that you associate with the wrong people. Squeeze called you that night to go after Nine and his people and you listened to him and now look. And I know how y'all used to stick people up and all of that... It's like when you're young and you don't know any better, that's one thing. But Promise, you can't look at the past and try to change it because the past is the past. The only thing that you can do is focus on the future. What I would say is just do you! Do you and stay away from the streets. Focus on finding your daughter and getting things straight legally. And I'm telling you, start praying! It works."

Candy reminded me so much of Audrey because she was telling me what I needed to hear, and she was right.

"You right Candy... And I'm a listen to you."

After I said that, there was this brief silence then Candy put the bible away and came close to me and started kissing on *my* neck this time.

"A nigga still wanna hit this?" Candy asked in a joking way.

We both laughed, and then I replied, "Nah, you killed the mood with all of that seriousness and the bible but I needed to hear it though."

Candy apologized for killing the mood but the rest of the night wasn't a complete waste as the two of us just chilled in her room watching a Sanford and Son marathon on the TV Land channel.

Sunday afternoon rolled around. Candy and I were in her living room chillin', listening to the radio and drinking some rum and coke. We had to turn down the volume on the music because it sounded like someone was at her door.

"You expecting somebody?" I asked getting nervous thinking it was the cops. I quickly realized that if the cops had any inclination to get me inside, there would be no way that they'd politely knock and ask to come in.

"Nah, I'm not expecting anyone."

"Just to be safe I'm a hide in your bathroom. I'll be behind the shower curtain," I said as I scurried off.

Candy's bathroom was situated right near the living room and the front door wasn't too far off from the bathroom.

I heard Candy ask "who is it?" and then I heard her unlocking the door.

"What's up Ma'? We sorry to just be showing up unannounced but..."

From the sound of the voice it sounded like Show. More than likely Squeeze was with him.

"Damn!" I thought aloud. I knew that I had slipped up because I didn't have my gun on me. It was stashed deep in Candy's linen closet along with the loot from the robbery.

"You heard from Promise?" Show asked.

There was a brief moment of silence before Candy spoke. "Squeeze, you gonna come in my crib and not even speak? And I ain't seen you in I don't know how long?" Candy said in what sounded like her attempt to play things cool.

"My bad. Let me give you a hug," Squeeze replied before adding, "I'm just kinda heated right now so you gotta forgive me."

"What's going on?" Candy asked.

"A whole lotta drama wit' Promise, is all. You seen him or heard from him?"

"Nah, actually, Show I haven't heard from him since that day I called *you* looking for him."

"You sure, Candy?" Show asked.

"Yeah, I'm sure..."

There was some more silence.

"So what's up? You was just chillin' for the day?" Squeeze asked.

"Yup. Gotta get ready for work tomorrow."

There was more silence as my heart raced.

"Candy was you by yourself all day today?" Show asked.

"Yeah, why?"

"I was just wondering why there was two drink glasses on your coffee table."

What da' fuck? He think he got damn detective? I cursed inside my head.

"Oh, that's from yesterday," Candy lied, a horrible lie at that.

There was some more silence. All of a sudden, I heard Candy scream and didn't know what was going on.

"Candy! Don't lie to us!" Squeeze barked. Candy said nothing.

"I'll choke the shit outta you, you lie to me!" Squeeze barked again.

I was ready to burst out the bathroom and get the showdown started but I nervously held my position.

"I'm not lying!" Candy said, followed by some coughing and gasping for air. She had probably just been freed from the grips of Squeeze's hand around her neck.

"So if the drinks are from last night, why are there still ice cubes in them?"

"I don't know!" Candy screamed.

"Squeeze, didn't that nigga, Promise, have on a gray Sean

John outfit at the club the other night?"

"Yeah," Squeeze responded.

My mind was racing because I knew they were definitely on to me.

"Candy, whose Sean John jacket is that?" Show asked.

"Look! Y'all gotta go! Y'all can't be coming up in my crib like this!"

"Show, I'm a check the apartment for that nigga. I bet you his ass is up in here."

"You are not gonna just be walking through my apartment!" Candy yelled.

"Candy! Just chill and let us check the apartment!" Show screamed.

"No! Fuck that! I'm calling the cops!" Candy yelled back.

"You pick up that phone and I'll kill you!" Show said real quiet like.

I was extremely heated and at the same time I was prepping myself for someone to come inside the bathroom so I could snuff 'em. From the sounds of things, Squeeze was already rummaging through the one bedroom apartment.

"You got anything?" Show yelled.

"Nah, the nigga ain't here!" Squeeze shouted back.

"I'm a check the kitchen," Show informed.

"Get the fuck outta my crib!" Candy yelled.

"Ahight, I'm a check the bathroom," Squeeze stated as they both totally ignored Candy.

I told myself to get ready.

Then I heard the sound of flesh slapping flesh. It must have been Candy attacking one of them because the slapping sounds were followed by an outburst of female threats and curses.

I could tell that Squeeze had just entered the bathroom, so Candy must have been fighting and cursing with Show. I was dead still, not even breathing.

"Get the fuck off me bitch!" I heard Show yell. His yell was followed by a scream from Candy.

"Squeeze let's get up outta here!"

I heard the hinges on the bathroom door squeak. Squeeze must have been checking for me behind the bathroom door. His next move had to be to check in the bathtub behind the shower curtain where I was hiding. My heart pounded.

"I know that nigga was up in here!" Squeeze shouted as he sounded like he was shouting into my ear.

He had to be standing right next to the bathtub. I still was not breathing but my fist was cocked and if the nigga pulled back that shower curtain, I was ready for whateva! Even if the nigga had a gun, I was ready to kill with my bare hands! I wasn't gonna go out easy.

If you grew up on the streets of New York then you have heard the expression, 'If you got it—flaunt it.' So if you floss in Brooklyn be prepared to defend yours, or get your punk-ass thugged. Out-of-towners, not up on how things go down in the largest borough of the city that never sleeps, don't stunt unless you ready to give it up. That's how Brooklyn really gets down.

It's the place where not even the senile or infirm escape the creed of the street. Officers of the NYPD are accustomed to seeing the end result of violent crimes motivated by greed mixed with endless lust. Like the KRS1 lyrics …*Manhattan keeps on making it…Brooklyn keeps on taking it…*

However, there are parts of BK where the only things police are exposed to was the odd combinations of luxury vehicles and the drivers inside them. On these streets, police often see a stately nearsighted retired politician making an illegal left turn in her BMW 745i, the teenage thug and his posse speeding to nowhere in his parents' Rolls Royce Corniche, the matronly civic leader blithely double parking a black Jaguar at the Chinese grocer on the corner. This is Canarsie in its sleepy quietness, an oasis for those who can afford to drink from its shores.

The investment made by the partnership of Squeeze and Show had begun to pay off. Squeeze wanted somewhere further away from the dope-dealers, the fiends and the hood-rats. He needed to live somewhere better and raise his family. Six months ago, it happened. He bought a million dollar mansion with six bedrooms and a heated indoor pool.

Squeeze and his family, a baby boy name Ahmad, and the infant's mother, Yvonne, were now far removed from the hustle and bustle of the city. He stayed on his daily grind and chilled here in Canarsie with the family.

Squeeze and Show sat in the Cadillac EXT high on twenty-four inch rims, a few posh pads away from where Squeeze called his rest. He was excited but cautious. Show knew he was acting distant and wondered why. They had stacked enough cheddar and Squeeze had relocated to this ritzy neighborhood when his son was born.

He'd always wanted his baby boy to grow up somewhere other than the hood where dad had come up. His son would be spared the harshness of living on the streets of New York as much as possible. To this end, Squeeze and Show parlayed cake money and seized the opportunity to invest in a legal business venture, a nightclub and bar known as *The Brooklyn Café*.

On any given night, the queue from its velvet rope entrance snaked around the block. While up in da club, the speaker system packed more than enough bass for any player's face and all the highs so that the wallflowers couldn't even standstill.

The ambience was seductive, enticing, appealing to the attractive beautiful and sexiest of the party people. It was equipped with a huge dance floor that was always crowded. Pretty girls with sexy thighs and dresses way too high ran up and down the stairs. The place was hot on any given weekend-night.

nig-gas for life

ANTHONY WHYTE

Squeeze and Show had taken to the life of nightclub owners as if it was their natural born hustle. It turned out to be a grand one up to this point. The club opened Tuesday through Sunday and the partners saw their papers grow longer. After the first year, they began seeing the benefits of Squeeze's push to legitimize their holdings.

They paid their dues on the streets of New York. Now Show and Squeeze paid taxes for a place that was no ordinary lounge. It sported a large VIP area that was always chock-full of Hip Hop celebrities. The massive dance floor and colorful lightshow allowed revelers to enjoy their fantasies. They could shake their groove without rocking anyone else's boat. Alcohol was always in demand and the club owners made sure it flowed generously from the bar into your gut and the money moved from patrons' wallets into their account. It was a great exchange. Everyone benefited.

Security was thought to be tight until a certain recent episode when Promise, an old friend to both partners, had scammed his way upstairs to the business office and robbed the club. This brazen act irritated them to no end. After all, Promise was like family. Along with Pooh, the four went all the way back to childhood like MC Lyte on the boulevard. But Pooh had caught a bad one and Promise had gone on the lam with his girlfriend. The pair ran like bandits on the loose, robbing a couple of banks down in VA until the girl, real name Audrey, was bagged by the feds.

Initially, the law kept a close watch on the nightclub but after Promise failed to come around, they cut back on the severity of the surveillance. Nevertheless, they continued to call and harass the business partners from time to time. It had been about a year and change later when Promise showed his face. His visit was met with contempt from the partners because the feds could still call and check or just show up when ever they felt like. If they found Promise in the club, it meant that the partners would be shut down for good. Yet, neither Squeeze nor Show gave Promise up to the feds despite the fact that not only had Promise visited; he had come back with some other Philly punk and robbed them.

Show and Squeeze gathered information and set out on Promise's trail. They were told by a reliable source that he had been holed up inside Candy's crib. She was an old friend of theirs who went back to when they were shorties. They thought they had found the hole where Promise had been hiding but after a search of Candy's apartment yielded nada, the frustrated partners left with the residual anger lurking in their minds. They were still out of their fifty grand and back to square one.

Squeeze was driving home in silence while Show nodded his head as he rolled a blunt and Jadakiss spit fire to tracks from the *Kiss Of Death* CD pumping hard through Clarions. Now as he and his partner gazed through smoked tints looking at the rows of expensive looking houses along the quiet tree-laden street, Squeeze wondered why they were being pulled over by the police. He was in the driver's seat chewing gum unfazed by the glare of flashing lights and tried to be patient as the officer took her time getting out of the patrol vehicle. Squeeze was sure he had not been driving erratically so what was it? Why was he being stopped, he casually wondered while lowering the thump of the bass.

"Nah man, don't turn that down, dogs. That's that *Kiss Of Death* joint. That's Jada, dogs."

Squeeze turned and glanced for a beat at his childhood friend and business partner. He glared when he noticed Show's eyes were closed and body rocking in time with the rhythm. It was very obvious that Show's mind was not really on their current police situation.

"That ecstasy must be working on you or sump'n, dogs. Don't you see po-po behind us?" Squeeze asked. Show opened his eyes with difficulty. The weed mixed with some dust made them look like slits on the side of his head. He'd been smoking all day and lazily glanced through the monitor to see the uniformed officer.

"Squeeze, what's up, son? Ain't nothing change, nigga. Fuck po-po," Show said raising a bent middle finger at the image in the camera on the passenger side.

"Fuck da police, huh? That's what's up? Like you don't give a damn about shit?" Squeeze asked shaking his head. "It never cease to amaze me, how sometimes you on point, Show, but there be times you sleeping, sun. I'm telling you, stop fucking with all that ecstasy dust and drinking that alcohol. I been meaning to speak on it so I'm a tell ya. You be going overboard, and that shit ain't right. It means that I've got to be one doing the thinking and all that planning shit all the fucking time while your ass stay stuck on E and booze wired to hip hop. It's stupid shit like this why da nigga, Promise, penetrated our security. Hide 'em burners, man."

"Whatcha saying?"

"I'm saying, Show, forget it, ahight, forget that I even brought that shit up. Forget we got burners up in da whip. Forget we wuz blazing haze and that shit smells, ahight. Forget all that." Squeeze was getting irritated and could no longer hide his feelings. He felt around for the guns under the seat with as little movement as possible. "You forget that we wuz just hunting da rat down with all these gats up in here? Po-po will throw our black asses in da a poky and I ain't trying to do no bid. You feel me?"

Squeeze seemed more annoyed than was really necessary, Show thought fixing his gaze on him. They had been friends for sometime now and Show understood what was not said. He nodded his head slowly and spoke.

"I ain't going to no jail, dogs," Show said as Jadakiss and Anthony Hamilton belted out *Why*. He could see the female officer finally getting out of her patrol scooter and approach the Caddy-truck from the rear. "This what you call black on black crime," Show added then reclined in the seat.

"What're you trying to say, fool?"

"I'm saying this black cop bitch is being pimped by the system and she coming and harassing us. I bet she ain't stop nobody else from round' here. They'd sue," Show said watching Squeeze slowly chewing gum. "She should be protecting our black asses from these devils," Show continued as the officer approached the driver's side. Squeeze let the window down.

"Driver's license and registration please," the officer said and peeked inside the Caddy. Squeeze handed over the requested documents. "Please turn the music off. You know why I'm stopping you, right?" she asked and glanced at the requested items.

"I don't know but I'm sure you're gonna hit me with that piece of info, right, officer?" Squeeze said with overt sarcasm.

"Don't be a wise-ass because I can be one too, okay, mister?" the officer warned in a testy tone before walking away. The traffic stop was no surprise for either man.

"I'm telling you, Squeeze, that's the reason po-po always getting wet up. It's for shit like this." Show became animated and slowly worked himself into being pissed. Squeeze nodded his head and demonstrated considerable restraint as he spat the gum out the window. Show did not let Squeeze's attitude slip. "Yo, dogs, I don't get you, man. Since you came outta the bathroom back at Candy's place, it's like you's a changed man. Tell me what's good?" Show turned to stare at Squeeze who avoided eye contact with his childhood friend by staring nonchalantly at the rearview.

"Five-Oh always trying to swing a brother's head low," Squeeze said, eyes locked on the patrol vehicle in the rearview. Show didn't hear the answer he was expecting and became a little too pushy.

"So tell me what's really good, Squeeze?" Show asked for a second time. This time, Squeeze glanced at him sideways from underneath arched brows.

"What?" Squeeze managed with a cold stare.

There was no anger but he was way out of sorts and his temper was short. Show knew it but didn't want to let up. He was trying to figure out what could possibly be eating at Squeeze causing him to look shook. Lately things had gotten a little out of hand, he thought as he glanced at the police through the video screen on the side mirror. He heard Squeeze talking but kept watching her every move.

"Show, you know you my man and all, right?"

"No doubt."

"So I'm asking you to drop it, ahight? I don't wanna speak on it just yet, dogs. Let me think this one over, ahight? You feel me?"

"You got it, Squeeze."

Through the corner of his eye, Show could tell that Squeeze was staring at him. He nodded without making further eye contact.

"Po-po's always taking they sweet ol' time. I tell you one thing though, honey better hurry before I change my mind and not take that damn ticket from her," Squeeze said. He resumed watching the officer from the rearview.

"Ticket? What's the ticket for?" Show asked.

"Dogs, I don't know. I suppose it's for driving while black," Squeeze answered mockingly. They both chuckled. The officer returned and handed Squeeze the summons.

"Officer, you mind telling me why I'm being given a summons?" Squeeze asked politely.

"You went to school, didn't you? You got a fancy ride here. Somewhere along the line you had to have learned how to read, right? I'm making a major assumption here of course, because all y'all ain't nothing but a bunch of goddamn illiterates. I recommend GED classes. Get some edumacation and stop being the sore eye of the race. Don't waste your money on another piece of bling-bling until you invest in some education. You have a nice day now."

She was out of earshot when Squeeze and Show shook their heads multiple times in an attempt to recover from her verbal assault.

"Yo, did that cop bitch called us a bunch of illiterates? I know she ain't trying to dis by calling me a…What was that ho-cop doing when I was a high school football star running through offensive tackles and sacking quarterbacks? Man, she don't know…she better ask somebody," Show said slapping his knee. "I was the man in high school!"

"Yeah? Who she gonna ask, huh? Your non-playing ass still can't read. She was real, straight up," Squeezed said with a smile. "I know *I* can't read nothing on this damn summons," his eyes squinted as he perused the form. "That cop bitch can't write to save her fuckin' life. Wha' she talkin' 'bout? She da one who need to take her non-writing-ass to class."

"Tell that cop bitch she can suck my Johnson and sleep tight, bi-yotch! How much is the ticket for?" Show asked. Squeeze handed him the paper. "Damn! They trying to balance the budget? That's straight up gangsta. Dogs, this shit way too much. See how she can check the dollar amount with no problem but anything else you can't make-out nada. That's mad game right there. They just geeing the black man out of his ends on some bullshit."

Show examined the ticket, crumpled it, and tossed it over his shoulder onto the backseat.

"You got the next one rolled up, Show?" Squeeze asked.

"Yeah, after all that bullshit I'm ready to spark it," Show said as he fired up the blunt and immediately started coughing. "You gonna pay that?" Show asked puffing away.

"Yeah, why? You know you gotta render to Caesar and all that bullshit. I gotta live here, Show."

"You right. If them politicians don't get pc, it'll be all kinds a drama for you and your baby mama. They'll…"

"Don't chat her up, dogs. I tell you, I need a break," Squeeze interrupted.

"I hear you, son. Fuck a bitch. I know I could use a long ass break from mine." Show said with a yawn.

"Yeah right. How you gonna take a break when she's prego again, negro? Pass that blunt, sun."

Squeeze's question had Show thinking long after handing him the blunt. He seemed to fall into an idea when he opened his mouth.

"Man, I still could go to South Beach for a hot minute. It ain't like I ain't got the dough. I mean, dogs, we got dough for all seasons, you heard?"

"No question, son," Squeeze added as he gave Show a pound. "We came off big."

"Over the fucking top with that nightclub and that strip joint is off da fucking meat rack," Show added.

"I told ya. I told ya that shit would happen. Y'all niggas fronted on a..." Squeeze started but Show wouldn't let him finish.

"Why you say y'all? I was wid it from jump. Never once fronted on ya. Squeeze, you say sump'n, I'm a listen cause we roll way back like muthafuckin' car seats. Ya heard me, son?" Show asked while he puffed. "Now that nigga, Promise, he fugazy fo sho. Smell me?" Show exhaled as he asked.

The combination of inhaling and speaking at the same time resulted in a coughing fit just as he passed the smoldering herb to Squeeze. They made brief eye contact and Show detected an immediate change in expression once Promise's name was brought up. Show watched his partner's lips twitch and noticed the contortion go from smirk to scowl.

Squeeze inhaled deeply, twice like he was hungry for more. He opened his mouth but said nothing. Show could tell that Squeeze was clearly plagued by the intensity of his thoughts. Squeeze looked away uneasily scratching his dome just as often as he puffed. He had long turned off the engine and the accompanying choke from the smoke was the only sound except for the spit of Jadakiss.

> *Why they gon give you life for murder*
> *Turn around and give you eight months for a*
> *burner...*

The message in the lyrics had real meaning for both partners. It opened a floodgate of emotions and made what followed vital to the success and growth of any relationship. Someone had to reach the road of rationality. Show felt it had to be on him.

"Yo son, you did what you had to do, ya heard? Promise jooks us for some short change. If this was a game, he'd be begging for forgiveness by the fourth quarter. You know that and I know it. Man, this ain't a game and our money's long so we could find that nigga in any arena, any ballpark and pull him out from the rock he hiding up under. You know we can, son. Just give the word and it's done, over with."

"Nah don't even say his name around me. Promise was ma muthafuckin' brotha, from anotha motha. We wuz tight till he pulled that shiesty shit on peeps who been down wid him since day one. Don't ever fuckin' mention dat nigga's name round me no more. His name's shit."

Squeeze spat out the window. Show stared out the window at the manicured lawn of the tony row of houses. He could hear the hurt in Squeeze's voice without looking at him. Instead, he stared out the window. A few mansions up, landscapers were at work. He knew what he had to do. Squeeze couldn't do it.

"That nigga scoped us out well before he hit us though. Sometimes I feel like there were more than him and his man. There had to be others watching and telling him shit." Show shook his head slowly side to side, puffed twice and passed the blunt.

"Fuhgit-bout-dat-nigga. He living on borrowed time," Squeeze said inhaling and staring out of a haze of smoke. "I know who wuz wid me from jump." He paused to stare at the fire on the tip of the blunt then crushed the tip as he attempted to knock the ash from it. "It just pains me to see that da nigga now wants piece o' da action after not trying to see us. Like da nigga wants a free ride. Nigga better know he ain't riding 'less he got snaps on da petro."

Squeeze had worked himself into a frenzy and exhaled to calm down.

"All that nigga does is handcuff his bitches. Whenever he gets one, then da nigga starts with that falling-in-love shit," Show said with disdain. He took a few tokes and slowly passed it as if sunk in deep thought. "Yo, Squeeze man, you figure Pooh was really right 'bout that nigga all along?" Show asked and the words exploded as Jadakiss flowed.

"Pooh's dead so get all that shit outta your head. You know we came up poor, busted out our grind, held shit down for some time and now we got this." Squeeze highlighted his statements by waving his arm around the vehicle and the neighborhood. "What da nigga got? Not a muthafuckin' thing." Squeeze coughed vigorously before he continued. "That nigga ain't no brotha of mine no more. That's it, over, done." Squeeze took a few more puffs on the blunt before he got out of the Caddy and started walking to the huge house. "Yo, you might as well come chill for a minute, play some pool, have a drink or sump'n," he said turning to Show.

"Nah, man, I got some errands to run before tonight. I'll see you later at the club." Show answered.

"Ahight my nigga. Lemme deal with this family thing and I'll see you later, my man," Squeeze hollered and held up a peace sign, walked up his driveway and disappeared inside his house.

Show jumped into the driver's seat and peeled out. He pumped the volume on the number six track from the *Kiss of Death* CD. It had quickly become his favorite. Yet for all the sound banging in his head, Show couldn't put his overactive thoughts to rest. He knew that something had to have happened at Candy's. Maybe Promise was really hiding out there in the apartment. He could've been in the bathroom. But the question that haunted his mind was why Squeeze didn't drop the hammer on him.

Jadakiss continued to spit and Show steered the whip towards the BQE. Several tracks later, he was pulling slowly to the curb until finally coming to a stop outside the club. He sat back glancing around as his chrome kept spinning.

Show was looking for Pooh's mother who had called him about possibly working at the club. He had asked her to meet him out front at six pm before the club opened. He didn't know what to expect. Most of all, he really didn't want the old earth of his former running partner working for him. Show sat tinkering with the remote to the Clarion stereo thinking that maybe he could just hit Pooh's mother with extra dough or let her wait tables on certain nights. His thoughts spun like the Spree's the vehicle was sitting on.

Something was definitely bothering Squeeze. That was for sure. Stevie Wonder could see that. The reflection rolled off the chassis of his intellect. I guess he'll talk about it when he feels like.

Thoughts ran through his impatient mind as he got out of the vehicle and with hands in his pockets began a somber gait to the club. He stopped many times to look up and down the avenue for Pooh's mother. Maybe Promise and his man, he was ready. She was nowhere in sight. He leaned against the wall outside the club, lit a cigar while waiting and thought of what could have happened with Squeeze in the bathroom. He did not want to say it but every time he thought of his partner, he wondered if Squeeze had been shook. It seemed that Squeeze had walked into the bathroom like a tough guy and a different person came out.

Show flicked the cigar away before going inside the empty club. Quickly, he disarmed the security system and the lights came on before he trudged up the stairs to the office at the top. He entered the clean office, closed the door and threw himself atop a black leather chaise. With a sigh, he stretched and unbuttoned his shirt exposing his wife beater. The phone rang as he was preparing to make himself comfortable. This had to be Pooh's mom, he thought as he checked the monitor and saw the woman's figure. Yet Show still screamed, "Who is it?" to make sure.

"It's Misty, Pooh's mother. I have an appointment with Show," she answered. Once identity was confirmed, Show buzzed her into the building.

"To the left is the stairs. Come on up, the office is at the top," he said over the intercom. He kept his eyes glued to the monitor charting her every move from his perch on the chaise.

"Damn, damn, damn!" He exclaimed with every step she took. "That's Pooh's old earth?" Show wondered aloud instinctively moving his hand to his crotch.

Show jumped to his feet and rubbed himself as he watched her walking around. He clapped his hands and walked briskly to a big executive chair behind a huge mahogany desk. He plopped himself down and cupped his head with his hands as the knock came on the office door.

"It's open, come on in," he said and when she walked in, his eyes became transfixed on her plump backside.

"Hi, Show. How're you doing?" she greeted with a smile. "I'm so sorry to be late," she continued as Show pushed past her outstretched hand and swept her up into a tight embrace. His dick was hard from watching her walk up the stairs. She immediately felt it solidly poking against her thigh. Without backing off, she gave Show a kiss on his cheek. "Oh, you're soo crazy," she screamed.

Show spun her around and again then he laughed until they were both a little dizzy.

"I wasn't sure if you were gonna make it. You called before and I told you to come through but you stood me up," Show explained.

"Lemme catch my breath," she said rearranging her dress. Its green color seemed brighter at the cleavage. The dress was fitted on top and loose on the bottom. The woman wore strapless three-inch pumps that helped to accentuate her girlish figure. Show blinked hardly unable to completely believe his eyes. Her figure enthralled him. There was no shame so he stared. "Like what you see, Show?" she asked with a casual smile.

"Yes, I like...ah..."

"You can call me Misty," she said and pranced from one side of the office to the next pretending she was on a catwalk. Show's eyes danced and as he followed her small waist and the fat ass, he began whistling. Misty whirled and whirled her body taking Show to dizzying heights. Each time she did, there were more thighs and ass revealed until she curtsied. His jaw dropped involuntarily as Misty's little tease left him in disbelief.

"Oh yeah, baby! You da bomb," he yelled after finally regaining control of his chops.

"So what kinda job you got lined up for me, Show?" She asked wearing her smile.

The question had Show going. He wanted to pull out his dick and give it to her right then and there but this was Pooh's mother. His man, Pooh, had been killed over a year ago and he and Squeeze had revenged his killing. Show had to bite his lip hard in order to regain his respect for Misty. Show's dick was swelling and he wanted her bad.

He thought for a moment before asking, "Do you wanna little sump'n to drink?"

"Sure, long as they ain't no rum or brandy in it," she answered smiling seductively. The quick glance at his crotch was not lost on Show. She seemed turned on by his discomfort even though he wanted her to see the effect she was having on him. "Well, I'm glad you're happy to see me," she said as she sat cross-legged toying with him.

Her loose skirt opened to reveal sexy olive toned thighs. Show smiled as he handed her the glass half filled with blue liquid. She winked when she caught him stealing a bird's eye view of her breasts. He sipped, swallowed quickly, and cleared his throat.

"No doubt, no doubt it's good to see you," he said swirling the liquid in his own glass before continuing. "I mean, you and I never really met besides at the funeral and maybe once at your place when we were all shorties, you know."

"That's because I don't make it my business to holla at my son's friends but now that we're all adults, we can do grown folks things. You feel me? Salud," she said raising her glass and sipping.

"Bottoms up," Show responded and threw the liquid to the back of his throat before speaking again. He took another look at her, scratched his head and then began. "You have the cocktail waitress job. With tips, you could earn up to about eight hundred to nine hundred dollars a week depending on how often you wanna work it."

Show watched how Misty held her head back as she sipped and peeked flirtingly at him from the corner of her eye. Show cleared his throat before continuing. "Seriously though, that right there's good for you. You'll have a little cheddar and with tips, you can probably max out to like a gee a week." He looked up when she moaned.

"Hmm, this is really good. Is it Hypnotic? I'm not used to all these fancy drinks. I've been a Budweiser woman for sometime now. What is this?" she asked with the anxiety of a schoolgirl.

"It's ah... Alize Bleu," he answered. "Care for more?" Show asked with the hope of a man trying to get his date tipsy.

"Nah, it's a little too strong for my blood," she said and wobbled a little when she stood. "I came for a real job. I guess I've got to prove that I'm working with a lil' sump'n, sump'n, huh?"

Misty licked her lips when she saw Show shifting in his seat. It pleased her to know that her presence had stimulated him sexually. She shook her tail fast when she saw his hard-on. Misty knew her actions were responsible. She thought that she was in control. Misty was thinking she could turn him on or off until unwittingly, Show threw a wrinkle in her plan.

"Well, that's taken care of. We can chill out and get to know each other better," he said standing and loosening all the buttons of his shirt. Misty was not to be deterred from her plan.

"Uh huh, I came here to audition for a job, okay? Not to be seduced by you. I mean you handsome and all but...but...you could be my son."

"Know what?" Show said sitting down, "you're absolutely right but I don't need to tell you that Pooh was my man. He was a brother. Someone I would die for."

Show spoke with open honesty and this took Misty for a loop. She had heard of her son's friends, Promise, Squeeze and Show. She was also very aware of their exploits on the streets. Show was supposed to be thuggin'. Misty was surprised by the ease in which he had exposed his emotions freely without any prompting from her.

"Don't tell me you're a humanitarian, Show?"

"I'm about the kids and survival." Show answered and had no problem exposing a softer side. "Pooh was my younger brother."

"He was my only son."

"I'd do anything to bring him back. You feel me?"

"One day you may have to prove that. He loved kids too. He always talked about having his own family. You're the family..." She stopped and turned away.

Show got up and held her. He stared into her eyes. She

wanted to cry but no tears came. Instead, she stopped in her tracks and listened intently. Misty's breasts heaved with each word. Show pulled away and lit a cigar and continued.

"You're his old earth so therefore you're like family too. All respect due, you know what I'm saying?"

"I don't know about being any old earth. What exactly does that mean anyway?" Misty asked hands akimbo and staring at Show as she waited for his answer.

"It's just another way to say you his mother, understand? I ain't meant no disrespect by it, ahight. All I'm saying is you don't have to do anything. Just say what you want and I'm sure sump'n can be worked out."

Misty placed a hand to her mouth as she pondered the offer from Show.

"Nah, I don't think so. I want a little more, babe. You sit back and chill. Let this play inside your head for now, you feel me?"

When Show heard her saying this, he was instantly disappointed. He had really wanted to get to know her better and now it seems that all she wanted was to audition for a job and then be out. She had refused a second drink, which he interpreted as things not going right for any opportunity to get her tipsy. Misty straightened the full length of her body with a slow bump and grind.

Show reached for the remote, switched on the music and became engrossed with her sinew body motion. He tapped his feet to the way she swung her hips. She reminded him of an Egyptian dancer. Show was enjoying it so much he hummed along to the song from Juvenile while he watched Misty's dance.

> *Hmm I like it like that she working that back/ I don't know how to act,*
> *slow motion for me/ Slow motion for me*
> *she's moving slow motion for me/*
> *Hmm I like it like that she working that back I don't know how to act./slow motion for me...*
> *I like the way your Victoria Secret fit...*

By the time Juvenile had completed sixteen bars from his *Juve the Great* CD, Misty had dropped it like it's hot and was down to her black thong with titties bouncing around in Show's face. He could hardly contain himself so rubbing his legs together kept him from exploding.

"You got a great body for an older..."

Show caught himself. He didn't want to say or do anything that might spoil the moment. He really wanted to please her. "You definitely got sump'n that will keep the customers happy while they drinking," Show said swallowing hard. "You're all that and much more," he continued as beads of sweat crawled down his spine.

"All that and much more huh?" Misty repeated with eyebrows arched.

"Yeah, you know? You damn sexy and all that... You feel me?" Show asked. Misty saw that he was clearly ill at ease and smiled. With her index finger, she signaled for him to come to her.

"You definitely got a nice body," Show said in an almost whisper.

Almost trance-like, Show got up. He pounced on her as if he had been wound up, fully charged and ready to go. Show groped her and rubbed her tits. He hastily ripped the thong from between her ass cheeks, spun her around and pushed her face first toward the desk. Misty's olive skin stretched thin to cover her fatty that was raised high. Show gave both cheeks a slap and slid his index finger between the cheeks.

"Ooh, be easy, big fella," she moaned but grunted and reached around to massage his package hard as rolled quarters.

Misty unzipped his pants and felt him coiled stiff and ready to strike. She placed a knee on the desk just as she heard Show ripped a condom from a package. Misty felt the hard thrust against her thighs. She reached for his dick and guided it deep inside her. Show felt the moistness and rode hard. He spanked her gently, rubbing her clitoris all the time.

"Hmm, hmm uh, uh..."

"Oh yeah, Show. Give it to me hard big boy, huh uh huh," she cried as Show kept shoving.

She felt his plunging getting deeper and the increasing rapid movement of his hips against her exposed ass. Misty heard him scream and held on for dear life as he pummeled her into the mahogany wood.

"Ah yes I'm coming, ma," Show yelled biting her earlobes and neck.

"I guess this means I'm stripping?" she asked as Show staggered backward from the desk.

Misty watched him remove the condom. She saw the shiny head and there was no hesitation. She dropped to her knees and glazed his dome with the curl of her tongue action.

"Yeah, keep doing that and you're gonna be running things round here. Oh yeah."

Show bucked as Misty worked her way past all boundaries and he could feel her stiff tongue in his asshole. He was screaming like a baby. "You can have whatever you want!" Show's body was thrown into convulsions.

Misty's jaw clamped his pulsing dick and her tongue teased his head until Show became caught up in throes of ecstasy. He kicked off his shoes, hoisted Misty over his shoulder and spread her across the chaise. Her skin glistened with sweat as he entered her with rapid strokes. Show beat her pussy with strokes from doggy style to the frog then he spun her over and buffed her voraciously.

"Oh yeah big boy you know what mama likes," Misty chimed in, singing praises, building his ego and spurring his tongue action. "Yesss! That's the way I like it. Ohh yesss!" Misty cried baring open her thighs as Show continued his assault on her inner flesh.

"You gonna come, mami?" he asked taking a whiff of air.

"Yess! Stay right there and keep licking and I'll come for you!" Misty screamed as if she was being tortured. Show bobbed his head and she began screaming so loud that he clasped a big hand over Misty's mouth smothering her, but that only made her wilder. With ease, she flipped over and was positioning herself on top of Show's pole. She was ready to ride. She did it with a smile on her face as he closed his eyes and moaned, his toes curled and his body shaking like a leaf in autumn wind.

"Oh yeah, mami that's the way I like it," Show mumbled.

He felt her put the sheath over his head and then slowly she mounted, her ass bouncing off his legs. Hearing the clap of her ass cheeks, he reached for her tits but couldn't hold them for long. Show reclined against the sofa, closed his eyes and enjoyed the ride. At full extension, Misty's arms rested on his shoulders.

The up and down motion brought her nipples closer. Show couldn't resist. He plucked at each like he was at a buffet. Nibbling and sucking, hearing her scream and at the same time, he felt a jolt like lightning rip through his midsection. He held on for dear life as Misty rode his dick to a volcanic eruption.

"Ahh, egad ugh ohh sheeeet!"

Show felt his body going limp and for a beat everything became blurry. He remained stationary, only blinking his eyes for a few seconds then closing them. His knees were weak and he fell completely backwards into the sofa. He could feel her mouth suction removing all the fluid from his body by using his dick as a straw. Show squirted skeet off in her face all the time stomping his feet from the intensity.

Spent, he closed his eyes as Misty wiped cream from her long black hair. She carried a crooked smirk and leaned over him. Show slowly opened his eyes. His breathing slowly returned to normal.

"I want a job as a stripper."

"Done. When can you begin?"

"I want a five thousand dollars advance."

"Done!"

"I'll begin next Tuesday."

"Done deal."

Show stayed on his back for a few more minutes while Misty rearranged her clothes, make-up and smoked a cigar then he also got up fixed his clothes. He walked to a framed poster on the wall. It depicted Malcolm X standing at the window with an assault rifle. The caption below the photo read, 'By any means necessary'.

Show tapped the poster and an opening appeared displaying the front of a safe. Misty grinned as he quickly opened it, pulled out five thousand dollars and handed it to her before closing it back up. "It's a tough life to lead but dancers make about twice this amount every month. Don't spend it all in one place," Show said as he handed her the money. Misty had a happy face on.

"That's all I needed to do in order to get five thousand? I will see you Tuesday."

"Be here at nine sharp," Show shouted and sprawled on the black leather sofa.

"See ya next week," Misty shouted over her shoulder.

"Nine sharp."

Show was exhausted but poured himself a drink and smiled as he toasted his dead friend's memory. He sipped, lit a cigar and checked the time on his Rollie. I still got another hour or so. I'll get me some shut-eye, he thought as he eased back with a crooked smile on his mug. Finally, not able to hold back the laughter, he opened his mouth and let it out. "Ha, ha, ha," Show bellowed before he closed his eyes and snoozed.

Hours later, Show was woken by the ring of his cell. He yawned and took a look at the caller ID. It was Squeeze. "Yo, what up, Squeeze?" Show inquired trying to regain his senses. He glanced at the time.

"Show, man, you sleeping, dogs?" Squeeze asked.

"Nah, nah I've been up doing my thing. Did that interview," Show said with a smile.

"Ahight, ahight, I hear you. How did it go?"

"It was bananas. I'll tell you about it when you come through," Show said not able to contain his enthusiasm.

"Yeah, okay but just to let you know I'm gonna be late. My in-laws are visiting. I got to take 'em back to the city."

"Ahight, I'll see you later then."

"Yeah, get that shit jumping, dogs. You know, open the bar and check if them crack dealers are outside. Them police sez we responsible for all that so watch the monitors carefully. Make sure five hundred in singles gets up to the strip bar cause people always looking for change and also make sure each bar have enough Cristal, especially the one in the VIP area. I'm expecting some peoples..."

"Yo Squeeze man don't worry. I gotcha with all that man," Show said interrupting.

"I'm just reminding you."

"Sounds like you don't think I know what I'm doing, huh?"

"C'mon man, ain't nobody never said nothing like that. What? I can't remind you of shit to do, dogs?"

"Yeah, it's all good but you kinda made it seem like you uptight and all."

"Show, just because I'm calling you to remind you about certain things, it ain't even like I never always do this shit solo. Now I'm callin' you tellin'..."

"Yo my man, stop stressin'. I got your back, like I said, ahight?"

"Who's stressin'? I ain't try to sound disrespectful or anything but right now, you sound like a fool."

"Yo Squeeze, man, chill. I'm saying, I gotcha your back always, ahight?"

"Yeah, whatever. I'll holla atcha later."

"Yeah, later."

Show closed the cellphone and immediately began wondering about Squeeze. What da fuck is eating at him? Maybe his girl's mother but they ain't married. Kick that bitch out if she stressing you. Maybe that's why he's so tight. He better get him a dose o' trim before he gets up in da club. Show opened the safe and counted out the money as Squeeze had ordered then he made the necessary calls to ensure the security staff was in place for the evening's opening.

After doing all this, Show paced the office thinking of what had gone wrong with Squeeze. There was something on Squeeze's mind and now it was beginning to rub Show the wrong way. Show rolled a blunt carefully as he thought about it.

'Money changes people, even the ones closest to you,' he remembered hearing from old heads in the streets. Maybe Squeeze was getting too big for him or sump'n.

Show lit the blunt and inhaled. He checked each security monitor, noting the conditions and then reviewed the line outside the club. He tried to focus on the faces and tried to pinpoint the faces of the neighborhood crack-dealers. If any were recognized, the bouncers would be alerted by radio and the dealer would be tossed off the line or asked to leave the club area. This was important because the community board members put this as one of the conditions that the club could operate by. It was the club's responsibility to clean up after itself or be shut down.

Satisfied that everything was proceeding smoothly, Show poured himself another drink. "Ain't no need for him to worry, I can run this," Show said as he called VIP security to inform them of the guests his partner was expecting.

In an attempt to take the edge off his thoughts, Show flushed the liquid down his throat but all of his contemplation kept popping back up. He knew something was bothering Squeeze but couldn't tell exactly what it was. Show thought about the possibilities as he poured another drink and decided he wanted to find out. Since Squeeze didn't want to talk about it, he would find out another way. He'd be damned if any bullshit destroyed his relationship with Squeeze.

His mind wouldn't let it go as Show clicked to his cellphone directory and shook his head after he had spent a moment browsing. He dialed the desired number and sipped as the phone rang. Finally his call was answered.

"Who dis?"

"Yo, this Show, my man. What's popping, dread?"

"Same ol'. Just trying to put more wood in da fire, you know, make it hotter. You feel me, Show?"

"No question. You da muthafuckin' man. When was the last you visit yard?"

"Who? Me just step off Air Jamaica yesterday at six in da evening. I man spend couple months down there. Now I man is back up in dis piece dat dem call Brooklyn."

"I feel you, Rasta. I know you wanna go back and check some other family members out, Rude Bwoy."

"Absolutely, big Show. Like you read my mind and all."

"Come through to the club. I've got sump'n I want you to check out for me, ahight."

"When you want me fi pass through?"

"Oh, come through tonight, dread."

"Any special time?"

"Any time after midnight."

"Me in deh. Irie, Big Show."

"Yeah dread, I'll see you later, Rasta."

Show closed the cellphone, sealed the safe and walked out the office. He paused at the top of the stairs and gazed down at the swelling club. He slowly made his way downstairs to the dance floor where he was greeted by waves of hugs and kisses. Glad-handing, he made his way to the bar where he spoke to the main bartender for a minute then walked away.

Show walked past the red velvet rope through to the VIP area. He spoke to the bartender and sent an expensive bottle of champagne to Squeeze's guests. Next, Show walked around the back to the bathroom area. Finally, he went outside and walked alongside the line. He smoked a cigar as he slowly paced himself trying to look inconspicuous as he searched for any sign of crack dealers.

"Show?"

He did not turn immediately when he first heard his name. It was the voice of a female patron standing on line. He remembered that the game was to holler his name out and try to get in the club quicker by talking to him. This is the reason I don't like doing this, he thought acting as if he did not hear his name being called.

"Show! Show!"

She was persistent, Show thought. Not looking usually would end it since the person would be too embarrassed to keep calling his name. All he had to do was pretend to be preoccupied. He looked in the other direction and then felt tugging on his sleeve.

"Damn, you wanna get in da club real bad? I bet you wanna use the bathroom real bad too, huh? But you just can't wait on this long-ass line, can you?" Show asked as he turned around with cynicism dripping from his tone. The uncaring look on his face turned into an embarrassed smile when he realized who had been trying to get his attention.

"Oh shit, Lindsay, is that you, girl? Hot damn! Pooh's lil' sis done grown up." Show exclaimed as the young lady threw her nimble body against him. Show caught her suppleness with the greatest of ease and wrapped her in his huge arms as everyone on line stared at their display.

"Yep, it's me in the flesh. Who did you think it was?" She asked, hugging Show and planting a wet-one on his cheek.

"I saw your mother earlier."

"She told me all about you and the club and all," Lindsay answered. Her smile made Show uncomfortable for a second.

"She told you about everything?" he asked sheepishly.

Show really wanted to know the details of what was told to Lindsay but asking that could reveal more than he wanted to. His curious gaze became more about what she had to say than the way she looked. He saw the smile on her face and it reminded him too much of the way her mother had looked earlier. Maybe he read too much in the situation, Show thought as he heard Lindsay speaking.

"Yeah, you know, she told me about the club," she said pouting and smiling. "Last week my girlfriend was here and she was boasting and talkin' bout how nice it was. Then my mother came here and she talked for hours on end about how big the inside was and how nice it was decorated. She said you had a nice office with expensive leather furniture. She was talking about it so much I decided that since it's my birthday, I'd to come see for real what all the fuss is about," Lindsay said.

She had Show's full attention and he beamed wildly when she told him about her birthday.

"Say what? It's your birthday, huh? Well a big happy birthday to you, lil' sis," Show said and kissed Lindsay. "Well, I guess you ain't that little if you came here, right?" Show asked flirtingly. He hugged and kissed her again.

"I'm grown, Show. I made eighteen. I'm legal and all." Lindsay said and shook her groove thang just enough to make sure Show saw her backfield in motion.

Show felt his eyeballs scrambling and he let off a long whistle to hold them in their sockets. Pooh's lil' sis had grown up and was looking well, he thought. Her animated behavior had attracted the eyes of every man on the line, much to the dismay of some of their dates.

"Goddamn, girl, easy now. You gonna start a riot out here. You better come with me," Show said. Lindsay halted him.

"I'm here with my date," she said smiling and pointing to a young man, impressive in a dark suit, waiting on line. He reached forward to handshake with Show.

"How you doin'? I'm Malik," he said.

"Oh yeah, Malik, this was my brother's best friend, Show," Lindsay said.

"Nice to meet you, Show. I've heard a lot about you," Malik said greeting Show with a firm handshake.

"Ahight, I hope she told you some good shit," Show said extending his arm.

"Nah, it's not only her. Everyone knows that you been doing ya thing with some live cats. Ya'll legendary when it comes to holding down da streets," Malik said.

It was clear for everyone to see Malik was daunted by meeting Show. Show made it clear he was no longer 'only a gangster'.

"No doubt, no doubt. Da streets raised us but right now it

ain't about da streets. It's about running da club. We serious bidness-men. You gotta stay 'bout your money, ya heard me?"

Malik gave Show a pound and they embraced. Lindsay smiled watching the two hit it off.

"Where's Squeeze?" Lindsay asked immediately.

"Oh yeah, he'll be around later on. He comes in later after I set things up, nah mean?" He winked.

"Oh you da man, Show. I mean, damn, that's probably a lot of work. You don't need an assistant?" Lindsay asked with a grin.

"Right now, we can pay someone to run things here and we sit back and count cheddar, you know wha' I'm saying? But you can't sit back and think other people gonna run things for you the way you want it to go. If you want it done right, you gotta go do it for self. You feel me?"

"Yeah, I hear. That's real, man," Malik said.

"See, I could tell already that you is a smart brother, Malik. Come, y'all follow me. Lemme set y'all right up in da VIP section. No birthday girl should be seen waiting on no damn line, understand?"

"I feel ya, Show," Lindsay yelled with a grin. She grabbed Show's arm as she continued. "That's what's up, Malik. Told ya someone would recognize ya girl," Lindsay said. She and her date were escorted proudly through the velvet rope that was held open by bouncers. Before going inside the club, Show paused to speak with one of the bouncers.

"Al-cakes, them two muthafuckas in da blue Yankee, throw 'em off da line. If they ask why: Tell 'em they can't be up in da club cuz the shit they wearing ain't upscale enough. If they give you any static, ya heard me? Any fucking static, holla at me on da walkie, ahight?"

"Yeah boss," Al-cakes said and quickly moved out.

Show joined the couple waiting at the door and escorted them inside. The blast of the music greeted them.

> "Let your body go all the fellas go move your body
> girls let your body go..."

Lindsay wore a big smile when she heard the heavy bass line

and saw the happy couples grooving to the rhythm of the night. She saw the waitresses busy rushing tending to customers running back and forth to the bar, keeping the drinks flowing. She was impressed by the size of the club.

"Damn, mommy was right. This joint is huge and it's off da hook up in here," Lindsay exclaimed. She was flying high as they were ushered through the club serenaded by the sound of Nina Sky: *Move your body girl*. Eventually they touched down in the VIP section.

"I don't have time to give you a full tour," Show apologized.

"This is great. It's all good," Malik said.

"You wid fam, nah'mean? So come out on a Tuesday or a Wednesday night and I'll give ya'll a full tour. What y'all drinking?" Show asked competing with the decibel level of the pumping sound. Realizing it was next to impossible, he waved off the question before adding. "I'll send a waiter to y'all, ahight?"

"That's cool, Show," Lindsay answered flipping an okay sign to Show. He shook Malik's hand once again and gave Lindsay a kiss on the cheek.

"Enjoy your birthday and have fun. I'll stop by later to see how y'all doing."

Unseen by Malik's eyes, Show quickly squeezed Lindsay's ass. It was shapely and round in her tight dress. He smiled when her round rump pressed back to his hand and his package hardened. When she licked her lips, Show sealed the deal in his head.

"Oh, Show, before you disappear cuz I know you busy and all, Malik got sump'n to say to you."

"I mean, if it's about a job he could holla at me. I'll give you the digits to the club and you can holla any time."

"Nah, it's not about a job. Its sump'n else. I told him to tell you and Squeeze but since Squeeze is not here..."

"Yeah, go ahead, you could tell me now," Show said sitting down with the couple.

He glanced furtively at Pooh's sister. She was a knockout with the same skin tone as her mother and they all shared the hazel eyes. Show knew Pooh broke a lot of hearts with his but Lindsay wore them best, hands down, he thought.

"So what's the dealy?" Show asked and tried not to stare at Lindsay. She assisted him by pointing to her date whenever he stared.

"Malik speaks Spanish and a lot of people don't know cuz he looks black and all. Anyway, he cops pounds from peeps in da heights and he was telling me about..." Lindsay paused as the waitress arrived. Show whispered to her and the waitress departed in a hurry.

"Before you tell me though, I just want ya to know I ain't fucking wid da weed but I got peeps who'll give you great prices. Ya heard?"

"Nah, Show it ain't bout no weed," Malik quickly said.

"Yeah, Malik, you explain to him," Lindsay ordered and smiled at Show. The young man stared off for a beat then cleared his throat before speaking.

"I got family who deal with these cats and they all Dominicans. Now these guys was bragging to him one night about a week ago saying shit in Spanish, right?"

"What were they saying?" Show's curiosity was peaked.

For a minute he thought about Promise. Someone had the goods on Promise. He wasn't sure why but Show was expecting to hear about where that nigga Promise was really hiding. Show really wanted to speak with him this time and maybe find out about what happened in the bathroom. Instead, he heard Malik saying something else entirely.

"Yeah, so they be bragging all the time that they had to shoot this *moreno* from Bed-Stuy because he robbed their girl of thousands of dollars and all."

A waitress bearing a bottle of champagne arrived. She filled two long stemmed glasses and departed. Show was frozen and besides a nod did not say anything for a beat. Both Lindsay and Malik sipped.

"Show, where's your glass? We're not large enough for you to share a drink with us? Malik has a job you know," Lindsay said jokingly.

"Yeah, that's good. Where do you work?"

"At the Footlocker on Atlantic," Malik said.

"Ah yeah, that's good to know. I'm always in need of sneaks. You got 'em new Jordan's yet?"

"Yeah, we got 'em in all sizes and colors. Come check us out. I'll hook you up."

"I definitely will do that. So you say these cats are from da heights, the ones that be bragging about killing some man?"

"Yep, that's where they be. They got a gift shop but it's a front for a weed spot. I've known them cats for a while and they were talking back then but when they heard that the other dude...ah, what's his name?"

"You talking 'bout that nigga Nine, and them?"

"Yeah, that was the cat I'd heard them say killed Pooh."

"I had told you that because that's what I had heard for the longest," interjected Lindsay. "So I started believing it too but I started having mad dreams. Ah, Malik and me, well from the start when me and him got together, I was telling him about the dreams with my brother, right?"

"Yep," Malik confirmed.

"What kinda dreams you were having?" Show asked.

"I used to see my brother's face a lot. Once I dreamt," Lindsay paused and sipped before she continued. "I dreamt that he was chasing me through the projects and I...I was naked and I just thought it was really freaky," Lindsay's voice trailed off.

"I told her that's because she a girl and she gonna be scared and all but that's life, right?" Malik asked looking at Show. Lindsay began speaking again, her tone strong against the music.

"That dream seemed so real. It stayed on my mind for days," Lindsay said as both Show and Malik drew closer.

They could not only catch her every syllable but also felt

her hot breath. There was fire in her eyes that failed to douse her tears that flowed when she spoke. "Right after the dreams started, I met Malik and we got to talking. I told him about my brother and his friends and all that happened. He was surprised to know Pooh was my brother." Lindsay wiped her tears and both Show and Malik reached for napkins. "Thanks," she said wiping her eyes sparkling with moisture. "Malik started to let me know how my brother and his friends were legendary OGs and that the wrong people died behind my brother's killing."

"Huh?" Show was taken aback by this piece of information. He pulled at the crotch of his pants and nervously shifted around in his seat. "Wait a minute. What da fuck you trying to tell me?" Show asked then exploded in heavy guffaws. "Ha, ha, ha, stop playing kids. This grown up shit you dealing wid. This ain't no Mickey Mouse shit now," Show said before continuing to laugh. "Ha, ha, you can't be serious...ha, ha, ha."

"Show listen, listen," Lindsay said reaching under the table and touching Show's large thigh. "Listen, Show, you gotta believe that ..." Lindsay started and then was surprised when she felt Show grabbing her hand and placing it on his crotch. She left it resting there because she knew Malik could not see what was going on. Through crushed linen and cotton, Lindsay rubbed Show's dick as she spoke. "When I met Malik, I told him he reminded me so much of my brother. Don't he, Show?"

"There is a resemblance," Show said glancing quickly at Malik.

The whole time Lindsay spoke she massaged his dick and it was almost ready to explode. He reclined with a sigh as she undid his zipper. Show noticed that Malik was too busy wiping away her tears to care about what was going on under the cover of the tablecloth. Show tried to appear calm without giving away the secret to his obvious pleasure and felt a rise of sensation when Lindsay's hand kneaded his dick. Show stared lustfully in her eyes as she continued speaking.

"I know all this is a surprise to you but I had to see you. I wanted to tell you and make sure you'd have to stay and listen, okay, Show?"

Show sighed as the sensation of the hand job took away his breath. "Whatever you say lil' sis," Show's answered came with the quickness.

"Malik got some information on these guys that you're gonna be thankful you heard, okay? Go ahead Malik," Lindsay said and continued massaging.

Show reclined further, shoving his legs all the way underneath the table. His actions allowed Lindsay maximum control of his shaft without Malik noticing. She took full advantage rubbing her hands up and down the shaft until Show whistled in an attempt to release pressure from the intensity of his swollen head. He leaned forward to hear exactly what Malik was saying. Show peered around in an attempt to hide lust filled eyes. Then he stirred and gazed at the dance floor as he tried to listen to Malik speaking. It was difficult but Show endured.

"These cats, they hustle and all that. I go with my man on occasion to pick up, you know wha' I'm saying? One day after Nine had been killed, I went over there to pick up. That's when I peeped their whole shit. They were in the back o' da spot drinking Henney and smoking sour-diese and all that. They had the newspaper and it was about Nine and they were just laughing. Word B," Malik said.

"Say word?" Show answered.

It was too much for him seeing as both his heads were being massaged by new stimuli. He tried to think but it was no good. Through the pleasure and his own thoughts, he could hear Malik's voice.

"When Nine got killed, they were clowning y'all like they kill da wrong muthafucka. They were laughing loud that day. Even when we were leaving, they were still ragging and carrying on but only with their Spanish friends. See, because my brother and his man are part Dominican, that's how I found out about it." Malik paused and looked directly at his girl, her hand still busy stroking Show's dick under the table. Without missing a beat, the unsuspecting boyfriend continued, "Once I started dealing with Lindsay, I had to let her know da real. You feel where I'm coming from?" Malik sipped and Show stared at him with a far off look. Malik thought Show was questioning his story. "You seemed as if you don't believe me or sump'n. I could let you speak to my brother but he's locked up right now. He calls home on Wednesdays. He'll be out soon."

"Oh, uh, yeah, definitely I feel you, young one. I hear that and ahhh," Show said as he popped off under the table. Lindsay released her grip and he felt the uncontrollable release of skeet. She wiped her hands on the tablecloth. Show grinned from ear to ear. Malik looked befuddled.

"I'm saying, if you don't believe, I could take you to the spot and you send someone you know who speaks Spanish and boom you'll see. They don't care. They'll say if you ask."

"Ahight, Malik, me and my man, we gonna talk about this and we gonna put all that shit you shooting to the test, cool?"

"That's cool and the gang," Malik said giving Show a pound. Show closed his zipper and waved at the waitress.

"Sweetie, bring this lovely couple another bottle of champagne," Show said to the waitress then he turned back to the couple whose company had been very enlightening. "I don't know but either of you driving?" Show asked his eyes smiling at Lindsay.

"I got a hoopty but I let my man hold it. He gonna…"

"No, Show, neither of us drove here. Maybe you can hook us up later with a ride, okay?"

Lindsay's wink served as her signature to a romp in the sack. Show smiled as he armed himself with that knowledge. He could have both mother and daughter. It was possible if he played his cards right.

Show turned and faced Malik. Lindsay was dead on the money. Malik at a quick glance held an uncanny resemblance to Pooh. Show tried not to stare. Instead, he smiled at the couple.

"If there's any truth to what you told me, I'll hit you off wid some dough and you can come up in here whenever you wanna. We owe Pooh and we'll check out if what you saying is on da real cuz you know how rumors goes round these parts."

"It's real. I swear on my mother's grave. I'm telling you, Show, it's da truth.

Show sat back in the chair when he realized that he had leaned forward to hear everything the young man said. Show nodded his head.

"So you know what these cats do all day?"

"They run da spot and that's it. They be pumping good too, you know. Mad customers be up in da spot seeing them. They open up about ten in the morning and close at ten in the evening. They be having shit like clockwork. So they were saying the bitch that your man robbed was a drop girl. She was the bitch that be picking up their money and dropping supplies off, you following that? So they say honey was supposed to have just picked up twenty five gees when they say your man, Pooh, robbed her."

"Robbed? You sure? Pooh ain't never told me he jooks down no Spanish bitch."

"I'm telling you, that was why they say they killed your man." Malik took a sip he looked at Lindsay who nodded in affirmation. His gaze focused again on Show as the questions kept coming.

"You sure that's why they shot him?" Show asked. Malik nodded without saying anything. Show wanted more, he tried to work through the confusion he felt. He was suddenly unsure if he wanted to fuck Lindsay or believe her boyfriend. He wanted what he had just heard her boyfriend say not to be the truth but Show could not dismiss it either. He stared at Lindsay as she began speaking.

"They was like, he robbed they girl and took money and drugs off her? So those fucking stupid muthafuckas killed my brother? Some damn platanos...fucking Dominican greedy asses shot my brother down in cold blood at the train station."

"But..."

"If I was a guy, they would not live to see another day."

"Chill, Lin. You gotta let the men handle things from here. Have some champagne," Malik said pouring the bubbly. "You gotta let the males do their thing," he continued speaking as he tipped the glass into Lindsay's mouth. She swallowed with difficulty. Malik spoke directly to Show. "See, I know if y'all had known, urrthing would've been put to rest already. I know y'all reps. The problem would've been handled."

"Show, y'all gotta do sump'n. I know if the shoe was on the other foot, my brother would've ride for y'all."

Lindsay stared at Show intently as she spoke. He seemed confused and spoke after wiping moisture from his brow.

"Pooh ain't never jooks on no bitch. And da bitch Spanish?" Show asked rewinding his memory of Pooh. It was hopeless. He came up with blank. "On da real, I can't remember at any point where Pooh robbed a bitch. That's some next shit. But saying that don't mean I ain't gonna check out your story. Them cats that you talkin' 'bout, they still around, right?" Show asked.

"They be opening on da daily running da spot. They carry that sour diesel and weed that's real hard to get like haze, purple, strawberry. They be having the exotic works, my man. The works, I tell you."

"Oh yeah? They got it like that?" Show asked.

"Off da hook. They be new customers in there every time I've been in there. They ain't selling nothing but twenties and fifties. You can't get a dime up in that piece. That spot is strictly for ballers."

"Good. That's real good."

"Yeah but Show, I want you to know in front of my girl that I'm a soldier and I'm ready to help y'all in anyway I can cuz what them cats did to Pooh was wrong. I'm on your side," Malik said glancing at Lindsay. Her face beamed a smile right back. For a second Show wanted to push up some more on Lindsay but dismissed the thought and excused himself from the table.

"Ahight, I'm gonna be back. Gotta check a few things. Running a nightclub ain't such an easy job as it seems. You've got to stay on it," Show said.

As he walked away from the table, he knew their eyes were on him. He stopped at the bar. "Gimme a double shot of Henny," he ordered.

He immediately downed it and kept walking to the next bar. He left the happy couple smiling and Lindsay bragging.

"I told you I know the owners. Told ya."

"Let's dance," Malik said as Elephant Man crooned. ...*pon da river ...pon da bank...jook gal, jook gal...*

Lindsay and Malik strutted and worked their bodies on the dance floor. Show kept an eye out as the young girl sashayed from side to side showing a firm developed ass anchored by a nice body. Buoyed by the heavy bass of the club banger, *I'm So Fly,* Lindsay pranced and shook her body.

Show grabbed his crotch and slung another double shot down his throat. Before moving on, he couldn't resist shooting another glance in Lindsay's direction. The drums scatted and the bass rolled as the raspy throated Lloyd Bank$ flowed from *The Hunger For More.* The club jumped and the dance floor overflowed with beautiful ladies shaking their rumps and well dressed gents on the hunt. Sipping his drink, Show leaned against the bar and eyed the party revelers getting down to their damn thing reveling to another hit from the Boy Wonder.

> *I'm so fly ...I've got money so that's good enough reason to buy the things I buy/ I'm so high... I'm on point and I can tell that you're jealous just by look in your eyes and I've got by... I don't care G-Unit's going straight to the top this year/ I'm so fly... I've got money that's good enough reason to buy the things I buy...Banks is fresh out the gutter too smooth to stutter...*

Show's eyes roamed along with the strobe lights on the dance floor and his pulse quickened when his probing eyes encountered Lindsay again. He focused solely on her. The way she danced and made her hips meander, it was clear that Lindsay knew she was putting on an irresistible act. Her lips were slightly opened and her face relaxed as if she was having an orgasm. She smiled when she peeked at Show and knew she had given enough to keep him open.

She saw the way he licked his lips and stared as if he was in a trance. She saw that he was walking away but Lindsay knew that he would want more of her. She held her hands high as she shook her waistline and watched him from the corner of her eyes as he moved on. Maybe later they would hook up, she thought as she backed her ass up to edge of Malik's protruding crotch. Malik's arms encircled her and he held on as Lindsay enhanced his fantasy. She wore a satisfied smile on her face and the sound of Lloyd Bank$ laced her every move. His rasping method paved the way.

Show went back outside the club before the crowd started *Stepping In The Name Of Love*. He shook hands and observed the patrons on the line. His eyes steady watched out for the crack dealers. Show prided himself in smoking ten-dollar cigars. He bit the tip off and lit one as he continued walking. He stopped when his cellphone rang and he checked the number before answering. The number belonged to his baby mama, LaToya. He continued his slow gait down the queue without answering the call.

I need a vacation. I can't be bothered with all her drama, he thought as he glanced down the line. A request for more time or money was always made with every word out her face. Show was in deep thought when he felt a tap on his shoulder. He searched in his bag of excuses for not letting him by-pass the queue. He whirled slowly thinking of the perfect reason and was surprised when he saw two familiar mugs from Flatbush standing in front of him.

"What's good, Nappy Head Don?" Show greeted.

"This my right hand man Rude Bwoy Rex."

"Nice to meet ya," Show said and shook hands.

"Him come straight outta yard, yuh no know?"

"Y'all came early. I expected that y'all were coming through much later," Show said embracing each man individually.

"But yuh done know that once yuh mention job, dollar signs start popping off in I and I head. I man can't sit down and wait when money's to be made," the one known as Nappy Head Don said. He flashed Show a gold toothed grin and tossed his long dreads about his shoulders.

"Ahight, ahight I hear that, cuz. Ain't nothing wrong with a little enthusiasm," Show said leading the way to the other side of the velvet rope. He stopped momentarily to shake hands and chitchat with some hotties.

"Go straight ahead and to the left are the stairs to the office," he said pointing. The two men moved on, silently being scrutinized by the club security.

They paused to get a drink and after paying the tab, continued their walk. Throughout the club, bouncers eyed the men suspiciously. Security had determined that they were a threat and watched their every move. The word went out that they were guests of Show and that fact made it seem as if security had relaxed except for the two standing on either side of the entrance to the stairs.

This was due to orders given by the partners after the burglary involving Promise. Both Show and Squeeze had concluded that no suspicious looking characters would be allowed upstairs. Security immediately pounced on the men and tried to apprehend them. A minor scuffle developed.

"This area is off limits. You can't go upstairs," a bouncer said in a gruff tone. He was pushing back Nappy Head Don while the other bouncer kept Rude Bwoy Rex at bay.

"Easy, bwoy. If yuh wanna eat lead, just keep coming," Nappy Head Don said. His hand was already in his waist gripping at the pearl handle of his nine. Luckily Show, a few steps behind, caught up.

"Oh, I see y'all have met," Show said as he reached close enough to see that the men had squared off and were about to scrap. "Gentlemen, these are my associates and guests," Show said and both security men backed off. "We're gonna have a meeting upstairs. You may let 'em up. If there's any problem, I'll call you," Show said with a wink.

He was thoroughly pleased with the performance of his security. After the incident with Promise, it had been his idea to place the security team at the entrance of the stairs. They were different than all other security in that all their orders came directly from Show or Squeeze. Nappy Head Don and Rude Bwoy Rex climbed the stairs and went into the office.

"We done know that security tighter than ever up in this piece, Show. Wha happen, man?" Nappy Head Don asked.

"Yo, you ain't supposed to know but I guess I could tell you. Remember that nigga, Promise?"

"The question should be more like; 'How could I forget Promise?'"

"Yeah right, he being so popular and all," Show said sarcastically.

"Every time you turn on the TV, that nigga on some evening news, he on *America's Most Wanted*. He all over, world-wide."

"Yeah, that's why you here."

"What? You want me and me bredren fi go ketch Promise. Promise is your friend. Man, he's a hero to me. Every time I see him on the news and know the feds or the police can't find him, I feel good. I'm thinking he disappeared like him Bin Ladin. You done know, me nah help no Babylon. Babylon have fi bun and me nah trow no water pon da fire."

"Nah, nah you wrong, dread. I don't want you to help us catch Promise. I know this honey he was staying with after he robbed us. Her name is Candy."

"Candy, you mean that crack head bitch from Queens?" Nappy Head Don asked. Show stared in surprise. "You forgettin' we go way back to shorties?"

"Nah, I ain't forget nothin'," Show said smiling. "I'm surprised that you remember her so well from when she was crackin'."

"What, I used to be her numero uno supplier, Show. You done know."

"Yeah well, the only thing that she gets supplied with now is bible verses."

"She turn Christian?"

"Yeah, after she came outta rehab, she started walking around telling everyone that she's saved and that she don't need no man in her life because Jesus is her man. Da bitch moved out to Rochdale and been out there ever since. People say they ain't seen her with no more pipes but you know once a crack head, always a crack head."

"Yeah Candy, I man remember her," Nappy Head Don said. "She used to have long hair and pretty too. Lots a fat cats looked out for her. Now she's looking forward to going to heaven, huh?" Nappy Head Don asked.

"That bitch got information that I need and I know she knows cuz peeps out on Atlantic told me she been shopping at Fulton Mall. She was seen buying men's clothing and all that. And from what I know of her, she ain't never had no brothers or male cousins. Mostly everyone in her fam is female."

"Yeah, I know her. She comes from a long tribe of females, my bwoy. But you done know, them all pretty. She got some nice cousins and her aunt I still see buying ganja from me bredren dem out on the Ave."

"I ain't got no interest in that old head. I'm interested in what that bitch, Candy, knows. I need some answers and she's the only one who could provide them."

Show was pacing the office. He had poured himself a drink and was sipping as he listened to Nappy Head Don.

"That sounds easy enough. What kind of problems you having man?"

"Da bitch, cuz she thinks she knows me and feel I won't touch her, she won't tell me nothing. She's loyal to Promise. That nigga always has bitches like that around."

"That sounds true cuz I heard that it was his girlfriend and him who was robbing them banks and she held that man down for sometime," Nappy Head Don said. "That man lucky you know," he added as he glanced over at Rude Bwoy Rex.

Show watched him nodding in agreement and stared at Rex for there was something peculiar about his features. Show also noted that he had not heard him speak all evening.

"Y'all want sump'n to drink right?" Show asked.

"Yeah, man, make mine a Guinness." Nappy Head Don answered with a laugh.

"Done," Show replied and picked up a telephone. Without dialing, he spoke to someone directly at the bar. "And what will it be for your man?" Show asked holding the telephone and addressing Rude Bwoy Rex but Nappy Head Don answered instead.

"Same ting, man, same ting for him. Cho, a Guinness we a drink, yuh no done know, man?"

"Bring up four cold Guinness stouts," he said and set the phone back on the stand.

Before Show could pour another drink, a waitress had arrived with the four bottles and steins. She was about to pour the drinks for the men but Nappy Head Don stopped her.

"Daughter, I man don't drink from glass that other people used, yuh no know. So if that's not a new glass, my brethren and I prefer to drink ours straight from da bottle, yuh no see it?" Nappy Head Don was close enough to whisper in her ear but he shouted instead.

The waitress exited the area with an annoyed expression hanging on her face. The office door slammed and Show began laying out the strategy.

"Ahight, here's the plan. What we got to do is scare this lil' bitch and she will sing. Everything that we do and say right now is strictly between us. Nobody else knows about this, ahight?" Show said.

"Not even your man, Squeeze?" Nappy Head Don asked.

"Especially not my man, Squeeze. I don't want him to know nada, ahight?" Show asked looking at both. Nappy Head Don nodded while Rude Bwoy Rex transfixed his gaze on the door. "My man, you understand wha da fuck I'm sayin?" Show asked Rude Bwoy Rex directly. He gave no answer. "Don, your man speak or understand English? Or, is he just in the goofy category?" Show asked in an infuriated tone.

"Him alright, Show," Nappy Head Don said.

"What'd ya mean he's alright? Da nigga sittin' here with a fuckin' grin on his face since he got up in here, man. I been watchin' him. Sump'ns wrong with his muthafuckin' ass. He's crazy or sump'n?"

"Da man deaf and him can't articulate words," Nappy Head Don said looking at Rude Bwoy Rex. "Me no know yuh never knew all dat but him cool. I can take him anywhere and leave him. He gonna find his way back home," Nappy Head Don said and pointed to the bottle of Guinness sitting next to Rude Bwoy Rex. "Drink it," he said.

He again pointed to the bottle then put his hand to his mouth simulating taking a drink. Suddenly Rude Bwoy Rex picked up the bottle and gulped. Show shook his head and smiled.

"You responsible for him. Ahight, dread?" Show said before he outlined the plan.

Payment was arranged and the three toasted with drinks in their hands following the talks. Everything was set and according to the agreement, they were to meet the following day outside Candy's home in Rochdale.

"I'm going back to Jam-down soon as I lay my hands on that ten gees. It's a done deal. We'll meet up tomorrow 'bout two or so at the girl's crib."

"Nah, listen up, man. You not hearing me right, Rasta man. It's gotta be at two o' clock. That's when she's home and I got errands to run."

"Yeah, I done know you big timer now so just bring cash money, alright man?"

"Don't worry any. That's as good as done." Show shook hands with both, still eyeing Rude Bwoy Rex. He wore a cruel smile the whole time and hardly touched his Guinness. "Ahight y'all, thanks for coming through. Y'all welcome to stay and hang but I got a nightclub to run, feel me? I gotta go do…" Show started but Nappy Head Don cut him off.

"Cool, you know? We'll see you tomorrow bright and early in da afternoon."

They were about to disperse when Squeeze dressed in a full black suit made his way into the office.

"Okay, this must mean we going to war," he announced as he walked in. "Got the Raas claat natty dreads from Flatbush all up in here," he said as he walked then came to a stop in front of Nappy Head Don. They scrutinized each other as if they were about to touch gloves but instead they embraced and shook hands. "Yo, what's up, dreadlocks bombo-claat rasta man? I ain't seen your Jamaican ass in ages. How's biz on the Ave? Still pumping that raw?"

"Yankee bwoy, Squeeze, you done know how we do tings pon da Ave. I still running tings after all this time, my man. I still going strong, you looking like a million bucks. I haven't seen you at all. You made yourself scarce like a thousand dollar bill, my man. But I see you running tings on this end," Nappy Head Don laughed as he embraced Squeeze.

"You know what they say, boy; 'Once a hustler, always a hustler', baby. And I'm a keep it that way." Squeeze went to the mini bar and poured himself a drink.

"I was telling Show, you guys did it right, man. Left the streets, went legit and now look at all this. Y'all big-timing now, bwoy," Nappy Head Don said and raised his bottle in the air. "Continued success and such, you hear. All da best, man. When people do good that makes me feel good. You done know, a long time now me know you and Show hustling out on da streets. Now you bringing it indoors, that's all." Nappy Head Don took another swig of the Guinness.

"Yo, dreadlocks, I was about to say the same damn thing about you, man. You just beat me to the punch. What's da real?" Squeeze asked as he walked over to the desk and sat. Show moved to the sofa and parked there with a drink in hand. Squeeze busied himself looking at the mail left on the desk before addressing Show. "Yo Show, them cats got here already, dogs?"

"Yeah, they should be sitting over on the left side in the VIP section," Show said.

"That's all good. Did you send 'em complementary drinks?" Squeeze asked.

"Yep, that's all done. I have a waitress with them. They good," Show said.

"Bwoy, Show deh pon da job. That's the way to be," Nappy Head Don rejoined.

"No doubt," Show said.

"I got to make tracks and travel back to da spot," Nappy Head Don said.

"You're not gonna stay? I wanted to hear what y'all plotting to take over," Squeeze said.

"Nah, they were leaving when you walked in. You know a hustler's work is never done," Show said.

"I'll pass through and spend some more time. Right now me have to run, irie?" Nappy Head Don readied himself to leave.

"Ahight, ahight, Rastaman, be well, my man."

Still seated at the desk, Squeeze raised his glass. Show walked both men to the door and shook their hands.

"Me will definitely see you, Show. Later on." Nappy Head Don and his man Rude Bwoy Rex turned and left.

"Yo, take care o' yourself. Come through anytime, man. I'll see ya," Show said and closed the door as both the men went down the stairs.

"Them muthafuckas wanted dough, huh? Don't loan 'em no cash without interest, dogs," Squeeze said.

"C'mon, man, you know me - always wheeling and dealing. I ain't trying to spend no money if you can't do shit for it," Show said.

"Yeah, but them muthafuckin Jamaicans, they be quick to bust they guns and let off on a nigga. Don't be bringing they muthafuckin' asses up in here," Squeeze warned, sipped and continued. "Niggas see the club and immediately it's like: Damn, these niggas sitting on sump'n, sump'n. Niggas be scheming trying to rob a nigga."

"C'mon, Squeeze, ain't no body else jooksing us for our cheddar, dogs. Believe that!" Show shouted.

Squeeze listened and swallowed the remaining liquid in his glass. He rose and said, "Keep your game up, my nigga. Lemme go do some biz with these muthafuckas. Where they at?" he asked as he headed out the door then returned to the desk, removed the .45 from his waist and put it in the desk drawer.

"They in VIP. You can't miss 'em. They all dressed in suits sitting on the left side," Show said and heard his cell ringing. He ignored it until Squeeze spoke.

"Answer your phone, dogs."

"I know who it is," Show sounded annoyed.

"No one told your ass to push no baby up in dat bitch. I told you da bitch was problems. Now she ain't gonna let go of your ass." Squeeze watched as Show bit his lips. "Ain't no use being mad. You gotta own up to your problems."

"I'm gonna take a fucking vacation to the islands. Acapulco, Mexico, anywhere; just gonna go somewhere this bitch can't reach me and stay there until this bitch dies. I can't fuck with her on any level, I'm telling you, son."

"Yeah, nigga, back in the days when Pooh used to tell you she got problems, you wasn't trying hear him."

"Man, even you knew the bitch was banging then. But as soon as a nigga start flossing a lil' sump'n, da bitch brings her whole family in a nigga's biz. They be telling her don't give up da milk if the nigga don't wanna buy the cow and cramping a nigga's game. A nigga need pussy. It's only natural and when a nigga can afford to have three, four pieces o' ass, a nigga should live. You feel me?"

"Yeah, I hear you, dogs, but that's just the wrong fucking bitch for all that shit. She ain't going for all that bull. You're doing real well and she trying to lock your black ass down. You can forget about all the other pussy and just marry her."

"Oh lemme guess, you met with her on some secret shit or maybe you ran into her while you up in da mall with your wifey?"

"Man I ain't trying to hang with your problems, nigga. I ain't got time for trifling ho's."

"Oh, that's why you banging Denise?"

"Which Denise you talking 'bout, dogs?"

"Light skinned bow legged shortie with da fatty."

"The waitress?"

"Yes nigga, the same one."

"Oh yeah, I remember her. See, that's a bitch where a player like me took one look at that ass and knew I had to do my duty. I had to hit that. She had a walk that used to get my dick hard. Damn!"

"Yeah, that bitch was trifling. She took the liberty of drawin' all over your fuckin' P2K with a damn key."

"Yeah but that's after we fired that bitch but before that... Hmm, goddamn, she had sump'n to keep my dick hard all night. She could ride and work that ass."

"Don't forget the bitch was stealing from us. That was one trifling ho."

"Fuck her. She someone else's problem now. Meanwhile you pushed a baby in your bitch and she's still your problem." The cellphone rang again. "Answer the shit."

"I don't feel like talking to my baby ma. I'm a spaz on da bitch if I talk to her. She is too fucking annoying. She'll blow any nigga's high." The phone rang and rang then stopped and began again.

"I'm gonna answer the shit if you don't."

"I'm telling you, it's LaToya and I don't feel like speaking to her whining ass. Yo, I swear, ever since she had my son, I can't get her to stop whining," Show said as the phone continued ringing. "She's always fucking with a nigga's high asking shit like; 'When you gonna come home?' or ordering a nigga to do shit. 'Do this and when you finish, do that.' This bitch better leave me alone," Show said still ignoring the call.

"I think you better answer your phone, nigga, before she

start calling me and the bars and all the other phones in da club. You know how she do? Bitch crazy. She'll have security hunting for you." Squeeze laughed but Show didn't find the joke amusing.

"Man, I don't give a shit. Fuck that bitch!" On cue, the phone in the office started ringing off the hook. Squeeze was exasperated.

"Answer the damn phone," he yelled. Picking up the telephone, he screamed, "Hold on. He's right here," then walked out.

"Hello what's up? Bitch, didn't I tell you not to call me at work. I gotta make money so your dumb ass can go spend it at the mall with your girls. Where's ma daughter? You left her with your mother. Oh, so you out getting drunk? That's all you fucking do. I be home when I get there. I'm a…" Show screamed into the receiver and realized he was talking to a dial tone.

He slammed the phone down and lit a cigar. He paused to use the toilet before going downstairs where the party was heating up. Air vents blasting cold air could not cool the high temperature radiating from the dance floor. There were beautiful ladies moving their legs and in skirts high and tight. All the players were iced-out, popping Cristal trying to wet breasts and staring at rumps bumping. There were bikini top clad dancers sprinkling the floor.

The beautiful ones were wearing low rider jeans displaying ass tats and cracks easily visible through colored thongs. Name brand fashion hogs and slaves to the rhythm were belly-to-belly and back-to-back, dancing, laughing having fun shaking it out to the pulsing sounds coming from six thousand watts of power. It was on a Friday night up in *The Brooklyn Café*. The speaker system was so deafening, the mixes came uncomfortable and quick for even the most trained wallflower.

Show stood on the balcony, his eyes on the floor. From this angle, it appeared as if the building was moving along with the stomping crowd wall to wall on the dance floor. Things were ablaze in the packed club and the dance floor bursting at the seams was common for a Friday night crowd. Show calculated mentally that they stood to make somewhere in the heavy six figures from tonight's take.

There were plenty of big ballers in here tonight, he thought glancing at the crowded bars. Everything had turned out well. He took pride in knowing he had done his part in getting this jump-off popping. He also knew Squeeze saw that he could run the place and could trust him even more. Show wandered by the security at the bar and the rear doors. All was secure.

He moved back to the dance floor area hoping to spot the current object of his desire, the five foot six olive skinned younger sister of his man, Pooh. Maybe I can get at that right here on this crowded floor or slip up to the office with her. He was convinced she was ready for him as his eyes paned the floor. She should be fully tanked, he calculated while his eyes scanned the floor.

The moment Show spotted Lindsay, his eyes drifted like the beads of sweat running down her back, culminating at her waistline. With lust in his eyes, he snapped his fingers like a miner who had found gold. His vision was stuck and never rose above her waistline. He salivated as he noticed the way her movements seemed well coordinated.

Her rhythm hugged the beat. Shaking her ass, Lindsay flirted with her dance partner's head. A thrilling feeling rushed through Show making him get down and he was soon bopping, his toes twinkled and he broke out into cheerful dance, his body led by a hardened dick that was cocksure that this young pussy was going home with him.

If you feeling like a pimp nigga
gon brush your shoulders off
ladies is pimps too
gon brush your shoulders off

No sir, he can't handle that. This me right hurr, Show thought and found himself being dragged in by her swirling ass in motion. He looked her up and down, measuring her petite frame with desire in his eyes. He was damn near twice her size, he thought. Show was planning to break her off and turn her young ass out. He smiled as he approached her dancing figure.

Niggas is crazy baby
don't forget that boy told you
get that dirt off your shoulders
you gotta get that dirt off...

He invaded her zone and found disappointment when he saw his partner must have had the same thoughts because he was also making his way towards her. Show reached them just in time to see Squeeze's big hand hugging and feeling on her tender ass. Disillusioned, Show turned to walk away but Lindsay wasn't having it. She whirled and grabbed the dejected Show and leapt in his arms. He caught her easily with his big frame. Lindsay hugged his neck. She was inebriated and ready to party hard.

"Don't leave. We could all dance," she whispered.

He wanted to leave the couple alone but Show felt the softness of her moistened thighs resting firmly on his arm and he couldn't say no. He found his fingers being interlaced with hers and his body danced away with Lindsay's. All three sweated together for a little, the men taking turns to ride the young girl's ass. Show's disappointment quickly turned into enjoyment as he took delight in rubbing her ass with his crotch and playfully pinching her nipples when the opportunity arose.

He tried to talk to her and get her in private but Lindsay would dance away. His only displeasure was watching his partner pushing up on the young girl's ass. Show held on to the smile pasted on his face pretending that he felt nothing but deep down inside he wanted this girl. He always had but he had known she had a thing for Squeeze.

"Let's go up to the office and have some drinks," he suggested knowing that Squeeze would want to leave soon or ask him to close up. Show had done that before and complained about it but tonight he would volunteer for the duty but Lindsay threw a wrinkle in the mix.

"I've got to go now. I've got to go to work in the morning," she said.

"Got a little job, huh?" Squeeze said hugging her. "You could still come up. I'll make sure you get home safely,"

That muthafucka is so greedy, thought Show as Squeeze led Lindsay off the dance floor. For the first time, Show was happy to see Malik. Lindsay slipped out of Squeeze's embrace.

"Hey, Malik, I guess you're ready, uh?" Lindsay asked. The young man appeared groggy and was slow to answer so she kept on talking. "Malik, we were invited to see their office. This is Show."

"Yeah, I met Show earlier. Remember?"

"Oh, that's right. Well, this is Squeeze. These are my brother's partners. They're like street buddies and close as family. They used to do all kinds of wild stuff back in the days. Show was always trying to, you know…" Lindsay was trying to shout over the music and Show hoped that she didn't mention anything about her mother or the hand job she had given him.

He watched her carefully but the noise of the music kept drowning her out each time she started. Finally, she quit. Squeeze led them to the entrance of the nightclub and spoke to a bouncer. Show watched as the young girl swayed to music, her hips hypnotically pulling him into her like a fly in a spider's web, where every resisting motion brought you closer to the end. Show walked over when Lindsay waved goodnight.

Malik was walking in front to the cab hailed by the bouncer. Show jumped at the opportunity to slip his tongue down her throat as he escorted her stumbling, drunken frame to the cab. Malik seemed inebriated also but as soon Lindsay was in the cab, they were in a lip-lock position. They stayed that way as Show and the bouncer smiled and waved.

"Boss, do you think he gonna tear that up or what?"

"I don't know if he can handle all that thurr."

"You might be right. He might need some help. She's nice."

"Hell yeah."

"But there's always plenty dimes up in here," the bouncer said as they walked inside. "Oh by the way, boss, Squeeze said to meet him upstairs."

"Ahight, I'll see him in a minute. Lemme check out some o' these hotties out here. Damn, look at the one in the short denim skirt. That's her panties, right?"

"Nah, boss that's beach wear," said the bouncer.

"Man, no way that's no beach wear. That's some pink underwear," Show said as he walked away. "Beach wear, my ass," he said laughing. "Get me her name and telephone number, e-mail, or sump'n," Show called out after he experienced an eyeful of her rotund derriere in motion.

He stopped at the bar to get a drink before proceeding up the stairs. Inside, Squeeze was sitting at the desk talking on the telephone. He hung up and Show started talking.

"Yo, man, that kid that was with shortie…"

"Which shortie you talking 'bout? Pooh's little sis? She got a body on that. Banging, dogs. She grew up real nice. I'd love to hit that one time," he said throwing a pound. Show returned the handshake.

"No doubt, fo sho, fo sho," Show said.

"You probably trying to bag that, huh? You used to like that lil' bitch. I remember Pooh always warning you about his sis. She's a nine and a half," Squeeze said.

"Nah, she a straight dime piece, nigga." Show said.

"That's because you wanna fuck that bitch. I know you. Once you fuck her, the bitch ain't shit no more," Squeeze said.

"It's all good. I'm just passing pussy around, nigga. You could hit it. I ain't on it like that," Show lied.

"I think I might bring her on the boat on Sunday. You going sailing with us, right?" Squeeze asked.

"Hell yeah, muthafucka. You ain't the only one who's gonna be living Hollywood here, dogs. I'm down with that too. Yo, man, but homey that was with her tonight sez he's sure we killed the wrong people."

"What? What da fuck you saying, dogs? Start from the beginning, man," Squeeze said. He moved to the mini bar and came back with a bottle of Louis IV and two glasses. He sat down and poured two drinks. "Speak on that shit."

"Homeboy that came with Lindsay, he speaks Spanish and he overheard some cats that deal with his cousins saying how we foolish for killing the wrong guy and one o' them told his cousin that they merked Pooh cuz o' some jooks he did. Something about taking money and drugs off some bitch."

"Wait up. Pooh ain't jooks nobody. 'Specially no bitch. That nigga stayed with me and we always see that nigga unless it was when everyone was laying low. Everyone on da streets knew that Nine was responsible," Squeeze argued.

"That's what I thought until homey started saying some shit."

"Da nigga trying to get a rep with us, you know. Like he rolls with us cuz he messing with Pooh's physical."

"Could be true but it's worth taking a look at."

"Why don't we get him to make 'em admit to it or sump'n like that?"

"Hmm, yep. He said he was soldier."

"See, that's a dead give away that the lil' nigga is trying to have a rep in da street for knowing us."

"Then we'll put him to our initiation test. We'll have that lying ass muthafucka go make a deal with them and get them to talk about that shit."

"Ahight, if you feel like then we roll like that," Squeeze said when the door buzzer went off.

"Who's that? You ordered sump'n from downstairs?" Show asked as the door opened and two women walked in.

"Come on in," Squeeze said as he stood up to greet the two ladies.

From where he was standing next to the desk, Show could tell that they were two ugly ducklings. This nigga just don't know when to say no, Show thought. He noticed that immediately after sitting down, one of them was already making herself busy feeling all over Squeeze's fly. I hope he doesn't mention we'll do train on these ugly bitches, Show thought. Tipsy as I am, I would surely earl up in here.

"Show you did real good, nigga. You came and did what you said you were gonna do. I've got to tip my hat to that, dogs," said Squeeze pushing the first ugly duckling down to her knees.

She wrapped her thick lips around his dick and you could hear the sucking noise her mouth made while tightly clamped to Squeeze's shiny dick head. All that and I don't envy the brother, thought Show as he shook his head.

"Why you acting like I'm dumb or sump'n, nigga? I can handle the opening. It's a piece o' cake."

"That's all good and...aah...all but I'm saying, pour a drink and choose one o' these ho's," Squeeze said but Show racked his brain for an excuse to leave.

"Ah...I'm kinda tired of all this running around. You know how it is when you got to open up the place," Show said but Squeeze was not accepting any excuses.

"Yo, I'm a make sure you get some real ghetto love in tonight, ahight. We can run a trizan on these bi-yotches. You feel me, dogs? It's all good."

"I'm feeling you and all that but I gotta go see my baby ma. You know that bitch been blowing up the phones all night so you know you can close down and all that. I'll holla." Show said making his escape before duckling number two could get down.

He walked to the door as Squeeze reclined with both ducklings swarming all over his dick.

"Ah yess...you can fuck 'em in da ass. They don't care. Ain't that right, mami?" Squeeze asked when he felt lips invading his package. "Oh yes...easy. Don't make me come too fast now. Easy does it. Ahhh..."

"Yo, man, just do you and enjoy yourself," Show said holding up the peace sign. "I'll holla at you tomorrow."

Show looked back to see one of the ducklings getting ready

to squat on Squeeze's dick while the other continued to lick his balls. Show smiled when he saw his business partner making funny fuck faces. Show gave the okay sign and the door slammed. He raced to the stairs and made good his escape. Since Pooh's death I just can't fuck with no ugly-ass bitch. Show was thinking as he ran downstairs.

I'd rather go home and fuck with my baby ma, he thought as he whistled a sigh of relief and bounded down the steps. Safe at the exit, Show spent a few minutes glad-handing before glancing at his rollie. It was damn near five-thirty when he finally left the club. Show walked down the block and jumped in his Caddy and rolled out.

Tomorrow he'd find out what had been eating at Squeeze's ass besides the bitches he had just left upstairs. He listened to the radio and steered the car towards the Belt. There wasn't a lot of traffic at this time of the morning. It would be an easy fifteen-minute ride home to Queens, where hopefully, his baby ma would have carried her drunken ass to sleep.

It was around midday when Show woke. He had to squint since the shades were open and the sunlight was smacking him straight in his eyes. He got out of bed, slowly rubbing his back and headed to the bathroom. There was a lipstick note on the mirror. He smiled when he read it. Da bitch had gone shopping for her mother's birthday.

"Yes!" he shouted laughing and pissing. "It's a good day! Yes, I can feel it."

Show ran to the living room, turned the television to BET, turned up the volume on Usher's *Yeah* and started doing push-ups. He managed twenty reps.

Next, he did some bent leg sit-ups. He accomplished the same number of reps. Then stood breathing hard and flexed his body in the mirror. Even though the fat content was high, he smiled nevertheless, threw a kiss at the reflection, scratching his balls and heading to the shower.

Two o'clock on the dot, he was at Candy's Rochdale address. He parked the Caddy across the street, got out and walked slowly to the apartment building. He recognized Nappy Head Don and Rude Bwoy Rex. They were on time. He nodded and without saying a word, the three made their way up the stairs to the second floor apartment. Show knocked twice and the door was answered by a woman's voice.

"Who is it?"

"Candy, it's Show."

The three waited in silence as Candy wrestled with the door lock. She stood partially blocking the door, the safety chain still attached.

"What do you want? You came here before and tore up my place and you know there's no one here, okay." Candy sounded annoyed and Show thought for a beat.

"Look, I'm here to square that all away. I brought you some money to take care of all that damage, aight."

"Is your crazy friend, Squeeze, with you?" she asked when she saw him pull out and flash the Benjamins.

Candy hesitated before opening the door but the money was in plain view and it was Show. He was cool. Even Promise had said that Show was aight and that Squeeze was the one you couldn't trust.

The moment Candy let the safety chain off she knew she had miscalculated. It was too late to turn back and she ran when Rex and Don invaded her doorway. Show turned the radio volume higher as Rex jumped and tackled her, knocking her to the floor. He pinned her against the tile of the kitchen floor and quickly subdued her.

He bound her hands and feet using duct tape then he sealed

her mouth with a piece, preventing her from screaming. She was dressed as if she was about to leave. They were right on time. Once they had her subdued, they sat her in a chair. Show addressed the woman with the terrified look in her eyes.

"I'm not here to kill you. We go too far back. All I want to know is if you've seen my man, Promise. That's it? The only thing I'm gonna say is before you answer, you better pray that you're telling the truth cuz I know there's only one right answer to that question. You know it and I know it and if you don't give it, I'll introduce you to your killers." Show reached over and lit a cigar on the stove before he continued. "When I remove the tape, you better have the right answer waiting for me."

Show stared into the whites of Candy's terrified eyes and saw her tears. Through the tape, he could hear her sobbing hard and her breasts heaved with each movement. While staring at her face, he reached out and removed the tape. He waited for the sobbing to subside then all he heard was more. Show smacked her cheek.

"I'm not here to play any games, bitch!" Blood dripped from her busted lips. "The last time Squeeze was the one who wouldn't pop off up in here. Fuck around and I'll do you, bitch."

Nappy Head Don came in the kitchen and signaled to Show. He threw a pair of Sean Jean jeans and an Echo buttoned down shirt in the mix. "Shit's getting thick." Show was about to continue but Candy spoke.

"Okay so you're Mister bad man now. I don't know where Promise is…"

"That's not the question. The question is, was he here the last time I was here?"

"What're you talking about? The last time you came here with Squeeze, you searched the entire place right? You were here."

"I'm asking the muthafuckin' questions and bitch, you better answer right cuz your life depend on it. Was Promise here when Squeeze and me came looking for him? Yes or no, bitch, and say the right one." The television blared loudly as they all awaited the answer.

"Yes, he was. He was here and Squeeze knew. He was in the bathroom hiding behind the shower curtain. He said Squeeze came close to pulling the curtain but changed his mind at the last minute. He's not here now. I don't know where he went. Leave me the fuck alone. I didn't want to help him but he forced me to!"

Candy's loud sobs competed with the volume of the television. Show walked away wearing a frown as if he'd heard something terrible. Like bad news, he knew it wouldn't go away.

"What yuh want done now?" Nappy Head Don asked.

"Kill the bitch," Show commanded as he walked out. He could hear her pray.

Rude Bwoy Rex closed the windows and sealed the kitchen then he turned on the gas on the stove. The escaping hiss was evident. He used the still burning cigar that Show had and placed it in Candy's mouth before racing out the door. Candy sat mumbling the Lord's prayer as time drew close.

"...though I walk through the valley of the shadows of death I will no fear no evil for though art with me thy rod and thy staff comfort me thou prepares a table in the presence of mine enemies thou anoints my head with oil surely goodness and mercy shall follow me..."

Back out on the street, Show gave Nappy Head Don a wad of cash as they sat in the Caddy. Before Nappy Head Don could reach his car, a huge explosion occurred. The lower part of Candy's dismembered forearm with the first finger still attached landed directly on his roof. Show got outside and used a rag to carefully discard it. Tires screeched as he peeled out leaving a great cloud of smoke and fire coming from the second floor. He quickly found a car wash and eased back with a cigar as the car went through the wash cycle.

Show rode back through and the Caddy appeared as glossy as a newly painted car. He called the number to Misty's place. The phone rang and he was about to hang up, when he heard the voice. He didn't know if it was mother or daughter.

"Who dis?" Show inquired.

"Who you want it to be? You're calling my phone so who are you?" He could tell that it was the mother.

"Hey, Misty. What's good?" Show asked.

"Ain't nothing happening too tough around here, Show. How are you?"

"I'm good. Trying to see what's poppin' wid you, mami."

"Show, why don't you slide through? Ain't nobody here but me, baby."

"Ahight, I'll be there shortly." Show was close by and he had wanted to see the daughter but the mom could be an appetizer for the real meal. Show stopped at the liquor store and purchased the biggest bottle of Alize Bleu. Since it had done the trick the last time, he was sure this time would be no different. He was guaranteed to get some ass fo sho. He smiled as he rang the doorbell and she buzzed him up.

She greeted him with a moist kiss wearing nothing but a sheer tiny black negligee that sat on either side of her shoulders leaving nothing to hide. Her naked body was bathed in the sunlight as she licked her lips and watched him react. Show grinned from ear to ear when he saw her blocking the doorway.

Her wanton nakedness exposed tits and ass to his full view. His gaze went from her throat and wandered past her plump tits to her stomach and finally to her mound, cleanly shaved and completely exposed. Show walked into the living room with his dick achieving hardness in record time. Misty reached out and tugged eagerly at his whole package. Show wasn't looking for immediate gratification. She laughed loudly when he produced the bottle of Alize.

"Oh, you remembered. It's kinda strong but I liked it," she teased while massaging his third leg and keeping it at total rigidity. Show moaned and fell against the sofa.

"Ah, oh yes..."

He closed his eyes and heaved a great sigh as Misty slipped the condom on him, hoisted one leg over his body and went to town riding. Her bouncing ass cupped by Show's big hands spurred her to increase the tempo. Misty held her breath and rode. Show slid his hand all over her body when she started to perspire.

"Oh yeah!"

Her cry was guttural. She strained for release. Show opened his eyes and saw her mouth open but no sounds came. Her face ripped to shreds by veins popping out from all angles, she bucked and went completely wild. Show tried to calm her by holding her tightly but he too became caught in the moment as Misty continued her fierce ride to climax.

"Oh yeah!" He yelled, voice shaky.

She came back in an almost church-like singing voice, "Oh, yes, daddy, spank my ass. Oh yes!" Misty sung with wild abandon.

Show needed no further encouragement. He raised his knees causing her ass to bounce higher then as she descended, he smacked her. When she landed on top of his dick, he smacked her again. She galloped and her ass shook like Jelly. By the time she screamed, "I'm coming!"

Misty's behind was bruised. She fell off and Show mounted her doggy-style. He could see the marks his hands made as he penetrated her moistness with intentions to crush. Show slid easily in and out wondering why some people enjoy pain. He was deep in thoughts when Misty reached under and rubbed the lips of her pussy, her fingertips grazed his balls. Show felt the immediate build up. His body jerked as he moved faster and faster. Suddenly he exploded.

He awoke around five o' clock in the afternoon to the smell of fried chicken and the radio blasting. Show licked his lips when he saw Misty in the kitchen naked with an apron over the transparent negligee. She wiggled her butt as she stirred the chicken. He couldn't resist and tried to enter her from behind. Show slipped his index finger between her thighs but Misty was ready for him.

"Uh uh, mister, you've got to go soon. Don't you have nothing to do?" She asked, slipping away from his probing digit.

"Yeah, I wanna give some more of this," Show exclaimed and grabbed his crotch. Even though he was wearing boxers, she could see the size through the slit.

"Hmm," she said licking her lips then it was if she had a sudden change of desire. Misty pushed him away as he came closer. "Boy, can't you see I got to go get my hair did," she giggled sexily and worked her body free of Show's weak attempts at fondling.

"Damn, ma, give me some more o' that" Show pleaded persistently but to no avail. Misty held up the tongs she used to remove the chicken to dissuade Show from getting closer.

"I've got a hair appointment, boy. Go do sump'n else with that big dick. Damn, that shit made me sore," she said doing her best to keep Show off her.

He gave up when she set a couple pieces of fried chicken and biscuits made from scratch in front of him. The smell chilled him so he sat and devoured the food ravenously. Misty munched a piece and watched Show going at it.

"I guess you were hungry. You could help yourself to more if you like," she offered.

"Nah, I want some more of you. That's what I want. You dig?"

"Yeah I dig but when I wanted more, you fell asleep. You snooze, you lose, baby. Come back some other time. I gotta go to the beauty salon," Misty said as she walked away. From behind, Show watched her hips sashay from side to side.

"You don't need no beauty salon. You too fine as it is," Show said enchanted by her good looks and sex appeal.

"Oh you so sweet," Misty said and turned around and blew him a kiss.

She disappeared into the bathroom as Show helped himself

to a few more pieces of fried chicken. After getting dressed, he pulled out five bills and left it on her nightstand then Show hollered at her from outside the bathroom.

"Mami, I'm out," he said.

A few seconds later, the bathroom door swung open and Misty in housecoat walked Show to the front door. He tried to cop a feel when they paused at the doorway but Misty shooed him on his way. She walked back to bedroom and saw the money. She smiled thankful that he had left the money. Her eyes widened when she counted. There were five one-hundred dollar bills.

In the Caddy, Show pulled out his cell and dialed the number that Malik had given him. He heard a gruff voice on the other end greet him with a question.

"Who dis and how did you get ma muthafuckin' number?"

"Yo, is Malik home?"

"I'm saying, dogs, I don't know you from Adam, you feel me? I just can't be giving out info like that. You better tell me who da fuck you is or I'm a hang up on your ass, you heard?"

"Yo, chill man, no need for all that. Just tell Malik that Show trying to holla at him, aight?"

There was silence. Show looked at the phone and realized the call had dropped. He started to redial but saw he was in a no service zone. Show set the phone down and decided to roll over to the park. He could enjoy the day and play a game or two of basketball.

On any sunny Saturday afternoon, the outdoor courts were crowded but Show was popular with his six foot four frame. He was meaty which meant he had down-low presence on the blocks. Show prided himself for being able to dribble the basketball well for a big guy. Sometimes, due to his competitive nature, he went overboard in displaying this skill.

He was labeled a showoff but Show brought something else to the court. He did work banging bodies down low and getting rebounds then making put backs. He racked up double figures in points and boards. Show managed runs with different teams and played for couple hours.

"That's game," he said after hitting a turn around jump shot. "Y'all better go get Shaq and them cuz ain't none a y'all can guard me one on one. Go get da next five…Next!"

Show sent the man who was guarding him on the court to the store for juice and when he retuned, Show took the juice and wandered away.

Off the court, he sat on the curb catching his breath and sipping the Peach Snapple Iced Tea. He saw Squeeze and some peeps rolled up. The silver P2K Jag was spanking fresh with rims that glittered in the evening sun. Show's ego took a blow when he recognized the other face in the car. Squeeze pulled to a stop and Show left the edge of the court where he had been sitting and walked across the street.

All that time Show spent on the basketball court had afforded his mind some relaxation. He had almost forgotten about Squeeze and the episode at Candy's but seeing Squeeze pimping in the Jag really ticked him off. The day they thought they had caught up to Promise, Show remembered the look Squeeze went into the bathroom with and the one he wore when he returned.

The vision of what occurred in Candy's bathroom flashed and although he did not go inside the bathroom with Squeeze, he could tell the look of a coward's face. Show wanted to call Squeeze on it. He wanted to know what really happened inside the bathroom but today he refused to listen to his ego. By the time he reached the car, the feeling that haunted him dissipated.

"What's really hood, Squeeze?"

"Show, what's popping, my nigga?" The two embraced and shook each other's hands. "How long you been out ballin'?" Squeeze asked pointing to the courts.

"Oh I don't know. Couple hours, I guess," Show said dabbing at his head with a clean, white towel.

"Yeah, your ass is sweaty enough. Looks like you've been running a few games. Back up nigga before you mess up my icy whites."

"Where you headed, now? Somebody's barbecue?" Show asked cutting Squeeze bragging short and nodding to the passengers in the car before they walked a little distance from the car.

"Nigga, all you think about is food, huh?" Squeeze answered but he knew Show wanted to ask about the passenger.

He was sure that Show wanted to know where he was going in the car. Squeeze did not reveal this to Show until he brought it up.

"Why you ridin' round with honey and homey, man?"

Squeeze stared at Show, holding himself back from flipping. Instead, Squeeze responded casually.

"Oh them?" Not waiting for Show's response, he stated, "I just picked them up when they called me and say they wanted to see you. I figured you'd be out and about ballin' or sump'n so I rolled through. Yo, homey sez he could take you to the spot where these cats operate at."

"Word? Which cats?"

"Those cats he claimed shot Pooh."

"Oh, you talking 'bout those cats."

"Go with him and see what da fuck he's talking bout then we see if they responsible for Pooh's body or not. If we wanna bring these cats down then it's good that you seen the spot for self."

"You going too?"

"Nah, dogs, I got things to do and I might be able to bone shortie while homey's with you. She's been trying to ditch him for over an hour now, dogs. He straight cock blocking, ya heard me!" Squeeze laughed at the revelation.

Show glanced at Lindsay sitting in the car. Malik was preoccupied with the basketball game in progress so he didn't see them scheming. Show figured if Squeeze hit Lindsay, she'd be the prettiest piece of ass he'd ever had in his entire life. It might bring some class to the coward ass nigga. Show listened as Squeeze continued his boast.

"Yeah, I went to Footlocker and spent about a gee up in da

joint. Bought honey some lunch and all but homeboy will not go. He's running up like it's nice to meet a real OG and all that cartoon bullshit."

"Word? That's all cartoon shit for you, right?"

"I'm saying, a nigga ain't got to suck me to get a rep, dogs. Fuck all that. I did ma thing back in da days, dogs. Now you wanna impress my ass? Go out there and do the deed then come holla atcha boy. Feel me? That nigga favors Pooh like a muthafucka. The shit's nuts. I be catching myself before I say, 'Yo Pooh'."

"Yeah, I feel you." Show laughed then they both laughed as Show spoke, "You know kids, they kinda, you know…impressionable. Always looking for some type o' hero, you know, someone to look up to and all." Show looked away as he continued speaking. "Some people ain't man enough to admit to their faults, you feel me? I'll roll with the kid. I'll get him outta y'all's hair. That way, y'all could go do your thing," Show said with a wry smile on his face.

"Ahight my nigga, that's what I really wanted to hear." Show and Squeeze walked back to the car. "Yo Malik, my man, ride with Show. You can let this nigga see where them cats operate from. Show, holla at me later, ahight. I'm a drop honey home," Squeeze said and got into the car.

Malik pecked his girl on the cheek and got out of the car. He watched Squeeze pull off, big pimping with his girlfriend. Show nodded and shook Malik's hand then walked with him to the Escalade.

"You ball here all the time?" Malik asked when he was inside.

Show glanced at the court thinking that homey was just a kid and had no idea or didn't care that Lindsay was gonna be up in some short stay motel having pipes laid in her in a matter of minutes. Squeeze wouldn't have picked her up from work and impressed her by spending a grand in Footlocker. A grand buying what? Sneaks and lunch? Show knew his childhood buddy and knew for certain he was tricking on Lindsay.

"Yeah, every now and then," he smiled answering as he

checked the rearview then gunning the engine. "Yo, I'm a go through that Wendy's drive thru up ahead, ahight?"

"That works for me. I had a long day at work. I'll get a lil' sump'n too," Malik answered.

"Ahight, I gotcha, kid. It's on me."

"Good looking out, Show. You mad cool."

They sat eating burgers and fries then chased down their lunch with Cokes and a cigar. From the way homey was stuffing his face, Show realized that Squeeze probably didn't buy him any lunch.

"You smoke weed, kid?" Show asked and pulled out a bag of Haze and rolled up something. Malik took time from eating and smiled then answered.

"Yeah, daddy, I be smoking that haze and dro."

"Ain't nothing wrong with that at all."

"I know but my uncle he be bugging the fuck out. Like I got my own job, I go to school. I graduate next summer on time. But because he caught me smoking weed, he be getting mad and telling me I gotta go to church. Can't nobody make you do nothing you don't wanna do."

"See but your father…"

"He ain't my father. My father's dead."

"Your uncle, he just think he's doing the right thing when he does shit like that. You gotta understand, shit goes wrong and the police coming to see him. He just trying to look out." Show sparked the blunt. "In the end, it's gonna be up to you. He's just doing whatever he can to prevent you from ending up dead or locked up."

"I'm sayin', I'm not out there doing nothing to go to jail. I know kids who be banging and they parents don't even know. They carrying burners and toasts to school and they parents don't even suspect a thing."

"Listen, you can't always look at what's going on with the next man. The only person you should be concerned about is you. Out here on the streets, nobody gives a fuck about you. They just know that you can do sump'n for them. They will use up until you're finished."

"Tell me, do you think that Lindsay loves me. I mean, her brother hung with y'all and she sorta thinks I'm like her brother and she expecting me to be big time but all I got is a sales job at Footlocker. I ain't nobody."

"Here, smoke some o' this," Show said as he passed the Dutch. "Learn one thing first, don't ever let anyone put you down and tell you that you're not somebody. You have dreams, right?"

"I do."

"Your dreams and the next man dreams are not the same. That's what keeps you going, kid."

"Word?"

"Word up, kid. It's that real. If your girl wants you to be somebody else, you could change for her or say fuck that stankin' bitch. She ain't for you cuz she has you but be wanting someone else. You just gotta let a ho be ho."

"That's the real. I ain't have no one break it down like that there but you Show."

Malik was overwhelmed with the advice passed on by Show. He gave Show a pound and sat back, blunt smoke streaming from his nostrils.

Later, Show cruised up and down the block before finally settling into a comfortable parking space. He could watch the operation of the weed spot without them being any wiser. He sipped on his Coke as traffic was heavy in and out of the small gift shop that doubled as a weed house.

"Things seem to be bubbling in thurr."

"Oh yeah, they be making mad cheddar."

"They got a lively customer flow going in and out real fast. You ever cop from them?" Show asked without removing his gaze from the storefront.

"Yeah."

"Ahight, good. Go in there and get me a fitty sack. Let me see what they working with," Show said and gave Malik a buck.

The teen jumped out the Escalade and raced across the street. He disappeared inside the weed spot as Show kept vigilante watch. Show removed the Nine Millimeter from its cache and sat it on his lap. The whole scene reminded him of when he used to rob stores like these for their drugs. Malik was the dead resemblance of Pooh. Show cocked the automatic weapon and checked the magazine. He took it off safe and reminisced about when Squeeze used to plan heists that brought down dealers and then they'd share great cash.

Pooh and him would sit in the car while Squeeze and Promise would case the joint. Even though the robberies usually went down without a hitch, Pooh was really shook the first time they went on a score. As the years went by, the crew got better and better at doing them until robbing dealers became child's play. That was all behind them and over the years, the stakes got higher. Both he and Squeeze had pulled themselves up from the gutter and were at the top of their game in the club world. Everywhere you went, people spoke respectably of the *The Brooklyn Café*. It was like gravy for soul food. You couldn't lick your lips until you had some.

Every time they went for a fresh cut at Nelson's barbershop, they catch up on all the gossip. Like the one about Promise, he was still on the run from the feds and every cop from New York to Virginia wanted him. Promise had breezed through about a month ago and pulled a heist at gunpoint in the club. He robbed his friends then instantly became a most wanted man to Show and Squeeze.

Show couldn't stand when Squeeze bragged about being a gangsta sweated by teens on the streets. He believed that all that was gangsta in Squeeze faded when he found Promise hiding in the bathroom at Candy's. Back at the barbershop he had stared at his homey's reflection in the mirror as Nelson's shears passed smoothly over his dome. Their eyes met and they held each other's stare. Show was convinced that Squeeze had to have seen Promise.

Show fixed his gaze on the reason why he was sitting, casing a weed spot with no intentions of robbing it. The answer was simple. Pooh lay rotting six feet under and Squeeze and him had hunted down Nine and shot him full of holes. Now Show was facing a grim possibility, he could've murdered the wrong man.

If this kid is right, these cats weren't just gonna be robbed, they were gonna be put out of business for good. But if he's wrong, I hope he's wrong, Show thought. Minutes later, Malik came out of the store and walked down the block before crossing the street. He got in the Caddy and pulled out the fifty dollar glass vial filled with 'dro. Show unscrewed the cap and sniffed. He smiled and gave Malik a pound.

"You did good, Malik. You did real good," Show said.

"I'm a soldier. I thought I told you before, Show. Whenever y'all ready to ride, you can count on me to be down, ahight." He gave Show a pound.

"That's good to know."

Under the setting sun of a warm summer day, Show drove Malik to Red Hook. When he reached the projects, he winked and they shook hands. Show stopped at the corner store to get a Dutch Master then sat and rolled a blunt from the vial that Malik had bought. He never saw Malik's cousins watching as he dropped the teen off or grilling him as he sat rolling. Show dipped back in traffic and drove around idly listening to the radio. He heard his favorite Nas classic and hummed along.

> ...It's mine, it's mine, its mine, whose world is this?
> The world is yours, the world is yours, the world is
> yours...

Show pulled into his garage, music banging, still puffing on a blunt.

> The world is yours the world is yours whose world is
> this...it's mine its mine it's mine...

He got out the car and walked inside the elevator feeling lifted. That weed was chronic, he thought pressing the seventh floor. He walked into the three bedroom apartment he shared with his year old son, Jay, and the mother, LaToya. Neither was home and Show jumped and hollered like he just made another quarterback sack. He grabbed the remote and found ESPN, snatched a beer from the refrigerator, kicked off his Nikes and settled into the plush comfort of the sofa.

In between highlights and sports scores, Show watched the college games. He followed his favorite teams, Notre Dame and Penn, religiously except when LaToya was home. Then he would just leave to avoid hearing her whine. The telephone rang once, twice, three times, and finally Show picked up.

"Hello," he barked into the receiver. Although the reception was not too good, he could identify LaToya's voice. He saw that his cellphone had messages. Probably LaToya, he thought as he listened. "You won't be home until later? Later when? Remember I've got to go open up this weekend at the club." He listened while the sports highlights and commercials were on but the moment the camera cut back to the game, Show yelled into the phone. "Ahight, enjoy your day shopping. Make sure you don't spend all my money, you hear. Say hi to your sisters for me. Got to go. Bye."

That bitch be always doing her hair and nails, trying to spend up all my dough. Fuck it! She's always finding a way to bother me, he thought. Show immediately switched his focus back to the college game where the announcer stated that Penn was down by a touchdown.

"C'mon, if I was playing, that quarterback would be in the mud. His uniform would be dirty...Man, they would have the back-up quarterback in already cuz I'd kill the starter... He's got too much time to sit back in the pocket. Someone better sack him or pick him off ...Do sump'n. Damn! You guys are Penn. You wear the blue. C'mon, make a play already...,"

Somewhere before the halftime whistle, he finally got his wish as Penn's defensive back went up and intercepted a pass. He ran it all the way back and Show went with him for the run and the resulting celebration. He danced around as if he was in the end zone celebrating with the rest of the team. Show was a prospect in high school when his ferocious pass-rush had disrupted the quarterback's timing causing the pass to be released too early. Now all Show could do was pretend to motion to his defensive back downfield to get the ball. After the interception, Show saw himself leveling the quarterback and having the opposition writhing in pain. He and his teammates were dancing going to the half. Momentum swung in his favor.

But real life hadn't ended quite like that. Show played high school football for three years and he was a sure thing for college. Many Division One programs were interested in him including Notre Dame, Penn, and the University of Wisconsin but Show had ruined his knee. After being scoped twice, once as a junior in high school and the other before graduation, no college scout would come close or even talk with him. He sadly lacked the academic grades it took to enter college without sports. Show joined the street hustle and after being busted twice before receiving his high school diploma, he hit a third and served a year in jail. After that, his football career was overlooked. Once the jury sacked him with the twelve-month sentence, he never really recovered.

I could've been a star in this league, he thought as his thoughts drifted back to game at hand and reality struck when he heard the broadcasters discussing his brief career.

"…Yes, siree, it's another fine day of football. A great day but not for Penn who is being hammered by the surprising tenacity of the Pittsburgh offense…Ah I think there's a gaping weakness in the Penn defense. They're in need of a strong linebacker presence…"

"Such as the once fast and furious Dashuan Grant AKA Show. The much sought after prospect so much for his potential. Wonder what he's into. Certainly not football, ha, ha, ha…"

"He had too many run-ins with the law. What a wash-out. A major loss to the college sports world."

"Certainly had a great future but…and Pitt has scored once more and will attempt the extra point…"

"These muthafuckin' reporters don't know me that well to be riding my dick. These muthafuckas know they can't fuck with me. I'm da muthafuckin' best!" Show caught himself screaming and decided to roll himself a blunt.

"Urrh-body wanna dawg Show. Even ma muthafuckin' partner. He still don't believe I could hold shit down."

Show was getting angrier and searched the bathroom medicine cabinet for some coke. He found some tucked away and proceeded to lace the weed. This cocktail should set me right, he thought. Muthafuckas' fucking with my equilibrium. He snorted some and laced the Dutch Master. He lit up and continued watching the television.

After awhile, Show was seething with anger. A mediocre team was hammering one of his favorite teams, a team that he could've easily represented, with an average quarterback. Show sat thinking that he would've somehow come out of this showdown with at least three sacks already in his pocket.

"Remember this," he said shouting angrily at the television. "No one could guard me then and they still can't, even fuckin' now. Fuck y'all! Y'all can't see me," Show screamed and rubbed his tummy. "Man, I'm eating well."

He pulled the shirt over his head and walked to the bathroom. He stood examining himself carefully in front of a full-length mirror. Then he sat on the throne before he showered. Later, as he was getting dressed, the phone rang. He let it ring and picked up just on fifth ring.

"What up?" He shouted. There was no answer. Show slammed the telephone down and continued to dress. Tonight, he would wear the all black Armani suit. It worked for Squeeze's ugly ass last night. Maybe tonight it would do the trick for him, Show figured.

Nightfall had descended on the city as Show lit a cigar and pushed the Caddy to a stop in front of the club. Perfect, he thought. He had managed to beat the Saturday night crowd and found terrific parking. Show walked to the entrance and attempted to enter. Three well-dressed individuals, two males and a female met him. They identified themselves as federal officers and walked upstairs with Show.

"Should I call my attorney? I've told you guys over and over again, Promise hasn't been around and he's..." Show started to speak as soon as they began ascending the stairs, however, an agent interrupted him before they reached the top.

"Listen Mr. Big Shot, we know for a fact that you've seen him and that he robbed you. You found where he was holding up. Then you went there and killed the girl. Now, we want to know where he is. That's the information we want."

Show was taken by surprise and struggled to find something to say. "Huh? What da fuck? You guys been reading too much o' that street lit. It's filling your heads with garbage, nah mean? I'm saying those shits turning y'all into fucking idiots. Man, I ain't killed no one so you better come with some real charges or drop the bullshit when you close the door behind you."

"You killed Candice Thomas or had something to do with her death. I'm sure if we go hunting down on the island of Jamaica, we can find us at least one witness to the fact."

Show walked over to the desk and sat without trying to be nervous about these accusations. These are the feds. If they were so amped about these allegations, I wouldn't be standing here. I'd been looking for bail so what was the deal? Show glanced around the office and saw that none of the officers were seated.

"So what d'ya want?"

The same officer walked over and pulled out a typed letter. He placed it on the desk and said, "We want Promise. This piece of paper contains information that could add Candy's body to a long list of bodies that he will be charged with when we find him. All you have to do is to cooperate. Give us the information she exchanged with you before she died and then sign your name to the bottom of the paper."

Show thought for a moment. These were the feds and he was from the streets. He knew he couldn't trust them.

"And if I don't? What then?"

The federal agent who had been speaking the whole time moved closer to Show's grill. "Then all the information we have on the murder of Candice Thomas also known as Candy will be turned over to the NYPD and you'll be arrested and go to jail for murder. The case is air tight."

"Can I think about this one?" Show asked. The heads all shook and he knew he had to make a decision. He picked up the form. It was neatly typed. He perused it. Most of it had Promise's name all over it. The female agent spoke.

"It's basically saying that you saw Promise in the last couple days and he killed his ex-girlfriend because she was about to inform on him. It's that simple."

"Ahight, if it's that simple then come back later and get this. I'll have it signed. I need time to digest it all."

"We'll be back in a couple hours. Have it signed by then."

Show watched them file out. He waited a couple a minutes before he opened the rest of the Club. Show ran down the stairs to the phone in the bodega on the corner. He dropped his quarter and dialed rapidly.

"Yo Sean-Do, what's good?"

"Show, what's up my dude?"

"I'm under pressure, my man. I'm calling from the store on the corner."

"What's the problem? You forgot the code to disable the alarm?"

"Yeah, yeah, it's the alarm system. Come down to the club right away."

"It's gonna take some real dough to make me."

"I got twenty grand for ya. How's that?"

"Twenty-five and I'm on my way."

Show bit the tip off a cigar and lit it as he walked back to the club. He puffed as the neon lights flashed but Show was not feeling right. He felt the feds had bugged the office and now he was sure they did. There was no other way to link him to the Candy incident. He walked around the club checking the security. Maybe the feds got these guys in their pockets, Show wondered as he drifted past them.

There were no more running jokes between them.

Tonight, Show was all business. He even rotated the guards at the foot at the stairway before Sean-Do arrived. Upstairs in the office, he checked the security monitors non-stop. Those bouncers are up to sump'n, I'll find out, he thought. The office bell sounded and Sean-Do walked in.

"What up, Big Show?"

"Sean-Do, tell me what's good?"

"Same ol'...Yo, can I go to work right away?"

"I gotta tell you about outside." Show said. He grabbed Sean-Do by the arm and went downstairs. They spoke and Sean-Do went back upstairs solo. He swept the office and disabled all the bugs then invited Show back upstairs.

"Pay me brother, I gotta go," Sean-Do said.

"Maybe you should check my place too," Show said as an afterthought.

"Maybe I should do it right away."

"What, you leaving without a drink?" Show asked. When Sean nodded, Show added, "Ahight, knock yourself out."

"I best do it right away because I got this fine chick coming later and I already stood her up once so there is no more room for error. I got to treat her right."

Show knew Sean-Do since high school. He was the smartest guy in computers he's ever known. Sean-Do made it through stealing credit cards. He did hundreds a year, siphoning off millions in goods and cash. He was a true baller. Sean-Do had wired the club's security system and made the whole thing computerized. He had also warned the partners that because of the feds' interest in Promise, they might bug the place. He had offered to sweep the place periodically for couple thousands a week. Now it was desperation time since the feds were one up on them and after finding the source, he was ready to leave.

"You were bugged, my dude," he announced with raised eyebrows. "But my dude, I located all of them and deactivated all of them. Now I'm gonna switch them. Here's the trick," he said and Show's ears perked. "I have this program which can put them to sleep with a western or turn them on with porn."

"Yeah, turn 'em on with porn. Do it, Sean-Do. Give these assholes some real sex."

"It's a done thing," Sean-Do said. He opened the laptop and punched in some numbers then closed it and smiled. "They'll be very happy tonight and mad tomorrow once they find out."

"Fuck 'em if they can't take a joke," Show said.

"Do you want me to run a check on your crib for you tonight?" Sean-Do asked.

Show put an envelope in his hand and Sean-Do counted his fee of twenty-five thousand dollars.

"Yeah, man, sweep it for bugs and clear 'em all out for me," Show smiled.

"Ahight, my dude, give me the address and leave the rest up to me. By the way, give me your cellphone."

Sean-Do took the instrument apart, checked it and put back together before returning it.

"Is the cellie good?"

"So far it looks real clean."

"Ahight then. Take care o' my crib. My girl should be home. I'll get on the horn and holla and let her know you're coming through to check the alarm, ahight? Good lookin', my nigga." Show embraced a well-dressed nine to five looking man. He was about to walk out the office, and saw the forms federal agents had left. "Yo Sean-Do, just double check this for me. I know that it's dealing with Promise and all but them feds, they be tricky so lemme get another opinion. Read this and tell me exactly what it says." Show gave the forms to Sean-Do. He glanced at the paper and immediately announced:

"I better take that drink you offered me, Show."

He left Sean-Do reading the forms. Show brought V.S.O.P. Sean-Do took the drink and sipped. He continued reading with a wry smile spreading slowly across his face. Finally, he spoke, "This is a prepared statement saying that you've seen Promise and that he's your friend. It also says he was involved in the murder of some chick and you know he did it. The important thing is, they can call you in and make you a witness against him. That's what it says down here at the bottom."

"Ain't that the same thing I'm saying?"

"Yep, you got it. You've got to watch these feds. They can be very slick. They probably have you recorded saying something or they could be bluffing," Sean-Do said finishing off his drink.

"Yeah, yeah, no doubt," Show checked the time on his watch. "But they be listening and watching porn for a minute, right?"

"Huh uh, at least until they check it."

"Tell me how they be able to do that?"

"What? Do you mean re-install another or update the system?"

"Yeah, you know what I mean, how can they come fucking re-install another one o' them bugs or sump'n. How da fuck could they do that?"

"They could send any ah...telephone maintenance or electrical types. They come in here and have access to your system. It's really easy for them to watch you. They can install cameras at different angles just like you're doing here."

"You mean they paying niggas like you to do shit like that, right? That's that shit they taught you when you were in the Navy, man?" Show asked.

"Show, the shit is not that difficult. Any kid with a computer can take over your security system and bypass it, get in your account, do anything they want to. The computer age has made all things possible." Sean-Do looked at the security monitor and then at the worried frown on the forehead of Show. "You ain't got a damn thing to worry about, my man. That's why you fucks with me, I made everything good."

"That's the reason I paid your ass that kinda money," Show laughed. "What...Twenty-five thousand? Now that ain't bad for a couple hours on a Saturday night huh?"

"Yeah, it feels good but you're also getting your apartments dusted off. Both places right?" Sean-Do asked.

"Yeah, but you gotta come by like next Wednesday or sump'n and I'll be able to do the other place, ahight? Right now my girl and my seed should be at the place out in Queens."

"You can tell when people gets large. They start having different homes in different Boroughs," Sean-Do said with a wink. He was leaving and Show gave him a pound.

"I got one in Queens for the fam and the stash pad out in Prospect. That's it. What?"

"Ain't nothing wrong, playa. Be easy," Sean-Do closed the office door leaving Show in a whirl of thoughts. Fucking feds always trying to bring the black man down on bullshit, he concluded and walked across to the mini bar.

Show poured himself a drink and phoned his home in Queens. No answer. Quickly deciding to call back, he nonchalantly leaned and became engrossed in the security monitors while sipping Hen. The bouncers were all in their places. The only thing to do was to open the bar. Show could see the queue of club heads beginning to form outside on the street.

Saturday night crowd wasn't rowdy and upscale attire was required for entrance to tonight's party. Unlike the Friday night crowd, he smiled knowing, it was one of those nights when you wouldn't be let in if you were ghetto.

No T-shirt or jeans and Timberlands with the bubble gum soles allowed. Snakes and Gators yes. For the gentlemen, a suit wasn't a must but if you were wearing any type of jeans, the bouncers knew well to tell you to move. Any static and they would throw you off the line.

If you were thinking about *The Brooklyn Café* on a Saturday night, you were warned to stay in the hood if you weren't dressed right. Tonight unlike Friday night, Gucci, S. Carter or G-Unit sneaks weren't getting you inside. Don't even think of bringing any type of weaponry because you'd be banned from ever coming back. All week prior the partners advertised on the radio.

Show felt the loud music pumping through the club, vibrating the place. The revelers were all outside and this allowed the sound to reverberate and freely echo from the walls. *Stunt 101* featuring G-Unit set the atmosphere.

This would be a heavy spending party. Show got on the horn and called the bar. He went to the safe located behind the Malcolm X poster. 'By Any Means Necessary', it read. Show inserted the special codes and took out a bulk of money and closed the safe. He quickly counted ten thousand dollars then Show separated it into piles of Jackson's, Hamilton's, Lincolns and Washington's. Minutes afterward, a cute looking waitress with a perfect fatty walked in.

"Hi boss," she said. "I brought you sump'n special from the bar." She smiled took empty glasses and the money on a tray and was about to leave when Show stopped her.

"Sanya is your name, right? How long have you been working here?" Show asked. He was unsure why but felt that he had to start being careful with everyone coming into the office.

"You mean total time working here?" She asked incredulously. She remembered that the only time Show or Squeeze paid any attention to her was when they wanted ass. She wondered if this was a new pick-up line. She decided to play along. "Why you wanna give me a raise, huh?" she asked batting her eyes cutely.

"Just answer the question, bitch! Why I gotta explain urrhthang to your ass." Show surprised himself by the blow up. He saw her smile changed to frown before she answered.

"I been here six months so far but if you keep yelling at me, it won't be longer."

"What? You threatening me, bitch? You fired. Don't nobody threaten me in my own club! You work for me! I am signing your fucking check, bitch."

"Well, in that case I'm supposed to get two weeks pay if you're firing me!" she screamed at Show. He reached into the pile and pulled out a wad. He rapidly counted the six hundred dollars, three hundred a week, and threw the money at her. She whimpered and looked at him with total disbelief registered on her face. "You bastard! I don't deserve this," she cried as she got on her knees and picked up her two weeks pay.

She sashayed out and slammed the office door. Show stood still not moving for a heartbeat then he poured another drink and prepared a cigar to be lit.

"Stupid fucking, trick ass bitch! Don't you know I'm da boss," he said aloud then checked his gun and walked out the office door with seven stacks of bills on top of the tray.

Show puffed as he walked by the security guards posted at the foot of the stage. He had known these cats from the hood but one couldn't be sure. No one could be trusted. The feds will penetrate the weakest link, he thought. His stroll ended at the fourth bar.

He glanced around and an uneasy feeling of seeing all the employees as potential FBI informers enveloped his mind. It was unnerving but Show held his anger inside and did his job. The feeling persisted like the wrong song trapped in your mind. He tried as hard as he could to forget about it but couldn't be free of the unrelenting loop.

He was finished making his rounds, and Show went outside to scout the party revelers waiting on queue. He bit another cigar and sparked it as he watched the line move. Show called the bouncers together and said, "I know this is Saturday Night crowd but make sure all ID's get checked and every single body and all bags get searched. Keep a sharp watch for the neighborhood crack dealers."

He walked around checking for undesirable drug dealers. So far, there were none in sight so far. But like hustlers, they were persistent and would reappear in another skin, another form. Like the next lethal drug, you can never truly get rid of them. Show just hoped to contain the drug dealing and using to the VIP section.

It was Show's job to identify the unwanted crack heads and dealers and get them away from the queue. He knew that once inside, they were liable to multiply like roaches. Pretty soon, the whole café would be just another crack colony. I ain't having that, Show thought as he continued to walk the length. The line was getting longer by the minute.

From outside, Show spotted Squeeze with Lindsay, his new flame, on his arm. I can't believe she's still hanging with that ugly ass nigga. Bitch gotta be gold-digging. She wasn't gonna get nothing here for free. She made Squeeze her main thing, even dropped homeboy she came in with the first time. Show's mind was on overdrive as he strolled to the front of the club. The couple had already passed through the velvet rope. Show paused briefly to throw his cigar away then went inside the buzzing nightclub.

He scrutinized the security at the bottom of the stairwell. "I pay y'all to work not to look at bitches' asses all night long," Show remarked sounding frustrated as he went by some bouncers.

Ego bruised and with a heavy heart, Show dragged himself upstairs to the office. To make matters worse, he walked in when Squeeze's tongue was down Lindsay's receptive throat. Show frowned when he saw them making out with wild abandon. They were loud and ugly.

"Huh hem," he coughed clearing his throat.

"Show, what's good, dogs?" Squeeze asked revealing pearly whites that made Show clench his fist as if he was ready to throw a punch.

"Y'all need dough for a room or sump'n?"

"If we needed that, Squeeze, could easily afford it," Lindsay smiled and teased. They had been sitting at the desk and Lindsay in his lap. She sprang up as she continued. "Furthermore, you should knock when you enter someone's office."

"Someone's office? This place's mines and Squeeze's. What you know 'bout that?"

"I know that you work for Squeeze and he's the boss so therefore this office belongs to him."

Lindsay looked pleased breaking the news to Show. It was

straight off the presses and very new to him. He looked confused as to what to say.

"Huh what?" he muttered then he looked at Squeeze. "What da fuck is this lil' bitch talking bout, Squeeze?"

"Lindsay, why don't you go downstairs for a drink and I'll see you in VIP, ahight."

She kissed him on the lips and strutted out the door. Show waited until it was closed before he began.

"Man, have you been filling this bitch head up with some nonsense. Gassing the bitch up or what?"

"Nah, it ain't like that," Squeeze assured his partner. "We were on this Riverama joint. That boat is ridiculous, dogs. It easily costs about a mill, son. You know me and them peeps from Key West? We balling. Them muthafuckas are big Williams's, ahight. So when they scope me and the shortie together, I had to give shortie the story of how I owned the club and you work for me so I could look real good. They muthafuckin' potential investors. And I knew she'd run her mouth and they'd be curious. Real connections, I'm telling you Show. I know shortie would be busy running her mouth there but I ain't know she would bring that back with her here. But it's all-good. Ain't nothing change." Squeeze gave the still shocked Show a pound and he barely saw it to return it. "You gonna leave me hanging, dogs?" Squeeze asked with his arm still extended. Show knocked his still balled up fist against his business partner's. "How're things going?" Squeeze asked. After pouring a drink, he poured Show a glass before he heard the answer.

"Yo, the feds infiltrated us. While you showing out with that bitch, the feds got to us. They got peoples planted. They got the phones tapped…"

"You ain't call your man from the BX?"

"Who that? Sean-Do? Nigga, I already took care o' all that."

"Ahight, so what they saying?"

"Them muthafuckas left some paperwork and shit saying that we saw Promise…"

"I thought I told you don't ever mention that muthafuckas name around me, dogs." Squeeze shouted and Show paused taking a breath.

"Squeeze, why can't I mention that nigga's name, dogs?"

"Cuz that nigga is a snake, you understand?" Squeeze swallowed as he said so and slammed the glass against the table.

"Ahight, ahight then if he's a snake, why don't' you rat him out?" Show retrieved the type sheet left by the feds.

"That ain't my steez, cuz. I don't trust the feds but I don't see no federal agents robbing me after knowing me and coming up with me all my life. Here, give me that shit. That nigga robbed us. That nigga should go to jail or sump'n. I ain't in his corner no more, dogs."

Squeeze looked at the typed form letter, picked up a pen and signed his name then crumpled the sheet and threw it across the office.

"Lemme ask you this for the record. When you went into Candy's bathroom, you ain't seen that nigga?" Show fixed his gaze on Squeeze.

He had known Squeeze so long and was aware that if the nigga's nose twitched, he was lying. It had been that way since they were kids coming up. This was just another quirk that Show understood about his long time friend and partner.

"I didn't know the snake was hiding up in the bathroom. I swear on my mother's grave, I ain't never seen him when I went in there. Furthermore, the bitch told us he wasn't around and since that bitch gave up cracking and became a Christian, she ain't lying for nobody but Jesus."

"Fuck that. The bitch was lying. She told me that nigga was there the whole time. When you went into the bathroom, she sez the nigga was in there. Now that place ain't nothing but yay wide," Show said his both arms extended. "How you miss him is a mystery to me, dogs?"

"So whatcha saying?"

"I'm saying, if you had a chance to get even with the nigga, why you didn't? And if you really didn't see him then Squeeze, you sleeping."

"That's how you feel about it?"

"Yep, that's how I see it."

"Then you can take it the way you wanna, nigga. You think I'm scared to clap a nigga? Man, I done put caps in countless muthafuckas."

"Yeah but nigga robbed us and he still in the hood like urrhthing good. You don't even buck him once. Not even in the leg," Show said as he stood in front of the desk speaking to Squeeze who was comfortably seated behind it.

Suddenly the office door opened and Lindsay walked in with two drinks in her hand. She sashayed past Show and handed the drink to Squeeze with a kiss.

"Is the discussion over yet?" she asked playfully. Squeeze smiled and answered.

"That's how this goes. We both got to work hard to hold it down," he said and drank.

"Cheers," she toasted. As the glasses clinked, Show spoke.

"Man I'm a break da fuck out and holla atcha later."

"Ahight, my nigga. Call me and let me know if you coming back."

Squeeze and Lindsay were lip-locked before Show was out the door. Show drove around in his car wandering aimlessly trying to make sense of all the nonsense he had been exposed to in the last couple of hours. With remote in hand, he flipped from radio station to next. He slowed and pulled to the curb. Show rolled a blunt and mixed in some coke then he blasted Mob Deep's *Twisted*.

He puffed away thinking about the day and the way things had played out with the feds. The line of thinking only made him a bit paranoid until finally, he felt the need to go home and hug his son. Fuck it, if I gotta deal with her to see my son, I will, he thought as he pulled to a stop and turned off the ignition.

Show was on the elevator trying to figure if Squeeze was really trying to get the better of him. He got off still trying to shake the feeling. Everything seemed blurred. Maybe he just needed time away to really think about it. There was a whole lot of money involved and he had worked tirelessly establishing the club from the jump. There were stretches back in the beginning when he never saw his son awake. Tonight, he'd just hug him.

He was inside the apartment moving quietly not to wake anyone when he heard moaning. Show saw the empty bottle of Lemon Patron on the coffee table surrounded by drinking glasses. Somebody was partying up in here. He could hear moaning and groaning was coming from the bedroom. Show crept with the hammer at the ready. He opened the door slightly and peeked. His jaw dropped and he felt as if someone had just kicked him in the stomach.

Show saw LaToya, mother of his child, her head down and her swollen naked breasts pressed against the head of the bed. Sean-Do's dick was sliding in and out of her protruding ass. They were going at it too hard to notice that he was standing at the door.

Sean-Do was fucking his baby mother in his bed. Show felt the cheap shot below the belt. His knees buckled and he held the door for support. A sickening feeling developed in the pit of his stomach. The stench of their lovemaking made him want to throw-up.

Distaste made his mouth go dry. Show watched Sean–Do's tongue licking her back and his saliva mixing with the tat on her neck. His dick was penetrating deep into her doggy-style. They were both groaning loudly and couldn't hear Show panting in sick disgust.

He crept and looked in on his sleeping infant. Their heavy breathing from hard fucking was sloppy and loud. Show became confused and didn't know what to do. He staggered away and wandered into the kitchen. He gripped a huge carving knife. His mind took over and he quickly dialed LaToya's mother on his cellphone while standing in the kitchen and staring at the knife's sharpened blade. He should leave the house and let the ho be a ho. This would be the reason he needed to replace her tired, spoiled ass.

"Hello,"

"Mommy, this Show. I'm trying to reach Toya but she ain't picking up her phone. Is she over by y'all?"

"No, LaToya should be home sleeping by now."

"Ahight, if she call, tell her I'm trying to reach her," Show said calmly. "Sorry to bother you. Have a good night."

"That's no bother, Show. Goodnight."

Show closed the cellphone and took a deep breath. He slipped a pair of black gloves on his hands then slowly walked back into the bedroom this time loud enough for them to hear him. They didn't because Sean–Do was too busy coming. He was spanking her ass loudly and thrusting deeper into LaToya.

Their juices mixed and ran down her thighs as Show walked over to where they were getting down into some serious ass-fucking. Show put the gun to Sean-Do's head and stabbed her, severing the carotid. With the gun still at his head, Sean-Do was dumbstruck. Trying to hold back his breathing and an orgasm, his whole body froze. Show kept the gun at his head and gave him the order.

"Go ahead keep fucking her, nigga. This the last pussy you're gonna have, muthafucka. How it feels?"

Sean-Do could feel that LaToya had gone limp in his arms and so did his dick. He struggled to offer an explanation.

"I...I...I can't do it no more, Show. Please forgive me. I'll pay you back for ..."

"Shuddafuckup, my man. I ain't told you to come up here and fuck my woman."

"She was the one who came on to me...She told me you was always out fucking everything else and she hadn't had sex in months. She had on a negligee..."

"Oh, so that gave you reason to jump in her, uh."

Show stepped back and pointed the weapon. LaToya was slumped bleeding all over the bedspread. Sean-Do looked as if he was about to faint.

"Please Show..."

"And you got the nerve to be fuckin' my bitch without a condom. It was good, wasn't it? Fucking someone else's wife without a condom is like Russian roulette, my man."

Show held the nine with the silencer in place. He picked up the knife and slashed Sean-Do's throat with violent intent. Sean-Do's dome leaned to one side of his neck like a slanted baseball cap on a thug's head. His body swayed then he collapsed on top of LaToya's bloody mess.

"You don't deserve no bullets, boy. You gotta feel what death is like when it's creeping on you, boy."

Sean-Do's body struggled in the throes of death. His hand reached out in a last ditch valiant attempt to seal the cut at his throat. But it was all for naught.

In a matter of minutes, Sean-Do's demise was complete. Show looked at the grotesque figures and took all the money he had given Sean-Do before he ransacked the apartment ripping out the telephone cord before leaving.

Driving away, he called the apartment again. Then he called LaToya's sister. He didn't like her either so she could go discover the bodies. He told her he was at the club and couldn't get her sister. Show asked her to check in on her. LaToya's sister lived ten minutes away. She'd be there soon enough then he would receive the call.

Show drove to his other apartment out in Prospect Park. All the time, thoughts spun in his head. Why did he have to hit my baby mother raw-dog? Why? "Muthafuckin' Sean-Do! Muthafuckin' Sean-Do! Fuck you playa," Show mumbled to himself.

The scene in his bedroom between LaToya and his former friend, Sean-Do was like a screen saver on his mind. He ran into the building as if someone was giving chase.

Once inside his one bedroom apartment, he quickly cleaned up and found fresh black duds. He stashed the other bloody suit in a paper bag and threw the bag in the incinerator. Show rushed back to the car and hastily drove back to the club.

He parked outside a little further away and checked himself

in the car mirror while smoking a cigar. Show was expecting that call and he steeled himself for it. Back inside the club, he stopped at the bar and took two shots of VSOP. The night's activities had been overwhelming and he was a bit wobbly as he walked away from the bar.

He could see Squeeze and Lindsay on the dance floor. Her dress was so short you could see her ass cheeks. Show was too tipsy to care when he saw Lindsay waving at him. He charged over to where she was dancing and started getting down with her. He loved the way Lindsay was shaking those hips. Squeeze did not try to keep him off her so Show held his hands high and shouted.

"Party over here...yeeaah..."

Squeeze closed in and let him know that he was taking a breather. Show kept dancing and grabbing at the teen with the bubbling fatty. She teased him jumping and shaking her rump to the sound of Elephant Man

"...*Shake ya booty... turn it round...wind your body...*"

She spun and Show was able to catch her in mid-air and carry her to the darkest part of the floor where he attempted to fondle her. He so badly wanted to win that he slipped his fingers between her upper thighs and felt her shaven mound.

"Stop Show," she pleaded and wiggled to slip away but Show was not letting go. He kept playing with her upper thighs until she gave in then he swept her to the back of the dance floor where only security could see him. Lindsay was drunk and even though she strained to keep her thighs closed, Show was able to paw his way in. "Stop, Show. Stop it now. Please."

Lindsay's attempt at keeping her thighs shut wasn't going very well. Show was a big man and wasn't going to lose a wrestling match against a small woman. He heaved Lindsay and sat her hard on his dick. "Ugh, you're hurting me," she cried. Show's hands roamed her body over her clothes. Finally, she turned around and kissed him real hard. He slipped a probing tongue down her throat. She relaxed and stopped fighting. He was winning. Show felt his tongue being bitten real hard and a knee to his groin dropped him to his knees.

"Ugh, you fucking bitch!" he yelled writhing in pain as Lindsay made good her escape.

Show recovered after a spell and walked back to the main dance area. He smiled when he saw other sexy ladies well dressed and hot. These girls were in the mood, ready and waiting for someone to dance all over the floor with them. Tonight, Show needed their kind so he would oblige them. He frolicked and danced with them for a while then offered to buy them a bottle of the best bubbly. He popped the bottle and escorted the ladies to the VIP section. They sat in a booth and sipped champagne until it spilled down their dress. Show graciously asked if he could clean it up and was doing exactly that when Squeeze tapped him on the shoulder.

"Man, I gotta holla at ya," Squeeze said pulling at the arm of his drunken partner.

"What is it? What is it, dogs? Take it easy with the linen suit, man." Inebriated, Show offered little resistance and Squeeze was able to pull him away from the booth with minimal problems. "Ahight, ahight, you got me, dogs. What da fuck is da deal?" The drunken drawl was evident.

"You need to sober up and call LaToya's sister, sun. Sump'n is up with your family."

"Yeah sump'n is up ahight. My girl won't stay home and always running the street. If my baby boy is not okay, I'm a kill that bitch. You heard."

"Show, man, I don't know no other way to tell you this except to say that somebody already did."

"Huh, you bein' funny, muthafucka? Whatcha mean by that?" Show asked.

"Show," Squeeze said and putting his arm around Show. "Someone stabbed your baby mother and killed this... some other man that she was fucking with. Her sister called the club a minute ago. The police and everyone is all over so be careful, stash the gats. You know the baby daddy is always number one suspect."

"You serious? Stop playing, dogs. I ain't trying to hear all that. What about my son? My son alright?" Show asked with concern.

"He's ahight. He's with his aunt and grandma. Show, I'm sorry, man. Let me know if there's anything I can do? I'm here for you."

Show held his head and Squeeze went back to the booth and addressed both ladies. They walked away patting Show on the shoulder. Show seemed lost in drunken sorrow. He looked like he needed help, Lindsay took his hand and led him upstairs.

"I'm ahight, I'll live," he said with a wink that she didn't understand.

Upstairs, he took some money from the safe and left the club. Squeeze offered to drive him over but Show wanted to do this trip solo. Lindsay and Squeeze walked him to his car and after embracing; he got in the car trying not to look intoxicated.

"Here's some spearmint," Lindsay offered. Show took the stick of gum and peeled out.

When he arrived on the scene, police were all over the place. Show walked up to the apartment with plans to hug his son immediately. The bodies were already transported to the morgue. With a distraught look on his mug, Show nodded to the police officers as he scanned the area for his son. Show spotted the boy sleeping in the arms of his aunt, LaToya's younger sister, Nicole. Silently, he hugged them then other family members joined in hugging the grieving father and his sleeping son. With tears in her eyes, one of the females, maybe it was an aunt, spoke.

"We're so sorry for what happened tonight..." she started but Show held his hand up.

"Right now, I don't want to be reminded. My man, Squeeze, already said enough about the whole situation. I'm just glad my son is alive. My main objective is to make his life better and forget all this."

"We'll take care of Dashaun until you're..." Her voice trailed off into sobs. Show turned to a detective who was trying to address him.

"I'm Detective Ramirez. I'm sorry about this," the detective said and offered a handshake. Show accepted and the detective continued to speak. "I know it must really be upsetting to you so we'll be in touch with you at another time. Did you know the ah…her lover?" The detective stared directly at Show looking for his response. Show gave him what he wanted.

"Yes, I knew the muthafucka but I didn't know he had been sleeping with my woman." Show let his tears slowly roll down his cheeks.

"They were apparently both surprised by an intruder and stabbed to death. We've got to do some more investigation but if you hear anything give me a call. You were at work I understand you were trying to reach her by telephone. Why were you calling at such a late hour?" Detective Ramirez said as he gave Show a business card and backed off looking at his reaction.

Show turned to his son and gave him another hug. Nicole kissed him and he hugged her. He pretended that this was all too much and everyone understood so they excused him.

"She was trying to call me and I had to open up at the club so it was the only time I had to talk to her. So, I called…" Show said and walked away leaving the detective to stare after him.

"I'll be in touch," the detective said.

"Do whatever, man," Show said and was out.

Monday afternoon, Show awoke with a sigh. He had slept some on Sunday but took the night off from the club and watched television all day with his son. He had dropped the boy back to the child's aunt earlier during the day. Show was thinking of going out to eat when his cellphone began ringing incessantly. He finally answered the annoying instrument with a bark.

"Yo, what up, nigga?" It was Squeeze. Show spoke immediately.

"I'm fit'n to go get sump'n to eat over at the steak house or sump'n."

"I need to see you, my nigga. Holla at me when you through with that. You ahight, dogs? You feel like ridin'?"

"Man, we got long money. We could get someone to do this for us."

"I wanna do this for my man, Pooh. I wanna be a man about this."

"Ahight, if you feel that way. Let me get sump'n in my stomach first."

"Don't be tryin' a go soft on me, Show. Hold yourself together, man."

"Is that the reason you calling me, Squeeze?"

"I just wanna know if you down. Holla at me."

"Ahight, my nigga. I'll holla."

Show closed the cell. He did his twenty reps of push-ups and sit-ups then he showered and left his crib. He wound up at Junior's for lunch. After devouring a couple of well done T-Bones with mashed potatoes and gravy, Show washed it down with some Heinekens, paid the tab and bounced. In the parking lot, he rolled a blunt and accompanied by The Roots, *The Tipping Point,* he drove to Squeeze's crib.

The sun shone bright and Squeeze was waiting outside for him. He pulled up in the driveway and they embraced when he walked up to the car. Squeeze seemed a little anxious as usual.

"Yo, dogs we really got to move on 'em muthafuckas. My mans and 'em told me that they used to hustle out on the corners until them Spanish muthafuckas opened up. Niggas sez all of a sudden five-oh was raiding on da reg. They busted everybody on da corner. Niggas think these muthafuckas dropped dimes on hurr-body hustling out there on da corner. Nobody hustle out there no more."

"That might be true cuz when I went out there I ain't seen no one on the Ave 'cept for they custies."

"Yo, it's our duty to ride on these Spanish muthafuckas and make things real hot for them too, you feel me?" Squeeze walked away and opened the garage. He jumped into the black Hummer. Show knew Squeeze was ready when he pulled the bulletproof vehicle out. "Yo I'm ready to make that block hotter than July. You ready to ride, nigga?"

Show stalled for a beat. Maybe this was what he needed to bring him and Squeeze close. This was the old Squeeze and he kinda liked the old Squeeze. The other one was nervous and acted as if he was a celebrity.

"Hell yeah, let's ride on these muthafuckas. They think they got away with merking my nigga, Pooh. Yes, let's go clap at these fools." Show jumped into the passenger side of the Hummer.

"Show, check these out, dogs. My man came from Iraq and brought me some o' these," Squeeze said and handed Show two U.S. Army grenades. Show examined the munitions carefully.

"All we gotta do is say what's up and pull this pin," Show instructed.

"Nah, don't pull that muthafucka, nigga. Not yet. You'd have to hold that pin down the whole time and that would be a bitch," Squeeze said and rolled out the driveway. "Let's bring the pain to these assholes of Flatbush!" Squeeze pumped some Mashed Out Posse, *Ground Zero* as they rode to Flatbush. They were burning weed as they drove when Show spoke.

"Yo dogs I'm glad we doing this together. This just like old times again, Squeeze," Show said checking and cocking his nine-millimeter. Squeeze gave him a pound.

"You know that we tight. Brothas from anotha motha, my nigga." Squeeze was hyped and that pleased Show. He smiled feeling the return of camaraderie. Then Show heard what he thought was Squeeze's reason for doing the mission. "Plus when we hit these muthafuckas, it's gonna make Lindsay happy and love a nigga more." Show shook his head pumped up the volume on the stereo and ignored Squeeze. "Show, Pooh was her big brotha." Squeeze added when he saw Show reclined in his seat smoking. It wasn't until moments later that Show raised his head.

"There it is. That's da spot right there on the left," he shouted. "Yep, that's them right there."

"Yo, they movin' shit up in there? What they selling, dogs?"

Squeeze asked, pulling to the curb. He parked the vehicle. "Let's go pay these muthafuckas a visit."

"They got two look outs one on each corner of the block. There they go now. That's the lookouts right thurr. That means muthafuckas pumping shit up in there."

"You take out that muthafucka at that end and I'll get the other nigga," Squeeze said and they both left the engine running in the Hummer and walked to opposite ends of the block. Show walked toward his target and shouted at him.

"Homey, lil' homey. Yeah, you nigga. Hold this, muthafucka!"

Show sprayed Heckler and Koch hitting the teen all over his body. He tried to get up and run but Show walked closer and shot him twice. He slipped a ski mask over his head, turned and saw the crowd running. Minor chaos had broken out by the time they both got to the entrance of the spot. Both Show and Squeeze were met with a fusillade of gunfire.

The partners looked at each other, pulled the pins from the grenades and threw them into the weed spot.

"Only one fucking way out, niggas!" Show yelled and took cover next to the car parked in front of the spot.

Five seconds later, the building was rocked by a series of explosions. There was panic in the street that had everyone running every which way. Like soldiers making their way to a rendezvous, Show and Squeeze were heading back to the vehicle. It was then that Show spotted a young mother lost in the confusion. She was totally oblivious to the shooter from inside the wreckage, who came out firing. Squeeze took him out with a couple of shots.

There was more shooting coming from the bombed out former drug spot. The mother, unaware of this shooting, was trying to escape but was pushing her baby in a carriage across the street in the direction of the gunfire.

Show realized that she and the infant were trapped in the line of fire. Squeeze watched in amazement as Show rushed to save her and the infant. He ran about ten yards and then dove on her pushing her and the baby's carriage out of the way. Bullets flew by them, narrowly missing the three.

"No, no Show," Squeeze screamed but it was too late.

Show somehow managed to accomplish his mission but caught a bullet in his upper torso. Squeeze dropped to his knees and let off on the shooter. While still firing in the general direction of the shooter, Squeeze yelled at Show, "Don't move, my nigga. I'm coming to get you."

He reached the Hummer jumped in and swung it into a u-turn. Tires screeching, Squeeze came to a stop by Show's prone body. Squeeze got out and yanked his partner in crime and friend inside the vehicle.

"Let's go! Let's get the fuck outta here. What da fuck you doing playing superhero, nigga? You ain't got to stunt for me. I know you got heart, nigga."

Breathing hard, Squeeze struggled to heave Show's heavy frame into the vehicle. Finally, with the aid of another street hustler from the block who was happy to see the spot crashed and burned, Squeeze was able to hoist Show's body into the ride.

"Good looking my nigga," he said.

"Nah, good looking to y'all nigga. Go on. Get out of here, sounds like Five-O is heading this way."

Squeeze ran around to the driver's side, jumped in the Hummer and peeled off with the quickness. Show was leaking from his chest and closed his eyes. Squeeze shook his homie trying to keep him from slumping.

"Don't pass out on me now big Show…"

"I ain't worried about passing out, just get me to the nearest hospital, my nigga."

"Don't die on me, nigga. We the last ones. We gotta carry this on, dogs. Don't die on me."

Squeeze was driving fast, swerving and getting around the slower moving traffic. The Hummer rocked back and forth, and side to side. He avoided other cars on the busy Brooklyn streets while holding Show's arm, trying to shake him to see if he was dead. Show didn't move. Squeeze yelled at him. "Show, don't die on me, please, my brother. You's all I got, dogs. Don't die. Not now. We'll be at the hospital real soon."

Show's eyes opened slowly. He blinked as if he was under heavy sedation. His eyes rolled back into his head. This freaked Squeeze into almost hitting an approaching car.

"Nigga, you better look where da fuck you going 'fore you kill both of us," Show rasped. With a crooked smile, he continued. "We did them muthafuckas up, right?"

The words made Squeeze laugh hysterically but when he saw Show slowly sliding away in the seat, he became really concerned.

"Yeah, we did them lovely. Show open your eyes, man. I wanna see your eyes," Squeeze yelled but Show did not move. His eyes stayed shut and Squeeze panicked again. "Show, man, stay with me, baby."

"Squeeze, I ain't goin' nowhere, dogs. This Show. I'm a just take a lil' nap till you get to the hospital, ahight?" He closed his eyes again.

"Nah, Show think about all the bitches that be on you after you sack a quarterback."

"Man, you got all the bitches...you got Lindsay, she's a fine ass right...?"

"Fuck all da bitches. You my nig to end."

"My nig," Show repeated. He clenched his fist before continuing. "Squeeze I really feel like I should take a nap," he said as his eyes rolled back in his head. Squeeze saw Show leaned way back.

"Nah, don't close your eyes. Don't die on me. Don't die, Show. C'mon, you all that. You can fight off ten other players and get to the quarterback... You da muthafuckin' man, Show. You da best friend anyone could have. Dogs? Dogs, please don't die on me. Just hold on. We almost there, stay wit me my nig," Squeeze pleaded.

Show reclined unmoving as they raced through traffic. The

Hummer was leaning dangerously as Squeeze maneuvered curves to get his man to the nearest hospital.

"Don't die on me, Show. Show...Show...Yo, Show."

There was still no change or little regard for his own safety, Squeeze continued driving at an erratic pace to the hospital. It was at this point that nothing mattered, not the cars, his house or the club. He would give them all up if he knew it would save his man's life.

the fall-out

ERICK S. GRAY

3:35 pm: Maryland

Brandon "Tooks" Miller stepped out of his pimped out classic BMW, a 1995 black 325i Cabriolet, one of his favorites. He was in front of the Maryland Correction Institution for Women where his niece, Audrey, was incarcerated.

He peered at the institution and a quick shiver ran down his spine reminding him of his quick bid he put in for the government ten years ago. He had given the government a total of fifteen years of his life. Since the age of fourteen, he'd been in and out of prison and been charged with everything the government could charge him with from petty crack possession to murder in the first degree. He knew how hard life could be behind them walls. That was why he had a bit of sympathy for his niece but at the same time, felt rage towards her. How could she be so stupid, he thought, I warned her.

He had gotten the news about his niece's arrest in Virginia when FBI agents came snooping around his business and starting asking him questions about Promise and other shit they hit him with. He was shocked to hear the news about his niece robbing banks in VA. He thought they had the wrong girl but when the feds showed him pictures of Audrey, pictures taken from the bank's security cameras, he damn near went into tears.

"I fuckin' warned that muthafucka!" he muttered under his breath. But Brandon also known as Tooks on the streets of Harlem knew nothing about Promise.

"I just met the boy for a few moments through my niece. She brought that asshole around and I fuckin' warned her about him. I don't know dat nigga!" he had told the feds through clenched teeth.

The feds believed him. That's why they didn't stress the issue with Brandon but Brandon couldn't get past it. "That nigga had my niece robbing banks!" he barked.

He wanted to kill Promise, rip his fuckin' heart out. Promise had disrespected him, his family, and his baby sister's wish for Tooks to look after her daughter when she passed away. And for that, he promised himself, if the feds don't catch him first, Promise was a dead man.

Brandon approached the facility smoking a Newport Light and dressed like a Don. He had on some black slacks with a turtleneck and a pair of classic wingtips. On his right hand, he sported a diamond pinky ring. There was platinum around his neck and a Rolex around his wrist but all that had to come off when he reached the security checkpoint and went through the customary searches. He put all his jewelry and other items of his into a small locker.

He waited for an hour to visit his niece. Brandon definitely stood out in the crowd of baby mamas, thugs, and other visitors that waited to see family and friends. Brandon was dressed like he was about to attend some business function, having lunch with high-class friends, than seeing his niece inside a lock-up. People in the room watched and observed his activities like he was the misfit.

Brandon paid the folks no mind as he kept to himself and thought about his niece. He prayed that she was doing all right knowing that Audrey wasn't built to stay in a place like this. His niece had been a happy and playful child—beautiful and charismatic. To him, she was the daughter he loved very much which was why this situation pained him so much.

Moments later, he heard his name being called and he stood up and approached the visitors' room with six other people. He sat down at a bare table with chairs and a room filled with people. Several moments later, he noticed his niece coming into the room behind three other inmates. She wore no smile as she came into the room clad in her dark blue standardized attire.

When Audrey noticed her uncle seated at the table, a small

smile appeared on her face and Brandon let out a small smile too. He was excited about seeing his niece even though it was under harsh conditions.

"Uncle Brandon!" Audrey cried out.

Her eyes were filled with tears of joy and at the same time pain. She embraced her uncle into a loving strong hug as if she didn't want to let him go. Brandon wished that he had the power to take her from this place.

"How you doing, kid?" he asked.

Audrey didn't answer as she continued to hug her uncle. But their embrace was short-lived, being that they had to be seated as per instruction of a corrections officer present in the room. They took their seats and Brandon peered over at his niece, observing her and already knowing the answer to the question he had asked a few short moments ago.

Audrey's long hair was in braids and her eyes appeared sad and disoriented while she sat unable to utter a word at first. Her beauty was still there, untouched, no scars, at least on the outside. But inside, Audrey felt torn apart and Brandon knew it too. He stared into her eyes and he knew that the choices that she'd made with her boyfriend were eating her up inside. She lived the kind of life that her uncle had separated himself from years ago.

"How they treating you up in here, kid?" Brandon asked.

Audrey sat with her elbows on the table, casting her eyes down at the floor and scratching her braids. She felt ashamed and couldn't look into her uncle's eyes.

"Audrey, look at me," her uncle quietly demanded.

She lifted her saddened eyes up from off the floor and peered into her uncle's dark black eyes.

"I'm sorry, Uncle Brandon. I'm so sorry," Audrey suddenly cried out.

"What's wrong with you? Huh? What the hell was going through your damn mind when you got with that punk nigga? He had you down there robbing fuckin' banks. Audrey, is you fuckin' crazy?

You're smarter than that. I know. I helped raise you. How did you let that nigga get in your damn head - not to mention your bed? I always warned you about niggas like him. Now where he at? He got every fed in the country looking for his ass while you're trapped up in this bitch!" Brandon chided.

"It just happened," Audrey weakly replied.

"It just happened?" Brandon countered. "Audrey, what da fuck, girl? I hate seeing you like this. That nigga...what da fuck his name is, Promises?"

"Promise," Audrey uttered.

"Well...that nigga put my niece in this predicament. I'm gonna kill him, Audrey. I tellin' you that shit. When I see him, I'm gonna gut da nigga like fuckin' fish," he threatened.

Audrey just sat there gazing at her uncle, knowing how violent and dangerous he could become. She knew that when he said something, he definitely meant it.

"Uncle Brandon, I didn't do it because of him. I did it for his daughter," she said in her defense.

"His daughter?" Brandon inquired. "What kind of man put you and his daughter in that kind of danger? That's not a man. That's a pussy nigga to do some shit like that. He couldn't do it himself!"

Audrey didn't reply. She just sat there and listened to her uncle's harsh approach. She knew he was right. What kind of man willingly put his woman and daughter in that kind of danger no matter how desperate and bad it was for them? She wanted to cry but tried to hold on strong in front of her uncle. She'd done enough crying.

"Audrey, no matter what, I'll always love you and I promise you this, I'm gonna help you get up outta here. You don't belong here. This ain't your world. This will never be your world," he assured. "But first thing, you know where Promise may be right now?"

She shook her head no. "The feds already came and asked me questions about him. I don't know anything."

"Ahight. What's done is done now you gotta move on and I'm gonna get lawyers for you to help appeal your case. We gonna make it look like you were forced to rob banks. You don't have a record so that's gonna help. I'm gonna get you through this, girl. You're not alone, ahight, kiddo? I'm a be here for you."

Audrey smiled. Hearing her uncle's words brought some kind of relief to her heart and she knew he meant it too. Brandon had connections everywhere. Underground and political—he knew people and he had done a lot of things in his life. He was a fifty year-old gangsta from way back when gangsta were gangsters. Tooks wasn't all talk like the young wannabes nowadays, having a rep and being loud. He had a good deal of clout in the streets and he was smart. He knew how to play things out.

"Audrey, listen, if you have any trouble in here with anyone and I do mean anyone, you let me know. You write me or call me collect anytime and I'll handle it for you. Okay?"

"Okay, Uncle Brandon."

"You made a stupid mistake but we gonna fix it," he assured her.

It was 5:30 p.m. when Brandon left his niece. He walked out of the correctional facility a stressed man. He felt sorry for his niece and knew that she deserved better than that. Promise edged into his thoughts again and a scowl loomed on his face. Brandon pulled out another Newport Light, lit it and took a long drag. Pulling out his cell-phone, he dialed one of his niggas from Harlem—Johnny.

Johnny picked up after the third ring and hollered into the receiver, "Tooks, what's happening man? It's been a long time my brother."

"Yeah, I know Johnny," Brandon returned. "Look, you up for a little work? I got a job for you."

"Damn, a job...I thought you was retired from these streets. What happened, man?" Johnny asked with serious concern.

"My niece is what happened. Some jive ass nigga got my niece into a fucked up predicament. Now she's wasting away in jail while this nigga lurks free in these streets eluding the feds and shit. I want him done."

"You mean Audrey? She was like a daughter to all of us. I got your back on this, Tooks, trust me. I got this. You hear, Tooks?"

"Yeah, I hear. Thanks, Johnny. Do what you can. I owe you."

"Nah, Tooks, you don't owe me anything for this."

"Thanks."

"I'm on it right now. I see what I can dig up on the streets about this nigga for you. I'm gonna talk to you, Tooks. You play it safe."

Tooks hung up and took another drag from his Newport. He hated calling up old friends for a favor but he knew shit had to get done. He'd been out of the game for ten years now but he still knew just the right men to call.

He took another drag, peered at his ride, and thought about death. Tooks was a Harlem nigga, born and raised over on 145th Street and St. Nicholas. He knew these streets like he knew himself. Even though he had gone legit, being a thug, the gangster still resided in his heart and when he felt disrespected about something, you best to believe somebody was either gonna get hurt or killed. When it came down to his family, it was death—nothing less.

He wanted Promise so bad that he clenched up his fist and shattered the driver's side window of his BMW with his bare fist. Blood spilled from cuts on his fingers and wrist but the pain and blood didn't bother him. Disrespect to his family, meant death.

Tooks leaned on the hood of his car and thought about justice for his niece. Justice for him was taking out Promise in the worst way and then having his niece released.

11:45 pm: Brooklyn

The nine-millimeter clip was quickly loaded into place, cocked back, and a deadly round was secured in the chamber—the gun was ready for death tonight. The nine was gripped in the hands of a fuming Dominican sitting in the back seat of a Cutlass Oldsmobile. He was seated in the back alone, while two of his homies rode up front. They were also heavily armed.

"Carlos, pass that." The man in the back seat spoke referring to the dro' they been smoking all night.

Carlos reached around and passed his nigga in the back the burning dro'. Nothing else was said as they crossed the Brooklyn Bridge into downtown Brooklyn. All three men had death in their eyes as they prowled for a kill tonight. The men felt disrespected and furious. Carlos, the leader of the three in the moving car, felt the most disrespected.

Three days ago, two unknown assailants ran up in his Flatbush spot and threw two grenades inside, like niggas were in Vietnam and shit. When Carlos got word that his cousin and his baby brother, Hector, were killed in the explosion, he became enraged and punched his fist through a wall. He started kicking over tables and chairs in his joint with everyone watching and no one attempted to stop him. They knew his anger and they knew how tight he was with his cousin and brother.

Everyone watched and the females tried to console him after but Carlos didn't want any consoling from anybody. He wanted blood to spill from the niggas responsible for such a horrendous act committed against his family and friends.

"These niggas blew up my shit and killed Hector and my fuckin' cousin!" he shouted as rage dripped from his voice.

Carlos along with two other men made it their business to travel from Da Heights into Brooklyn to wage war on his enemies. He had heard the name, Squeeze, once maybe twice but he didn't know the face. Squeeze didn't really ring any bells in Carlos' ears. The name wasn't as popular in Da Heights as it was in Brooklyn. New York's a pretty big town.

Nevertheless, Carlos got wind of Squeeze's establishment, *The Brooklyn Café* that was located right off the Brooklyn Bridge. So tonight, Carlos and two of his henchmen were making it their business to fuck his shit up.

"I'm gonna fuck Squeeze's ass up!" Carlos uttered. He

clutched a loaded MP7. "These niggas wanna come wit' grenades then I'm coming wit' machine guns."

"Don't worry Carlos, we gonna fuck these puta's up real good," the driver said.

Manny, seated in the back seat, took a long pull from the burning dro' and added,

"I hear one of his peoples is shot up real bad in da hospital, Carlos. I think it's his right-hand. Some fat clown nigga named Show. We need to do dat nigga in. Make him not come out alive. You feel me, Carlos?"

"Manny, you set dat up for me. Dis fuckin' puta wanna come at us hard like dat then we going to war on dat muthafucka. Everybody dying, his mamma, son, sister…I want niggas to feel death coming tonight," Carlos furiously proclaimed.

The Oldsmobile reached around to the *The Brooklyn Café* and slowed up near the block. Outside was calm and warm as all three men sat in the car and watched a crowd of people outside the club waiting to be let in. The line of folks outside the club had no idea of the carnage that was about to take place in a short moment.

Men and women stood outside clueless of the negativity that the *The Brooklyn Café* was about to attract. For the men and women in the crowd, it was about having a good time, mingling and partying at one of New York's most popular nightclubs. Laughter and excitement filled the air as male partygoers dressed in their best, socialized with sexily clad ladies revealing thighs and cleavage. Carlos took one last pull from the dro' and then flung it out the car window. Manny passed Miguel a second MP7 and he locked and loaded, getting ready for the kill.

Carlos peered over at Miguel and uttered, "I want this nigga, Miguel. I want this nigga's nuts hanging over my dashboard."

"It's gonna happen, Carlos. Dis nigga, Squeeze…the muthafuckin' puta don't know who he fuckin' wit'," Miguel replied.

It was the beginning of a war between the two groups as far as Carlos was concerned. Squeeze shot first so now he had to retaliate for his fallen brother and cousin. All three men had no idea about Pooh or why Squeeze and Show threw two hand grenades into their business. They may be trying to take over but they didn't know Carlos. He was a new era. Before anyone disrespected him, he was ready to clear out a whole city block first and put fear in niggas heart the worst way possible through carnage and death.

All three men masked up and the Oldsmobile sped off down the block. The quick screeching of car tires caught almost everyone's attention outside the club. The abrupt burst of rapid gunfire into the night caused chaos fast as people began to rapidly run for cover, scampering like scared cattle. The sound of death filled the air as those hit by gunfire dropped like falling insects.

The two MP7's were loud and effective. Carlos gripped his hand like a toy and he didn't care who got in the way of the deadly spray. To him, it was sending a message to Squeeze and everybody else that he had started something that he would be not able to finish.

Two beefy bouncers quickly pulled out two black Glocks and returned fire. Miguel and Manny jumped out and opened fire. They had the men outgunned. Bouncers caught rapid shots into their torso tearing up their chests and dropping them quickly.

Panic and horror could be heard everywhere. It seemed like the shooting went on for hours but it was only a little over a minute. Aware of the police coming soon, Carlos and the rest piled back into their Cutlass Oldsmobile and quickly sped off into the night leaving behind a massacre.

A few people started to rise up and look around in total awe. Women and men began to cry, seeing their friends and loved ones sprawled out against the hard cold concrete, crimson spilling out onto the street.

"Ohmigod! Ohmigod!" a lady shrieked at the top of her lungs while covered in her dead boyfriend's blood. Dozens of police sirens loomed from a distance. It was like a scene out of a Rambo movie. Bodies were just sprawled everywhere.

"Shit! What da fuck!" a scared man shrieked. He had been shot once in the arm.

Folks began to console and aid each other as they waited for New York's finest to converge onto the horrifying scene.

Tonight, the *The Brooklyn Café* had been cursed and no one would ever forget what had gone down this night. Many that survived would never return, some would sue, and some would be fucked up for the rest of their lives.

Carlos succeeded in what he had planned to do—shutting shit down for Squeeze and whoever because *The Brooklyn Café* would no longer be the same hot spot that it used to be. From that night on, it would be known as the club that topped headlines in every paper. Even the surrounding states would be talking about this shit.

The war raged on. Many innocent lay dead and many more would soon follow.

Show was still in critical condition with three shots embedded into his limp frame. The doctors weren't sure if he'd last the week. They were doing their best but it was now in God's hand if he lived or died.

Squeeze stayed by Show's side and hoped for the best. Show was the only nigga—the only family he had left from the streets. Pooh was dead and gone and Promise was on the lam, and Squeeze felt betrayed by someone who used to be his right-hand man. Squeeze, feeling alone, started to shed tears as he peered down at Show with tubes in and out of him and breathing through an oxygen mask.

"Don't die on me, nigga. I need you, baby," Squeeze quietly uttered, clutching Show's still hand. "We about this money. We a team, my nigga. You can't die. We're in this for the long run."

He wished Show would wake up and answer him but the room remained silent. Only the steady hum from the machines working to keep Show alive were audible.

Squeeze navigated his Cadillac through the Brooklyn streets early in the morning as he drove from the hospital. He had paid the nurses a few extra hundred so he was able to stay past the regular visiting hours.

While Squeeze pushed his way down Ocean Parkway with a loaded .380 resting in the passenger seat, his cellphone rang and vibrated in the seat. He picked it up and saw it was Lindsay hitting him up. He was on his way to see her so he didn't bother to answer her call.

Lindsay had a place in Coney Island. It wasn't big but it was comfortable and Squeeze felt that it was the perfect place for him to hide out until everything blew over.

He was stressing his man Show real hard and his mind wasn't right. He hadn't been down to the club in days. His man, Anthony was taking care of things down at *The Brooklyn Café*, until he felt right to come back and handle things. Squeeze had no idea about the carnage that had taken place in front of his club earlier. He hadn't answered his phone in hours. He had turned it off when he was in the hospital. When he turned his phone back on, he noticed he had 10 missed calls and 8 new messages. Squeeze pulled up to the projects around two in the morning. He parked his car, stepped out and activated the alarm to his ride.

Lindsay stayed in a notorious housing community called Gravesend housing. She had moved there a few months after Pooh's death. It wasn't perfect but it was home for her. Squeeze walked up to her third floor apartment. He had his .380 in his waistband and his cell in his hand. He never once checked his voicemail because if he had, he woulda known about what went down earlier.

Squeeze knocked on Lindsay's door and within a half minute, Lindsay came to the door wearing a long white T-shirt and some fuzzy slippers. She still looked good. She was a very beautiful woman—

young and very attractive. Squeeze took advantage of shortie, making Lindsay his trophy. Even tho' she wasn't a virgin like he wished, her pussy was still nice and tight. Squeeze didn't give a fuck about her supposed to be boyfriend, Malik. To him, Malik was nothing but some young wanna be gangsta who craved Squeeze and Show's attention. He wasn't a threat.

"Hi, baby," Lindsay gladly greeted him, hugging Squeeze as he stepped into the apartment.

Squeeze sighed and took a seat on the couch with Lindsay all over him. She had the stereo playing loudly as Chante's song, *"Bitter"* blared through the speakers placed around the room.

"So how's he doing?" Lindsay asked concerned about Show's condition. She knew what it was like to lose someone so close to you. She knew that Show was like a brother to him so she massaged his shoulders, kissed him around his neck, and tried to console Squeeze the best way she knew how.

"He ain't too good," Squeeze stated leaning back against the couch allowing Lindsay to do her thing. Lindsay climbed on top of his lap and straddled her legs around him. She slowly began to kiss him, tasting his lips, feeling his breath, and feeling his manhood slowly rising between her legs.

For Lindsay, this was cloud nine for her. She had had a serious crush on Squeeze since her early days in junior high school. She remembered the days when Pooh first brought Squeeze around during the summer. She used to think to herself that Squeeze was the sexiest man alive. He had that young thug quality about him and since she could remember, Lindsay was always attracted to thugs and roughnecks—ones who reminded her of her brother. In her mind, Promise was the nice and cute one, Show was the big and mean one, Pooh was her brother who was the wild and quick tempered one, and Squeeze—Squeeze was the smooth, sexiest and the most intriguing one that caught her eye. She'd held onto her crush on Squeeze for so many years until recently when she reunited with him and Show a few nights back at the café.

Lindsay never told Pooh about her crush on Squeeze, fearing what Pooh's reaction might be. She had kept her desires hidden from Squeeze for all these years but now, he knew what was up. Lindsay held nothing back as she slowly unbuckled his pants and pulled out his pulsating erection. She slowly jerked his manhood in her hand while Squeeze threw his head back and grunted. Squeeze tossed his cellphone and .380 to the side and enjoyed Lindsay's hand massage.

"I love you, Squeeze. I've always loved you since the day I first laid eyes on you," she proclaimed.

He smiled. Lindsay stood up and removed her T-shirt revealing that she had nothing on. She was stark naked and standing in her fuzzy house slippers. Her body was so soft, so easy to look at, and so fuckin' desirable.

"Eighteen, huh," Squeeze uttered, gazing at Lindsay with sexual hunger in his eyes. For the first time in hours, Lindsay was able to remove his mind from his dying friend and onto her and he loved her for that.

"Come and get it, baby," she said, teasing him by sliding her hand in between her moist legs.

Squeeze stood up and went over to her. He clutched her in his arms and fondled her phat ass and sucked on her breasts. Slowly, she removed his jeans, dropping them to the floor, and then took off his shirt and everything else. They fell to the floor where Squeeze positioned himself in between her smooth thighs and began to thrust.

An hour later, Squeeze's phone began to ring. He looked at the number and saw it was Anthony. He was concerned as to why Anthony, the head of his security, was calling him so he answered the ringing phone. His missed calls told him that Anthony had been trying to contact him all night.

"Yeah, Ant....what you want?" Squeeze spoke as he stared at Lindsay's luscious body.

"Nigga, we got hit... Some niggas shot up the club tonight," he informed Squeeze. "I'm down at the 88th precinct. Cops are holding me down here for questioning. You need to get your ass down here quick. They looking for you."

"Fuck you talking about, Ant?" Squeeze asked in shock.

"People died tonight, Squeeze. Innocent people died tonight. Why....I don't know why but I do know you need to handle this. I been fuckin' calling you all night. Where da fuck were you?"

"Ahight, Ant...I'll be down in a minute," Squeeze assured him and closed his cell. He quickly got up and reached for his shit.

"Baby, what happened?" Lindsay asked.

"I don't know," Squeeze returned. He quickly threw on his jeans, timbs and reached for his .380, placing it in his waistband. "I gotta go take care of something, Lindsay. I'll be back."

"Okay." Lindsay said. She lay across the floor and watched Squeeze disappear out of her apartment.

Half an hour later, Squeeze made it down to *The Brooklyn Café* where he noticed that the cops had the entire street closed off with yellow tape and marked and unmarked cars were everywhere. He saw police and detectives swarming all over. It was like a bomb blew up or something. They had the K-9 out and the ESU out as well.

Squeeze quickly jumped out of his ride and rushed toward his club but he hadn't made it within fifty feet from the place when a uniformed officer stopped him.

"You can't pass, sir," the officer stated. "You see this area is closed off."

"Fuck you talking bout'? This my shit. I own that club," Squeeze informed the officer. "What da fuck happened here?"

"This is your place?" the officer asked.

"Yeah, muthafucka. Who da fuck did this? What da fuck happened?" he shouted.

Moments later, a detective dressed in a gray suit approached Squeeze and asked him, "Excuse me, this is your establishment?"

"Yeah, why?"

"I'm gonna need for you to come down to the station with me. We want to ask you a few questions," the middle-aged detective informed him.

Knowing that it wasn't wise to resist and bring speculation upon himself, Squeeze agreed and followed two detectives to a nearby unmarked car and rode with them down to the 88th.

When he arrived at the precinct, he was greeted along with many other people who the cops were also holding for questioning. Squeeze saw no familiar faces. He just saw the look of frightened and terrified faces as one by one, NYPD questioned them about the tragic incident that had unfolded a few short hours earlier. They wanted the identity of the shooters but all the witnesses could give 'em was that they were in a late white Cutlass Oldsmobile and there were three men wearing masks and they all were heavily armed. No one could give the cops a motive for the shooting. The victims were just as clueless as the police.

Squeeze sat in a private room alone and a million and one things ran through his head. He looked around for Anthony but didn't see him anywhere. It was a good thing he left his gun in the car, Squeeze thought to himself. As he sat, his cellphone went off again and it was Lindsay calling him. He answered her call.

"Baby, you okay?" Lindsay asked.

"Lindsay, now is not the right time. I'll call you back," he told her then hung up. She called back but he didn't answer.

After being seated alone in the room for nearly an hour, two detectives entered the room and took a seat across the table from Squeeze.

"Yo, what da fuck happened tonight?" he barked.

"We need to ask you a few questions," the black bald detective spoke up.

"About what? What da fuck...am I under arrest? I don't even know what da fuck happened?" Squeeze shouted.

"Look, a lot of people died tonight," the white detective explained to him casually. "Three masked men took it upon themselves to shoot into a crowd of people who were standing outside your night club. Twelve people were violently killed tonight."

"Damn!" Squeeze uttered. He was shocked.

"Now what we want to know from you...do you have any indication of anyone that might want to harm you? Do you have enemies?"

"Nah!" he replied.

"You sure? Any recent arguments with someone?" he sternly repeated.

Squeeze sighed. "What I say? Everything's peace with me. I run my business and then go home to my girl and lay in some pussy."

"Well, have there been any fights or beefs between anyone of your bouncers or staff?"

"I don't know they business. Ask them about their personal life. Don't come to me," he barked.

"Listen, you ain't gotta be a hard-ass. We're just doing our job."

"Then do it quickly!" Squeeze protested.

Both detectives scowled at Squeeze then one asked, "Okay, now we need your contact information."

"For what?"

"Contact."

"Man, listen, I wasn't there. I ain't witnessed shit, detectives, so I'm sorry to say but I ain't no help to y'all."

"You don't care about the innocent lives lost in front of your night club?" the white guy asked.

"Listen, if I knew shit then it would be a different story but I don't know shit. I just got wind of this a few short moments ago. Now, am I under arrest or do I have to call up my lawyer and have him put his foot up y'all asses!"

"You shit, why you gotta be such a fuckin' hard ass? We trying to help you out. What happened tonight won't go away."

"Man, I don't know nothing," Squeeze repeated himself.

Both detectives stared at him with contempt and anger. They knew he was a hard ass but they let him be. They left the room and left Squeeze alone in the room for the next five hours.

When the detectives finally came back in, Squeeze was livid. He started cursing and carrying on before the cops said that he was free to go. Squeeze knew he should have been let loose hours ago. It was their way of fuckin' with him.

Squeeze came from the school of hard knocks. Never go to cops with your beef. You either handle it or you don't handle it. But he was still clueless as to who shot up his club and put him out of business. He knew that there was no way he could recover from an incident like this. One death, two deaths maybe but when twelve innocent lives are taken in one short night and so violently, he knew the city was gonna be on his ass. They would be determined to shut his shit down.

Now with Show in the hospital and his niggas no longer by his side, Squeeze definitely felt alone. He knew he had to do something and fast. These streets, they see an opening and won't hesitate to come for you.

He walked out of the room and headed for the exit. Before he walked out, he noticed Anthony still seated in the precinct waiting to be questioned. But Squeeze uttered nothing to the man. He treated him like a stranger and went on his way.

The club shooting made the headlines in New York. It traveled through every borough and beyond. The horrendous incident was broadcast on every news channel, made front page in every paper and the public was shocked to hear of such a gruesome and random shooting.

Cops went on a citywide search for the Oldsmobile. If you were black and young and riding in an Oldsmobile, you were getting stopped, harassed, and searched. You didn't even have to be riding. If you were walking, especially around the area in downtown Brooklyn, you were gonna get fucked with by the police.

Squeeze sat in Lindsay's apartment watching the news and

hearing witnesses tell the world of their horrifying experience that night and how they were able to survive. Squeeze listened to a man saying, "It just happened so quickly. I was standing there minding my business, waiting to get in, and then suddenly this car came speeding around the corner and opened fire on everyone. I took cover behind a car and heard the chaos going on. I mean, I heard machine guns being fired and everything. What kind of men would do such a terrible thing?" The man on television gave his grizzly testimony.

Squeeze shook his head and uttered, "Fuckin' coward!"

"Baby, you okay?" Lindsay asked coming into the room holding two glasses of juice. She passed one to Squeeze and took a seat next to him. "You know who did that to your club?" she asked.

Squeeze sighed and replied, "Nah but believe me, I'm gonna definitely find out."

He took a sip of juice and then leaned against the couch. He thought about possible enemies that were bold enough and stupid enough to pull such a stunt against him. The recent months had been quiet until him and Show pulled that stunt with the Dominican boys that ran shop on Flatbush. He thought about them long and hard and they became number one on his shit list. He thought it had to be them because him and Show hit that place hard wit' grenades and everything. The hit had made the nightly news and police ain't have a clue to what was going on. Fuckin' cops thought that it was about drugs.

Squeeze looked over at Lindsay and said, "Lindsay, your friend, Malik, where he at? I wanna holla at dat boy about sump'n."

"Malik, he probably at work or sump'n. I ain't talk to him in days," she said without looking at Squeeze. Her eyes stayed glued to the television.

"Hit him up for me."

"For what?"

"Cause I need to ask him sump'n important."

"Now?" she asked looking bothered.

"Yeah, now," Squeeze chided.

Lindsay sucked her teeth, got up off the couch and went for the cordless that was in her bedroom. Squeeze had a hunch and if his hunch proved right then them Dominicans were dead yesterday. He meant war. They had come at him hard and now he was gonna return the favor.

She came out the bedroom with the cordless in her hand and she tossed it at Squeeze. He caught it and asked Lindsay for Malik's number. She gave him the number and Squeeze quickly dialed. The phone began to ring as Squeeze continued staring at the TV.

"Hello?"

"Yeah, this Malik?" Squeeze asked.

"Yeah, who this?"

"Squeeze. You remember me?"

"Oh, what up, Squeeze. What's going on?" Malik gleefully exclaimed.

"Nuthin'. You tell me?" Squeeze said with the seriousness in his voice. "Yo, listen, I need to holla at you about sump'n. Sump'n really important. Where you at right now?"

"I'm about to get off of work right now. Where do you want me to meet you?" Malik asked.

"I'm over at Lindsay's crib. Meet me over here."

"You at Lindsay crib?" Malik asked sounding surprised, "Her number didn't show up on my phone."

"That's not relevant right now."

Malik was quiet. Truth was he didn't like the sound of Squeeze being at his girl's crib especially with it being so late.

"Malik, you still there, baby?"

"Yeah, I'm here," Malik said offhandedly.

"So as soon as you get off of work, come down here. I gotta holla at you."

"Ahight, Squeeze. I'll be there," Malik said and hung up.

"What you want with Malik?" Lindsay asked.

"Where did you meet this kid?" he asked.

"I met him a few months ago where he work at, Footlocker.

We talked, he took me out, and that's it. He's nice. Reminds me of my brother in a way. He just don't have a hot temper like him."

"So where is he from?"

"I know that his family is from Spanish Harlem but he lives out in Brooklyn with his grandmother, I think. Why? What's wrong, Squeeze? Did Malik do something?"

"Nah...nah, we cool. I just got some questions for him, dats all."

Lindsay stared at Squeeze. Damn! He's so fuckin' sexy, she thought. She loved the way he was in charge of things. His demeanor was just too ill for her. Here he was chillin' in her crib all nonchalant and cool after his club done got shot up and he was determined to find out who the culprits were and handle it in the streets like a man.

There was no hiding it. Lindsay was in love with Squeeze. As for Malik, he was just something to hold her down these last few months. She wasn't in love with Malik. He was nice and had his ways but he was nothing like Squeeze, Show and the others.

Lindsay walked up to Squeeze while he sat on her couch and started to touch on him sexually. She kissed him slowly across his neck down to his chest and then she placed herself down on her knees, opened up his pants, and uttered, "Baby, I got you tonight."

Squeeze smiled and grunted, "Damn, do you, baby."

Lindsay gripped his erection gently, massaged his balls, and then gradually placed his hard-on between her glossy lips and sucked him down to the balls.

Squeeze threw his head back, clutched the cushions with both hands, and grunted loudly as Lindsay put him in complete bliss with a smooth and rapid blowjob.

An hour later, Lindsay was asleep on the couch. Squeeze glanced at the time. It was 11:30 p.m. and that kid wasn't there, he became suspicious.

Squeeze knew that if he had to go to war, he needed help and Show wasn't capable but he knew other muthafuckas who would be perfect for the job. He scrolled down a bunch of numbers in his phone until he came across the right one. He smiled and pushed the call button. The phone began ringing in his ear and someone picked up.

"Who dis?"

"Squeeze, baby."

"Squeeze, mi glad to hear from yuh again, brethren." Nappy Head Don spoke. "Mi hear 'bout your Bwoy, Show. Him good people. Mi gwan pray fi di bredda, Squeeze, yuh hear! Whatever yuh need, Squeeze, mi have you."

"I'm glad to hear dat," Squeeze said. "I need a favor."

"What di fava, Squeeze? Anyting yuh need, mi deyah."

"I've been hearing about these Dominican cats from Flatbush. That's over by you, Nappy Head Don. You know what goes on around there. Niggas don't operate unless you know about it. What can you tell me about them? They shot up my club something serious da other day."

"Mi hear 'bout dat on da fuckin' news, brethren. Innocent people get kill, yuh hear. Mi frien' was on dat line. Dem Bwoys dem gots no fuckin' respect, Squeeze. Dem Dominican Bwoys, dem crazy. All mi cyan tell you is dat dem from Da heights up in Manhattan."

"Oh word? You got a name for me?" Squeeze asked.

"Not yet, brethren, but a wi find one fi you. Mi promise yuh dat, Squeeze."

"I'm ready to war wit' these nigga, yo. I need you, baby. I'm willing to pay healthy for your help. You down, Don?"

"Brethren, Show's like a bredda to us. Him forever showing mi love. Mi people ready when yuh ready fi give da word, brethren, and we gwan stick dey blood claat ass in a fuckin' hole."

Squeeze smiled knowing he could always depend on Nappy Head Don and his wild Rasta crew from Flatbush to come through for him.

"Ahight Nappy Head Don. One my, nigga."

"Respect, Squeeze. One," Nappy Head Don said and then hung up.

Squeeze thought about the Dominicans. If he had to travel

up to the da Heights for blood to spill for his retaliation then so be it. He had the right killers to do it with—Nappy Head Don and Rude Boy Rex were niggas you don't want as enemies—crazy ass Jamaicans.

Respect was big with them and you better show 'em much of it because if you didn't, they'd be quick to stick you in the eye with an ice pick and leave you on your mother's front porch with a note. Plus, Nappy Head Don was not too thrilled about hearing that the Dominicans that ran business on his turf, shooting up innocent people at a nightclub. To him, that was disrespect. Innocent people died over nonsense and that brought down the cops hard on him and his peoples. So for him, it wasn't about pay for Squeeze. It was about the disrespect.

Carlos and his niggas sat in a standard two bedroom apartment up in Washington Heights, each of 'em taking turns blazing from a burning L. Carlos was sprawled across the couch, looking nonchalant and shit, thinking about the death of his brother and his cousin. The room was calm with small chitchat here and there. All three men, Carlos, Miguel, and Manny were focused on the evening news as they watched their grimy work air on the news. It was the talk of the town and police didn't have anyone in custody.

They also had no luck finding the car. That was because Carlos and the rest had set the car on fire far off in Jersey somewhere. The public expected an arrest of the cowards and soulless monsters that committed such a crime but the police's hard work and interrogations were to no prevail—they had nothing to go on. The only person they had to work with was Squeeze and whatever he could give 'em. But since he wasn't cooperating with the law, there were no indictments coming down the pipeline anytime soon for the public.

Carlos took a long pull from the dro' then blew the smoke

out his mouth as he watched the 21 inch monitor plaster their horrific event across the screen once again. They watched a poor widower from the night give her gruesome deposition about how she lost her husband. Miguel smiled then joked, "Bitch, your man shoulda ducked!" Manny and Miguel started to laugh at the twisted joke.

"Muthafuckas, I wish dat nigga Squeeze was there. I want dat nigga, Carlos. We gotta get dat nigga."

"Carlos, you alright?" Manny asked, peering at his friend.

"I'm cool, yo. Chillin'."

"Yo, don't worry about Hector and Jose. Dey good right now, yo. Dey at peace but we gonna handle it."

Carlos didn't answer. He missed his younger brother and his cousin. He'd promised his mother that he would take care of Hector but Hector was hard-headed and wanted to be just like his brother. Jose, he was Carlos' right-hand, smart and a bout' it, muthafucka.

Jose had hooked Carlos up with a strong connect from Connecticut and helped him get the money out there on the streets. Jose had been on the streets since he was ten and he and Carlos had been getting down for a minute. They ride and die together. But Carlos resented Hector getting in on the game but his younger brother would always beg him to get down. He became a constant nag so Carlos put Hector on a year ago and things were going along smoothly until the incident with the grenades.

Carlos was the one that had to go break the news to his moms that her youngest most adorable son had been violently killed. He had been in tears as he approached his moms and his aunt while they were cooking with friends and family. He didn't know any other way to break the news to his family without being straight forward so he walked up to his moms who'd had a smile on her face all day. When she saw Carlos approach her with the somber look, Ms. Rodriguez predicted the news already.

"Mami..." he paused gazed into her inquiring worrying eyes then uttered, "Hector and Jose are dead."

Ms. Rodriquez and her sister, Jose's mother, let out ear

piercing screams as they clutched Carlos and collapsed to the floor. His aunt started screaming in Spanish as she banged her fist against the table.

Carlos hated it. He hated seeing his family weep and sob. He hated seeing his family, especially his mother, in so much pain. That's why he hadn't wanted his younger brother in the game. He had known that Hector wasn't built for it. Jose was a different story. Jose had taught him the game.

Unable to see his mother in such a disturbed condition, he had quickly left the apartment and met with friends outside. He vowed to find out those people who were responsible. He wanted blood to spill no matter how many.

The next day, a little birdie had told him of the men responsible for the deaths of his homies. The snitch had also informed Carlos about Show's condition and let him know which hospital the nigga was laid up in. Carlos paid for all this information, a very reasonable price that had led them to *The Brooklyn Café*. There was no remorse. Carlos lost family so now niggas were going to lose much more. Carlos remained seated on the couch, lost in his own thoughts as he continued to blaze.

"What we gonna do Carlos. These niggas are still breathing out there. Dat can't be. Fuckin' puta's gotta go," Miguel said. "Hector and Jose were like fuckin' brothers to me too, Carlos."

Carlos nodded, peering over at Miguel. "Get your peoples to handle Show. I want dat muthafucka to be breathing through his fuckin' neck."

"Ahight, Carlos." Miguel nodded.

"And Manny…." Carlos didn't get to finish talking because his girl Tara walked into the room catching the men's attention. Tara was an exquisite woman, standing 5'7" and decked out in lavish jewelry and clothes from head to toe. Everything she wore was expensive, even the $100 pink thong she had on—and all of it from her generous lover and man, Carlos. He loved Tara and was very jealous of his woman. Any man looked at her wrong and he was ready to murder them.

Tara strutted into the room with her long black sinuous hair, her size 9 Fendi high heels, Fendi skirt, and a Fendi bag to match.

"Hi, baby," she greeted.

Tara took a seat across his lap and kissed him on his lips. The men watched and tried not to drool at the sight of her. She was gorgeous but they knew she was hands off. Tara was Carlos's prize and he took care of her like she was a queen.

"I thought you was going shopping?" Carlos asked.

"I am but I need about five hundred, baby," she said pleasantly.

Carlos sighed, glancing at his niggas. He knew and they knew that Tara was a gold-digger. The bitch was probably born asking the doctor for a dollar but Carlos loved her and the sex was great. She gave blowjobs like a porn star. Carlos reached into his pocket and pulled out a wad of hundreds and pushed into her hand a grand.

"Thank you, baby," Tara said, giving him a loving hug and kiss on the lips then she quickly got up and strutted out of the room, leaving the men behind to talk about business.

Miguel and Manny peered at her luscious body longer than usual causing Carlos to shout. "Y'all niggas got a problem wit' y'all fuckin' eyes?"

Miguel and Manny snapped back to reality. "Nah, Carlos. We ain't got no problem," Manny said.

"Then stop staring at my bitch so fucking hard."

Manny stroked his trimmed goatee, leaning back into the chair. He meant no disrespect.

"And Miguel, I want Show out of business soon. Really out of business. Who you got on da job? I don't want this shit getting linked back to us, ya hear? But I do want to send these fuckin' niggas a message."

"Carlos, don't even worry. I got this old head that's been doing this shit forever. He knows how to handle things correctly. I'll call this nigga tonight. But he might want ten grand up front for the hit."

"Miguel, don't even worry about the money. I just want it done ASAP."

"Got you, Carlos."

Carlos peered at the TV. Even if it meant his own death, he vowed revenge against the men responsible for his brother's murder.

7:45pm: Kings County Hospital

Show's condition wasn't improving and the doctors wondered how much longer he had to live. Show lay in bed, barely alive but he was able to open his eyes and move his head a little. Squeeze came by as much as possible to visit his right-hand and every night when he left, he would shed tears for his crippled friend. Squeeze walked out of the elevator and headed for his car.

He wondered if he could continue to stand seeing his friend in that condition. As he strolled out the hospital lobby, he didn't pay attention to the 6'1" medium built man that walked into the lobby and came to pay Show a quick visit.

"I'm here to see a Deshawn Grant," the tall stranger uttered.

Security at the booth looked up at him and asked, "And you are?"

"I'm his uncle."

"Your name?"

"Ronny Maywood."

"You have I.D on you, Ronny Maywood?"

The stranger pulled out a fake driver's license and passed it to the security at the desk. He wrote his name and information down on the visitor's sheet and passed him a visitor's tag.

"Here you go. He's on the fifth floor. Room 528."

"Thank you."

"You're welcome."

The stranger walked off toward the elevator. He was dressed in black and gray—black slacks, black buttoned down shirt, and a gray sports jacket over it. He looked sharp as his shoes shimmered and his thick black beard and dark skin caught the attention of the female staff. But he wasn't concerned about the ladies' attention; he was there to do a job.

He walked down the hall of the 5th floor looking for room 528. He found it, last room down the hall. He glanced around for a quick moment then stepped into Show's room. When he walked in, the room was quiet and he saw Show resting in bed, looking helpless. He noticed his huge frame covered the entire bed and the stranger thought if Show had been in full health, he'd be a worthy adversary. The stranger knew that this man was fearsome before he was bound to a hospital bed. But he also knew that Show had information he needed so he walked up to Show's bed and gazed down on him.

"Nigga, you up? Can you hear me?" he asked.

Show didn't respond. His eyes were barely open. The stranger pulled out his weapon and placed a silencer on the barrel to quiet the sound of gunfire.

"Before you die, I need some information from you. If you answer me right, I'll make it neat so you can have an open casket funeral. You can talk right?"

Show looked up at the man. He knew it was the end for him and he wished that he didn't have to go out this way. He would rather go out in the hail of gunfire than the helpless state he was in, laying vulnerable in a hospital bed and staring up at his attacker. He was barely able to speak or call for help. But he was a soldier till the day he died and before he begged for his life, he'd rather go out with dignity. He wanted to shout out "Fuck you!" but his condition wouldn't allow him to.

"I'm looking for your friend, Promise. You know where he may be hiding at?" he glared at show then added. "Yeah, nigga, you know, right. He's your boy."

Show didn't answer.

"Nothing, huh?" The stranger said, taunting him as I gripped the gun in his hand and waved it around.

As Show stared up at the bearded man, he couldn't help but

to shed a tear as it trickled down the side of his face. He thought about his life, his son. He thought about the things he had done while he had lived. He'd had it all and now he was about to lose it all.

"Fuck you," Show was able to mumble but it was a bit incoherent.

The man scowled down at him and pointed the gun to his head. "Goodnight," he uttered and fired three silent shots into Show's head. As fast as he came, the middle-aged gentleman casually walked out of Show's room, acting like everything was all right.

In room 528 laid Show's bloody mess. There were three shots embedded into his skull, one between the eyes, one in his forehead, and the last shot into his left eye. The first nurse to find him would let out a shocked scream. It was a gruesome sight.

The stranger traveled down the almost vacant hallway, approaching a hefty nurse in white garments who was heading his way.

"Hello," she greeted the attractive gentlemen.

"Excuse me. I'm on the wrong floor. Can you direct me toward the nursery? My first grandchild was born today," he said.

"Ah, that's wonderful." She gleamed. "Boy or girl?"

"Boy."

"It's on the sixth floor. In fact, I'll show you," she volunteered. He followed behind her giving him time to find a secure exit out the hospital before the body was found.

Squeeze got the call the following day about his boy's violent and ghastly murder. He became enraged.

"Niggas are fuckin' cowards," he yelled, tossing a chair against the wall of Lindsay's apartment. "How they gonna murder my man like dat? He was already helpless. What da fuck he gonna do to a nigga!"

Lindsay stood off to the side, her eyes were fixated on Squeeze's violent rage as he tossed and tore up shit in her apartment. She stood there, not stopping him because she was also saddened by Show's sudden murder. Tears trickled down Lindsay's face as she folded her arms across her chest feeling like she had lost another brother.

After about fifteen minutes of ranting and raving, Squeeze finally calmed down and dropped himself down on the floor with his back against the couch and started to cry.

"My nigga, yo... My nigga! Yo, dat was my nigga...what da fuck is going on fuck yo. Fuck!" he cried, his face buried in his hands.

He felt weak and he felt alone. There was no one else. Even though Promise was still alive and out there somewhere, Squeeze still felt alone. Him and Show had ruled with an iron fist and now his right-hand man was no longer. He was saddened that it had to end like this but he knew what had to be done. Despite the businesses he had and the club he owned, bottom line was Squeeze was a fuckin' gangsta—a fuckin' thug and he knew death was inevitable for certain niggas—Dominicans especially. It was on. He no longer gave a fuck.

Lindsay finally came over to comfort her man. She had never seen him like this. In her eyes, she always saw Squeeze as a thug with little emotion about anything. But tonight, she was taken aback and saw that he was still human behind the guns, the attitude and the tough talk. She respected him. She loved him.

Squeeze didn't fight her off as she sat down crying next to him. She placed her arms around him saying, "I'm sorry, baby. I'm so sorry."

Dozens of folk showed up at Show's funeral. Distant family and friends come by to show their respect. Even his son's mother's family came by to pay their respect. They still had no idea that it was Show who had murdered his baby mama in the first place.

Squeeze sat off in the distance with his mind aloof from everyone around him and the funeral. Lindsay stood next to her mother; tears trickling down their cheeks as they stared at the closed casket.

Our Father which art in heaven: hollowed be Thy name, Thy Kingdom come. Thy will be done on earth

as it is in heaven. Give us this day our daily bread and
forgive us our debts as we forgive our debtors. And
lead us not into temptation, but deliver us from evil.
For Thine is the Kingdom, and the power and the glory
forever....Amen.

The men and women at the funeral recited the Lord's Prayer in unison. Squeeze didn't participate. He sat alone in his seat, contemplating his revenge. He had his .380 concealed underneath his Armani suit jacket and wanted to use it bad on the men responsible for him being here today.

He had shed his tears for his friend in private and only one saw him cry. Now he wanted to shed blood. His eyes were cold and no one approached him. He sat in the back of the funeral peering at the closed casket. They couldn't even allow Show to have an open casket funeral. He felt that was disrespectful. He wasn't able to see Show's face one last time. But he said his goodbyes and now it was time for him to move on and do what was necessary.

Lindsay turned around and looked over at Squeeze. She was worried about him. She left her mother's side to attend to Squeeze who looked like he needed someone to talk to or be there for him. Everyone treated him like an outcast. Maybe they were afraid of him, knowing his reputation, knowing what he was about but not Lindsay. The past few days, she had gotten to know Squeeze very well and she wanted to continue to get to know him. In fact she was so in love with Squeeze that she was willing to have his baby.

Lindsay came over to Squeeze and asked, "Baby, you okay?"

"Go be with your moms right now. I'm good," he lightly replied.

"You sure, baby?" Lindsay pressed.

Squeeze looked up at her, giving her a blank look and Lindsay knew not to press. Instead, she took a walk outside to get some fresh air.

Squeeze continued to sit for a few moments and then he got

up and walked outside knowing that the service was about to end in a few minutes. When he walked out, he noticed two detectives standing outside and he knew they were waiting for him. They stood by a black Sedan dressed in slacks, ties and shoes. He glared at them wishing that they would just leave him the fuck alone.

"Fuck y'all want?" Squeeze asked.

"We need to talk to you, Squeeze," the black detective replied. He had short dark hair, a goatee, and wore dark shades. He was tall too; 6'2". His name was Detective Daly.

"C'mon, don't you see that I'm at my boys' funeral? What, y'all ain't got no fuckin' respect?"

"Come with us now cuz all we gonna do is keep coming and making your life a living hell. I'm sorry about your friend but we need to clear up some things with you. Now you can call your lawyer…"

"Yeah, I'm gonna do that?" Squeeze countered.

The white detective glowered at Squeeze, not liking his sarcastic street attitude. He was from Long Island and hated the way these young black males conducted themselves in front of police and everyone else, feeling like they were always invincible and so fuckin' tough all the time. But Detective Haywood did his job and he did it to perfection. He'd been on the force for twenty years and had locked up many people who thought they were smarter than him.

Lindsay saw that cops were taking away her man so she rushed over to Squeeze as he was getting in back of the Sedan.

"Baby, why are they taking you?"

I could hear the concern in her voice.

"I'll be alright. Just going somewhere," Squeeze said not wanting to get her to get involved. Both detectives glanced at her but paid her no mind as they jumped into the sedan and drove off.

Squeeze rode in the backseat nonchalant, knowing that he was their only lead into solving the 12 bodies that they had on their hands—that's why they kept fuckin' wit' him. Squeeze knew that NYPD was pressed about the murders. The mayor, chief of police, and governor were on they asses about solving the case and they were gonna pursue every little clue, piece of evidence, and word of mouth on the streets. Squeeze was their target but he knew the routine having been through this type of shit wit' five-O dozens of times.

The cops realized that they weren't dealing with a new-jack. Squeeze wasn't the type of nigga to bitch up and start squealing every time a cop got in his face and pressured him about a crime or threatened giving him hard time. Squeeze would glare, bite back and hold his own.

Within no time, he was at the precinct and quickly escorted into a private room. He took a seat at a barren desk and stared at the dull gray walls and rocked back and forth in his chair. He wanted to call his lawyer but he knew before that happened, both assholes were going to come into the room and question him for the umpteenth time. So he sat and waited while rocking his chair.

Moments later, Detective Daly walked into the room with his white counterpart, Detective Haywood, following right behind him. Daly took a seat at the barren desk, scowling at Squeeze, and Haywood took a seat in the second chair.

"Look, let's not make this difficult," Daly proclaimed. "It was your club they shot up. It was your club that twelve people got killed at. It was your beef, Squeeze. I don't mean to bust your balls but work with us here and we'll help you out."

Squeeze looked up at Daly and uttered, "My lawyer."

"Fuckin' nigger! Fuck your lawyer...! This is between you and us," Detective Haywood barked. "You wanna be difficult? You wanna end up like your friend, Show with three shots in the fuckin' head, huh? Squeeze, we know you went after Hector and Jose up on Flatbush a while back. You and your right hand, Show. Your truck was spotted at the crime scene. Plate numbers match and everything. Grenades, muthafucka. We know it was you."

Squeeze smirked and uttered, "Prove it."

Detective Daly shook his head. "Listen, I'm about to retire soon and either way, I'm ending my case with one of you assholes behind bars. Now it can be you or it can be Hector and Jose's peoples. I'm willing to work with you here if you just give us some information to work with and I promise you, the men responsible for this will definitely pay. I'll show the judge you cooperated."

"Listen, I don't know shit. Y'all here interrogating me when the real killers still roam free. What? Y'all muthafuckas got a crush on me? Get on your jobs, Detectives!" Squeeze emphasized the word detectives as he glared at both of them.

"You fuckin' prick. You're just like the rest. You sit there in your Armani suit and prance around in your fly gear, driving the nice cars, wearing fly jewelry, and having the nasty street attitudes with the baddest ho's under your arms and think you're above the law? You think you're smarter than us, Squeeze? Huh, nigger?!" Detective Haywood chided. "You think you can't fuck up like every other nigger I done locked up and had begging for a plea bargain. You think you got street savvy, you're too much of a man, too fuckin' ill to snitch? Well, listen, I fuckin' know you. I've been around muthafuckas like you forever. I see niggers like you come and go and when the next one jumps up to replace you, I'll smack his black ass right back down and just wait for the next drug kingpin to lock up. But I know you. You're too proud to come to the police to help you out. Nah, you're going to handle things yourself cuz you got a reputation to maintain, baby. You got guns to fire and people to go after. You got to retaliate for your fallen boy, right? That's the way it goes down in the streets…that's how Squeeze gets down. So you can sit here and play Boyz n' da Hood but we'll be waiting for you to fuck up. I'll personally be waiting to lock your black ass up after you done went out and did some dumb shit because the one thing I figured out about y'all street savvy niggers, y'all niggers do the same shit day in and day out. They come at me, I'm gonna come at them," Haywood proclaimed, smirking at Squeeze. "Squeeze, go ahead and continue playing the tough guy because it's all about respect. You niggers are ready to kill each other over the smallest amount of disrespect. Better yet, end up like your boy, Show, and his closed casket funeral. In the end, I'll be the one still standing and you, you'll either be dead or in jail like every other drug-dealing fly ass nigger I had sitting in front of me. You're no different."

Squeeze looked over at Haywood and blew air out of his mouth as he continued to rock in his chair and remained unconcerned. "Whatever man! My fuckin' lawyer, please," he smiled, mocking the two.

"Nigger, don't be a fuckin' asshole," Daly chided.

"Yeah, we already got two in the room," Squeeze countered.

"Fuck you!" Detective Haywood shouted as he started to lunge for Squeeze but Daly held him back, saying to him it wasn't worth it.

"Niggers like you don't have any concern or morals about human life."

"That's right. It ain't worth losing your badge, you cracker. You're smarter than me, right?" Squeeze mocked.

Detective Daly glared at Squeeze and then surprisingly kicked the chair from underneath him, causing Squeeze to fall flat on his ass. Haywood let out a quick chuckle, watching Squeeze fall.

Squeeze stood up, clutching the back of his head and uttered, "Oh, y'all muthafuckas are definitely gonna be hearing from my lawyer. You fucked up!"

"See you in lock up soon," Daly threatened.

"Yeah, like cat and mouse, baby."

Both detectives left the room but not before Haywood uttered, "They will never change."

An hour later, Squeeze's lawyer came in and told him to leave. They had nothing on him but they kept pressuring him and his lawyer was getting annoyed with the NYPD's harassment of his client.

Squeeze went back to Lindsay's crib. He knew he shoulda went to see his family but he wasn't in the mood for the drama. He knew that at Lindsay's place, he could relax and chill out without his baby mom stressing him the fuck out.

When he walked in, Lindsay was all over him, hugging him,

kissing him, and trying to relax his mind.

"Baby, you okay? What did they do to you?" she asked.

"I'm good," Squeeze replied. He took a seat on the couch and stared up at the ceiling.

"You sure, baby. You need anything?"

"Nah, I'm good."

Lindsay went over to him and sat across his lap, throwing her arms around him. He had a lot of shit on his mind. For the first time in his life, his conscience was running wild. He thought about Promise, Why did I leave him alive that day in Candy's bathroom? Squeeze saw himself back in that apartment, knowing that Promise was hiding out in the bathtub. But something stopped him as he had the gun gripped in his hand and finger pressed slightly against the trigger. He could've ended the drama that day with Promise but he didn't. He left him alive. It was the first time in his criminal life that Squeeze had detoured from putting a bullet in a nigga. Show had his speculations about what went down in the bathroom. Squeeze knew he shoulda came clean with Show but he hadn't. Now he asked himself why. Maybe he was slipping in da game and becoming soft. He didn't want to show that side of him to anyone, not even his niggas from day one.

All his life, Squeeze had always been a fly gangsta. Squeeze thought about his life when he was young, growing up in Newark with his moms and abusive stepfather.

"You okay, baby?" Lindsay asked again, cuddling against her man.

Squeeze didn't answer her and continued reminiscing about his childhood days. When he was eight, his moms married some punk cab driver named Freddie. They seemed to be in love but Squeeze hadn't liked him from the jump. Freddie was a nigga who dressed like he was still living in the seventies and always had a bottle in his hand after he got off of work.

Soon after his moms got married, Freddie didn't waste time and started beating on Squeeze just because he could. When Freddie got tired of beating on Squeeze, he would turn his fists toward his mother and start whooping her ass. Squeeze tried to stop it but Freddie always overpowered him and continued to beat on his moms.

Squeeze, born Jeremiah Dinkins, never knew his father and never had close family to count on during the times of trouble. It was always just he and his mother.

Unfortunately, he and his mother endured two years of the abuse until she finally came to her senses and moved herself and her son away from Freddie to reside in Brooklyn, New York. What she thought would be a better life for her son turned him into something of the opposite. Jeremiah began hanging out with the wrong crowds of people and started hustling when he was thirteen. If you dared to challenge him, you'd lose because the one thing Squeeze hated was feeling or looking weak in front of his peers. He hated being vulnerable. He hated disrespect. Squeeze learned at an early age that there was power behind a gun. He'd held his first weapon, a .22, when he was twelve and he learned how to shoot in empty Brooklyn lots and alleyways late at night when he and Show would shoot at brick walls and garbage cans.

He loved the way a gun felt gripped in his hand and how it felt when a round was discharged. Squeeze would get so carried away firing off the weapon that he wouldn't hear the police sirens heading in their direction because he was too enthralled by the way of a gun giving him the nickname, Squeeze. Show would damn near have to drag his ass off and they'd run like bats out of hell, laughing and clowning around, while Squeeze still had the gun in his hand. He liked to have control and he loved the respect he received when he took control of things.

Squeeze would listen to himself and no one else. His moms had lost control and he was absorbed in the street life. He loved the hustle, respect, and the wealth it brought. He would tell himself that he would never be that scared little boy again when Freddie used to come home and whoop his ass. Never again, he thought. Today, if he came across Freddie again, Squeeze wouldn't hesitate to put a bullet in his head. Freddie was the last man to make Squeeze feel weak and scared. After him, he began to fear no one and he walked away from no beef.

He had kept his word until now. He kept wondering why he walked away from Promise. Usually, the nigga would be toe-tagged and buried six feet deep but the problem went much deeper than that. He began feeling guilty as his conscience for once started fuckin' with him. Promise had been there for him. That was his nigga; dogs for life. So what da fuck had happened, Squeeze pondered while he remained seated on the couch.

He thought that maybe it was his fault that Promise was on the run. Squeeze had called him up that night knowing Promise wanted out the game and that he wanted to be at peace with his daughter but he still came down to Brooklyn because his niggas had beef. Pooh got shot and that was real, that was family. Promise never turned his back on his family, no matter how rough, complicated, or deadly it got. Promise was there. He'd been bout' it since back in the day.

Even when Promise's baby moms, Denise, got killed, Promise still stood strong by his niggas. Now, there was no one left. Shit, no one he could trust anyway. Yeah, he had Nappy Head Don and Rude Boy Rex but he didn't trust them niggas. He had soldiers but they wouldn't ride or die for him like his niggas from back on the block.

"They hit me hard," Squeeze faintly uttered. "Fuck this!" His face was hard as he stared at the wall ahead of him.

"Baby, talk to me," Lindsay pleaded, still cozying up to him.

"I let him go because I owed him that," Squeeze said confusing Lindsay.

"Let who go?" she questioned.

"I couldn't do it. I couldn't take him out like that. Not like some scared rabid dog. I didn't want him to go out like that. We were boys." Squeeze tried to resist the tears but couldn't and they trickled down his cheeks. He thought about Pooh then Show and no matter how gangsta he tried to be that night, it was hurting him—the deaths were fuckin' with him.

"Show hit me hard, baby," he sniffled. "What happened?

We had this shit on lock. The streets were ours. Now my niggas are gone."

"Baby, you're gonna be okay. You're strong, Squeeze. Ever since I met you, you always have been strong. You need to remain like that. Them bitch ass niggas that did that to Show and got at my brother, they gonna get theirs, baby. I promise but you gotta keep your head strong, baby. You gotta maintain things like how you been doing. Don't start falling apart on us now, you hear?"

Squeeze didn't comment on Lindsay's statements. He continued staring at the wall. He thought about Brooklyn and he thought about the beef that was escalating between him and them niggas from Washington Heights who came and set up shop in his borough. Brooklyn—this was his fuckin' hometown.

Niggas shoulda stayed they asses uptown and none of this shit would've happened. Squeeze refused to believe that his reign was over, that he was losing control of the streets. If he did lose control and the respect that him and his niggas had fought so hard to maintain then that meant Show and Pooh died in vain. And Promise, Squeeze thought, he was a different story.

"Lindsay, I gotta go," Squeeze said, pushing Lindsay off his lap and rising up.

"Go? Where?"

"Like you said, I'm gonna handle things," he proclaimed, staring at Lindsay with fire in his eyes.

Lindsay smiled. She watched Squeeze collect his weapons; a loaded .45 and two loaded .380's from out her bedroom, stuff them into a small black bag then leave. Squeeze drove back to Bed-Stuy over by Fulton and Nostrand Ave. It was late but still warm out as Squeeze cruised down Fulton with 50 Cent blaring from his stereo. He recognized a few heads but there were a lot of unfamiliar faces out on the streets. He drove in a new car. That was why some folks didn't know who he was but he was still well respected around there.

Squeeze stopped in front of a 24-hour bodega where he noticed a few men gambling at the side. He knew them but didn't pay 'em quick mind. Not yet, anyway. He watched as one dude in a blue velour sweat suit and a Yankee fitted jiggled the dice in his hand and tossed them against the side of the store as everyone gawked waiting for the numbers to appear.

"Yeah, dat's what da fuck I'm talking about. Y'all niggas give me my fuckin' money. Pay up muthafuckas!" the man in the velour shouted.

Everyone shifted bills in their hands, anteing up their losses, and passed the money over to the winner.

"Niggas tryin' to take my money. Y'all muthafuckas must be going fuckin' crazy! Dats right, pay me my ends!" the loud mouth winner exclaimed.

Squeeze sat in his car and thought that now was the time to make his presence known. He gently pressed down on the horn alerting all and they turned to stare at Squeeze's lavish ride.

"Oh, shit!" the winner exclaimed staring into the car and finally realizing who the driver was. He quickly strutted over to the car, leaving behind the game, and a few niggas with broke pockets.

"My nigga, Squeeze. Long time no see, nigga. What's good wit' you?"

"Same old, same old. Different day, dat's all," Squeeze stated.

"Yeah, well, what you doing back in dis part of town? I thought your fly ass stayed up in Canarsie wit' the fly crib and shit."

"Nigga, you know dis still my hood. You know I'm gonna always come back."

"Yeah, it's still love. Yo, I heard what happened to Show. I'm sorry about dat. I know he was your boy and all."

"You know...dat's all part of the game we play. I'm gonna handle it though."

The guy smiled. "So what you want from a nigga, Squeeze? I know your ass ain't drive into Bed-Stuy to say what's up to a nigga. What's really good wit' you?"

"Hop in. I wanna holla at you for a sec."

The young man turned to his boys and shouted out, "Yo, Nat, hold da game down for a nigga. I'll be right back." He jumped into the passenger seat and Squeeze drove off. Squeeze drove down a few blocks before he said anything.

"You still got peoples dat be up in Da Heights?"

"Yeah, I still do some business out there. Why?"

"I just need some information."

"About what?"

"Who's a major playa out there? I mean, who's a nigga dats crazy enough to gun down twelve people in front of my nightclub?" he explained.

"Damn, I heard about dat shit. It's all over the news everyday. Cops steady fuckin' wit' niggas over dat shit...I mean, damn, they messed my man up da other day thinking he a suspect and shit. But da only nigga I can think of right now dat be holding firepower like that is dat nigga, Carlos. He crazy, yo, but he be holding mad paper. Matter fact, his fuckin' brother and his cousin used to be out on Flatbush running coke and weed till someone blew they shit up and killed both of 'em. Da game is fucked up," Pete chuckled. "Niggas throwing fuckin' grenades at each other now."

Squeeze glanced at him as 50's *Massacre* CD played low through the speakers.

"Niggas like Carlos and Miguel, them niggas don't play. They fuckin' crazy, Squeeze," he repeated again. "Why? What's up? You got beef wit' them?"

"Don't know yet," Squeeze uttered.

Squeeze made a quick right on Myrtle and drove past the Tompkins houses. He stared at the buildings while he drove and thought about what had gone down there a year and a half ago; the beef, the murders, and Promise killing that cop. He was still on the run. Slick muthafucka, Squeeze thought. The feds and the state couldn't catch that nigga. Squeeze had to give Promise respect for that. It seemed Promise was always one step ahead of them like Harrison Ford in 'The Fugitive.' Promise was just as good, maybe even better.

"Pete," Squeeze uttered. "I'm gonna keep it real wit' you. I think Carlos and whoever are responsible for Show's death might have shot up my club."

"What? Say word? You serious, nigga?"

"Nigga, do I fuckin' joke?"

"I know you gonna handle dat. You got to."

"I got this but I wanna ask you sump'n. When I need you, are you gonna be on call for a nigga?"

Pete looked at Squeeze long and hard then answered. "I got your back, nigga. Don't even worry. You need me, I'm here. I know where dem niggas mostly be at up in Da Heights. I know Carlos got a bitch out there. Some chicken he fucks with."

"Ahight, ahight," Squeeze said, nodding his head. When Squeeze stopped at a red light, he reached under his seat and pulled out a small manila envelope. He passed it over to Handsome Pete.

"What's this?"

"For you. Thanks for da info. It's a lil' sump'n for your help," Squeeze stated.

Pete slowly opened up the envelope and revealed twenty crisp hundred-dollar bills. "Word nigga? Its love like dat?" Pete exclaimed, smiling broadly.

"It's your winning night, nigga. You on top of the world tonight," Squeeze proclaimed.

"Squeeze, we gonna handle things. I got your back fo' sure, nigga. Just let me know when and Carlos, his shit's in the wind. I never liked the nigga anyway...faggot muthafucka!"

"Ahight."

Squeeze dropped him off a block from where he had picked Handsome Pete up. Pete gave him a dap and said, "One, my nigga. I'm on call for you whenever."

Squeeze nodded as Handsome Pete stepped out of the car. Now that he knew who was responsible, Squeeze vowed to end it quickly and painfully for Carlos and whoever had helped. Squeeze knew his name was hot around town especially with the cops. He knew he had to be careful particularly when it came to Detectives Haywood and Daly. He knew both men had it out for him. One fuck up and they were gonna quickly stuff his black ass in some county jail way upstate.

Now that he had a name, he had motive. He knew Handsome Pete for a few years now and remembered when Pete used to brag about getting money uptown with them Dominican niggas. He was always bragging about how good that Spanish pussy was and how quick a Dominican hoe could make him cum. Handsome Pete never stopped talking about uptown and how much money was out there. He blabbed about bitches he'd fucked and how they always cheated on their mans when he was chilling out there.

Pete was a handsome nigga in his early twenties. He had so many kids in New York that the nigga done lost count. Last time he remembered, he had about eight kids with seven different baby mothers but he forever boasted about his kids and how he keeps a bitch pregnant. That's why da nigga hustled because him having a regular nine to five wasn't gonna support all his kids. Child support would kick his ass.

Squeeze picked up his cellphone and dialed up Nappy Head Don's number. After the third ring, Nappy Head Don picked up.

"Bredren, mi jus bout' to call yuh, yuh know Squeeze. Mi have a bit of surprise fi yuh," Nappy Head Don proudly announced.

"Oh word!"

"Can't talk too long now, bredren. Meet me tomorrow evenin'."

"Where at?"

"Flatbush and Church at five."

"Ahight."

Squeeze hung up and proceeded to his home in Canarsie. He needed to see his kids and his shortie. It had been a long day for him. Soon the days were gonna get even longer.

"Squeeze, Bwoy," Nappy Head Don greeted Squeeze while he sat in his car.

Squeezed looked up but he didn't smile. He nodded his head and got out his ride parked on Church Ave and followed Nappy Head Don and Rube Bwoy Rex to their parked truck on Flatbush.

Nappy Head Don was saddened by Show's murder and he felt what Squeeze was feeling. They quickly embraced and vowed revenge for Show's death. They drove off riding north on Flatbush.

"Squeeze, mi promise yuh, we gwan get di men responsible, yuh hear?"

"I want dem to suffer, you hear me, Nappy Head Don? These Dominicans...I want dis nigga named Carlos."

"Don't worry, brethren. Mi have a likkle gift fi yuh," Nappy Head Don informed him. "Squeeze, we goin fi a likkle ride."

Squeeze rode in the 2003 Denali truck as they sped off to Atlantic Ave. A short while later, they stopped in front of a Footlocker and Squeeze was surprised.

"What we doing here?" Squeeze asked.

"Dis here da gift, brethren," Nappy Head Don said.

Nappy Head pulled out a black Glock 17 and Rude Bwoy Rex pulled out the same. Squeeze was about to see how crazy these two fools got down.

"In der is da gift, bredren. In der a fi yuh informer."

"Fuck you talking about?" Squeeze barked.

"Follow mi, brethren," Nappy Head said.

Everyone got out of the truck and headed into the Footlocker. It was late evening out but there still was a flock of people outside. Nappy Head Don and his partner strolled into the busy store with their guns discreetly held down and Squeeze followed behind them. They walked in and immediately, Nappy Head Don's eyes scanned the store for his victim. He spotted who he was looking for and quickly walked up to him.

"Can I help you, sir?" Malik spoke, seeing Nappy Head Don approach him so suddenly.

When he looked passed him and saw Squeeze and another deadly looking man standing next to him, Malik panicked and tried to run for the back exit but Nappy Head Don raised his gun and fired off a quick round at Malik, striking him in the leg and dropping him abruptly. The sound of a single gunshot caused an uproar in the store and shoppers and staff dropped everything and scurried for the nearest exit. Malik lay on the ground, crying out as he clutched his bleeding leg.

"Yo, what da fuck y'all want? I ain't do nothing."

"Then why yuh run?" Nappy Head Don barked. "Rex, come help me carry dis faggot to da car."

They picked Malik up and dragged him to the truck as a dozen witnesses stood off to the side and watched the crazy event. Squeeze was shocked but he liked how these two got down. He watched them carry off the bleeding and crying Malik to the truck and stuff him in the back where Nappy Head Don already had plastic bags scattered around. He made sure no blood got on his carpet. Quickly, all three men jumped into the truck and sped off, leaving moments before the police arrived.

Malik continued to cry out as he lay helpless in the back. "Yo, Squeeze, I ain't do nuthin' to you. What's up?"

Squeeze turned around and looked at him. He ain't never trust Malik for a second. The nigga always seemed too eager and friendly and always wanted to know nigga's business. A nigga like that Squeeze never trusted. That was why he had asked Lindsay about him and wanted to meet with Malik beforehand.

"Why you ain't come see a nigga, Malik?" Squeeze asked.

"I got caught up, Squeeze. Believe me, I was gonna come see you that night but shit happens. You know how that goes," Malik cried out.

Squeeze knew he was lying and he knew that there was something funny about Malik that he didn't like. Show dealt with Malik mostly. Lindsay introduced the nigga to Squeeze. He knew the nigga was front'n about his character.

Nappy Head Don drove to an abandoned building that was in an isolated area. It was a three-story dilapidated building that looked like it hadn't been lived in for years. Rude Bwoy Rex and Don carried the resistant Malik into the building's basement where they tied him to a chair and roughed him up a little.

"Fuck y'all!" Malik cursed, spitting phlegm at Nappy Head Don.

Nappy Head gave Malik an open handed smack across his face causing Malik's face to turn red slightly. Malik's eye was black and blue and his lip was split and swollen thanks to the work of Rude Bwoy Rex who loved his job—killing, torturing, and maiming.

"What's up wit' this pussy?" Squeeze asked, glaring at Malik.

"Dis here is da man who have been spreadin' yuh biznez to dat blood cleat, Carlos. Him is da one who give him da info bout' da club. Him is da one who give up Show," Nappy Head Don informed Squeeze.

"Squeeze, dis nigga's lying. I just met you. I don't know shit about you," Malik argued.

"Shut da fuck up, nigga," Squeeze yelled.

Malik squirmed against the ropes and spit blood from his mouth. "Dis some bullshit!" he uttered.

"How you know dis, Nappy Head Don?"

"Him an informer fi Carlos. Him deal wit' dem Dominicans."

"You tryin' to play both sides of da game, Malik? Huh, nigga?" Squeeze demanded to know. "Answer me, nigga!" Squeeze shouted. Grabbing Malik's neck powerfully, he pulled out his .45 and pressed it against Malik's temple.

Malik gasped for air as his face darkened and he tried to break free from Squeeze's tight grip as the cold steel of the .45 pressed against his battered face.

"Fuck you, Squeeze!" Malik cried out. He smelled death coming and tears began trickling down his face. He accidentally began to pee on himself.

"Damn nigga!" Squeeze said losing his grip around Malik's neck and backing away.

"You think I don't know," Malik blurted out.

"Know what?" Squeeze asked.

"About you and Lindsay. You fucking her, Squeeze, behind my back. You fucking her and then you come and smile in front of me like everything good."

"Nigga, you trippin' over a bitch?"

"I love dat girl."

"You set me up over Lindsay? Nigga, fuck going on with you?" Squeeze asked.

"She only eighteen, Squeeze. You could have any bitch you want. Why you gotta go after her?"

"So you know Carlos?" Squeeze asked.

"They came at me!" Malik proclaimed.

"Who came at you?" Squeezed asked.

Nappy Head Don nodded over to Rude Bwoy Rex who was standing behind the bound Malik. Suddenly Rude Bwoy Rex pulled out a thick 6" blade, put it to Malik's neck and carved open his throat. Malik squirmed and gasped for air as blood gushed out from the knife wound. He was dead within seconds.

"Damn nigga, what da fuck!" Squeeze shouted.

"Bredren, we need to finish biznez, yuh, hear. Him a snitch and him get what him deserve. Carlos, him da man we have fi kill. Him gets no respect," Nappy Head Don said, looking impervious to anything else.

Nappy Head told Rude Bwoy to dispose of the body properly. He didn't want Malik's body being found. Squeeze left with Don while Rex stayed behind to clean up the mess.

Rude Bwoy Rex cut loose Malik's limp body and his lifeless body collapsed to the floor. He got the equipment needed to dismantle Malik and got to work. First he started with the arms, cutting them off by the elbows with a chainsaw and then he worked on the legs, cutting them off at the shins. The head was left for last. Next, Rude boy Rex punctured Malik's lung so that when he dumped the body into the river, it wouldn't rise up. He also poured acid over the tattoos.

He removed anything that would identify Malik. The entire process took him a few hours because he did his job to perfection, leaving nothing behind for anyone to find.

After the body was completely dismembered and unrecognizable, he put Malik piece by piece into separate black trash bags and tied each one down carefully. He then loaded each bag into his truck that was inconspicuously parked in the back and drove the body down to the river. He dumped a few pieces of Malik into the East River then he drove down to the Hudson where he dumped more pieces of Malik there. Lastly, he drove Malik's head to Long Island and buried his head in an open field.

11:50pm: Washington Heights

"Ahhhhhh…Carlos…fuck me, baby…papi, I love you…I love you papi!" Tara cried out. She lay across her back with her legs spread out as Carlos thrust his pulsating erection into her moist vagina.

Tara straddled her legs around Carlos's waist and dug her manicured nails deep into his back as his 9" erection filled her completely.

"This my pussy, right, bitch!" Carlos proclaimed, sweating, thrusting and gripping the green satin bed-sheets.

"It's your pussy. It's your pussy, Carlos!" she shouted, closing her eyes, biting down on her bottom lip, and continued to decorate his back with love scratches.

Carlos gripped both her legs and positioned them upwards as he continued to pound into her. He was saturated with sweat. He'd been fucking Tara for a good hour and he still ain't cum. He was far from a one minute man and Tara loved every minute of her man — she couldn't get enough. She never faked it with Carlos because she didn't need to. Carlos was always on point and his dick was big enough. Unlike men she'd been with before, Carlos knew what the fuck he was doing and he laid down the pipe fo' sure in the bedroom. He had money and a fierce street reputation — Tara wasn't leaving that nigga Carlos anytime soon.

"This my pussy, right bitch...you cumin' for your man, right?" Carlos said as he fondled her breasts and gripped her thighs.

"Um, mm...take it baby...take my shit....fuck me!"

"You ain't fuckin' no other nigga but me. Pussy belongs to me, right!"

Tara moaned, clutching the satin bed sheets and feeling herself about to cum a third time. Carlos looked down at her then unexpectedly slapped her across the face. It wasn't hard but it left a tingling feeling in her cheek. Tara opened her eyes and stared up at Carlos but she didn't utter a word because the dick in her was still feeling too fuckin' good.

"What I say, bitch? You ain't fuckin' no other nigga but me. This my pussy, right?" Carlos scolded.

"Baby, you know who the pussy belongs to," Tara said.

Carlos thrust harder causing Tara to scream out. She straddled both legs around him tightly as she felt another orgasm about to come.

"Cum for me, baby. Cum for me," Tara begged.

"I'm gonna cum in your mouth," he stated. They both panted and pressed against each other forcefully, sweating and grunting. When Carlos felt himself about to let loose, he quickly pulled out, seized his erection and jerked himself off as he leaned over Tara's face. Forcefully, he shot out a load of semen onto her lips, mouth, tongue and jaw. He grunted and shuddered as he leaned over her on one arm, still gripping his big dick.

"Swallow them babies," Carlos partially joked as he collapsed on his back and stared up at the ceiling.

His body glimmered with sweat. Tara huffed, feeling a bit paralyzed. The dick did her justice and she didn't rush to wipe Carlos's semen from off her face. She let it sit there then licked some of it off with her tongue. She was a freak nasty bitch and Carlos loved every minute of her.

"You fuck another nigga and I kill you bitch!" Carlos proclaimed, still looking up at the ceiling.

"Damn, papi, why you so sensitive tonight?" Tara asked, looking at Carlos.

She couldn't help but to take in his generous features. He had smooth brown skin that was lined right with a pencil thin beard and goatee and he had dark silky hair, thick eyebrows, and a chiseled rock hard body. Tara had come across gold with Carlos and she loved every inch of him. He always spent money on her so she looked past certain fucked up qualities about him like his abuse, verbal and physical, and his fucking around with other bitches. While they been together, he had two kids by some other hoe but she still loved him though. She still wanted to be with Carlos despite the negatives.

Carlos had her staying in a legit two-bedroom apartment over on Indian Road across from Inwood Hill Park where she had a view of the Hudson River and the George Washington Bridge. Plus, her apartment was laced out with the finer things like imported Italian furniture and a Persian rug. She had a 50" Panasonic plasma TV in her living room with damn near every movie DVD out cause the bitch loved watching movies and cuddling with her man late at night. Tara was living like a queen and she wasn't about to give that shit up especially when she had never had nothing growing up.

Carlos turned and looked at her before answering her question. "Because you got some good fuckin' pussy, love, and I ain't about to let no other man enjoy what belongs to me." He let it be known.

Tara moved closer to him and began cuddling against him. "Baby, why you worry so much? Ain't no other nigga touching my precious punanny. My pussy got your name written all over it."

"Ahight...respect a nigga, Tara."

"Respect," she smiled. "I'll show you respect."

That said, she slowly started to kiss him on his stomach and made her way down to his soft but still big dick and grabbed it in her hand. She swallowed his dick down to his nuts, deep-throating that sonofabitch and causing Carlos to groan again as he threw his arms behind his head and enjoyed the blowjob.

This was why he loved her and would kill any man that dared to disrespect him and his woman—the fuckin' sex. Tara was the only woman who made Carlos feel the way he felt and cum like there was no tomorrow. He'd kill a nigga quick for this pussy.

As Carlos rested and enjoyed getting head, his cellphone went off.

"Shit!" he uttered. "Baby, stop for a minute."

But Tara didn't stop sucking his dick. She truly enjoyed that shit.

"Baby, stop...fuck!" he chided.

Tara lifted her face from off the dick and stared over at Carlos who had an irate expression on his face. He reached for his ringing phone, glanced at the caller ID and saw it was Miguel.

"Nigga, what?" he barked.

"Carlos, cops came looking for you at your mom's crib," Miguel informed him.

"What? For what?"

"Don't know."

"My moms okay?"

"Yeah...I think so."

"What da fuck you mean you think so? Is she alright or not?"

"I think so, nigga. She keeps asking for you," Miguel said.

Carlos sighed. "Ahight, yo, I'll be there in a few."

He tossed his phone across the bed and leaned back against the headboard.

"Everything okay, Carlos?"

"Nah."

"You want me to finish sucking your dick?"

"Tara, go take a shower or something. Just let me be right now," he said to her.

She didn't want Carlos getting upset with her so she left him his space and retreated to the living room. Carlos got up and collected his things. He quickly got dressed and headed out the door.

He got to his mama's in no time. He walked into her apartment and his moms started ranting, "Carlos, la policia! They come looking for you, Carlos." Then she mumbled something in Spanish.

"What dey want?"

His moms explained to him in Spanish about how they wanted to ask him a few questions.

"Mami, I'll be back. If they come back, you never saw me," Carlos explained.

He stepped out into the hallway and called up Miguel and told him to meet him over at one of his fronts. Carlos walked out of the building and he didn't get to take three steps when out of the blue, numerous police cars swooped up on him on St. Nicholas with their sirens blaring.

The police quickly jumped out of their cars with their guns out shouting, "Get down! Get the fuck down now!"

Carlos had nowhere to go and nowhere to run. He stood there with his arms in the air not looking worried. He even smirked a little at po-po but he did what they told him to do and got face down on the ground. Within seconds, cops jumped on him, pressing their knees against his back and forced his arms behind him. The iron bracelets were thrown on and he was quickly escorted to a squad car.

Several moments later, Carlos found himself handcuffed to a table in a dreary gray room staring at the walls and waiting to be interrogated. He remained nonchalant about things and knew he'd be out on the streets soon.

Three white detectives came in and they didn't look too happy but Carlos wasn't worried. He had a three hundred dollar an hour Jewish attorney and he knew he had done nothing wrong. Cops knew Carlos's rep out in Washington Heights and they were forever fucking with him and his crew so this was nothing new to him. He just thought of them as underpaid ball breakers with nothing better to do with their time.

One detective spoke up. "Fuckin' Carlos, you know out in Brooklyn, they got your name coming out of everybody's mouth? You're popular out there, guy. They're saying you're the lead man to go to about the twelve dead bodies the city's got on their hands right now," Carlos sighed.

"It wasn't me."

"Well, that's what we're not hearing. You know a Squeeze? He's got a serious reputation out there too and from what we hear, y'all two are clashing together. Y'all two got beef? What can you tell us about that?"

"I don't know no Squeeze and I think it's time for my lawyer. I know y'all are familiar with William Stein. He's put his foot in y'all asses many times for fuckin' wit' me. What? Y'all waiting for me to take out a suit against the NYPD?"

"Carlos, we know you're responsible in some way."

"Fuckin' prove it. I don't know nothing about no people getting killed in front of no nightclub. Yo, I was with my girl that night and we stayed up late watching movies. Fuck y'all talking about? Don't try and pin shit on me. I saw what went down on the news and y'all muthafuckas know I don't drive no fuckin' Oldsmobile so fuck y'all. Get Stein on the phone or I'm gonna have y'all fuckin' badges soon. Who killed Hector and Jose, Carlos?"

Carlos glared up at the detective. He didn't appreciate his brother and cousin's names being brought up. He said through clenched teeth, "Shit happens!"

Carlos knew what it was and he knew how to handle things. He wasn't no small fry with no clout or knowledge on how this game worked where cops would keep him for hours and try to force a confession out of him. See, he knew they fucked up because they hadn't even charged him with a crime yet. They had nothing. Carlos lived miles away from the crime scene and he knew that the detectives probably had some bullshit confidential informant who knew names on the streets and had knowledge about certain beefs and somehow spit Carlos's name out his mouths to evade a charge.

The most they could detain a nigga was for twenty-four hours. After that it was a wrap. The D.A. had nothing sufficient on him to present a case to a Grand Jury and he knew it was a waste of his and their time. There was no car, no weapons, and no suitable witnesses to pinpoint him to anything. He also knew Tara would back him up on his alibi.

His lawyer came through and cleared everything up. That same night, Carlos walked out a free man. He was a nigga who knew how to work the system. Since he was young, Carlos had learned that with money comes power and with the right Jewish attorney, you could probably walk away from any crime. He didn't say too much and he let cops know, I ain't the one to fuck with! Carlos continued to do him and ruled Washington Heights with an iron fist and a fearsome crew to back him up.

Handsome Pete got on the phone and dialed up one of his old flames from uptown—a pretty young girl named Laura. She was a shapely young Dominican girl who was in love with Handsome Pete. Pete hadn't spoken to her in months and he hoped her number hadn't changed. Handsome Pete wasn't calling Laura for a booty call. He was calling her for some information.

"Hello?"

"Baby, what's up?" Handsome Pete smoothly greeted.

"Who dis?"

"Damn, Laura, you don't know a nigga's voice?" Pete said jokingly.

"I think so…Petey?"

"Dat's right, love. So what's up wit' you? How you been?"

"I'm okay. Why you ain't call me in so long?"

"Love, I've been busy in and out of town. You know…tryin' to do me and make dis paper. But I've been thinking about you. So what's good wit' you?"

"Nothing. I'm glad you're calling," Laura said.

"I was missing you, baby."

"Really?"

"Yeah, you know how you and me get down. I wanna see you soon."

"Dat's not a problem. Let me know when."

"Ahight but listen, I wanna ask you sump'n," Pete said.

"About what?"

"Remember that shortie you used to hang with? What's her name…um, Carlos's girl?"

"You mean Tara?"

"Yeah her. What's up wit' her?"

"Why you wanna know about her, Pete? You know how Carlos feels about her."

"Yeah but this is about business."

"Business?" Laura inquired. "What kinda business you got with her?"

"Laura, listen, I ain't tryin' to fuck her if that's what you're inquiring about. You know I ain't crazy enough to fuck wit' Carlos's bitch like that but yo, Laura, on da real. There's five G's in this for you if you just give me some information about your girl," Handsome Pete persuaded.

"Five grand, Petey? Damn!"

"And you know I'm good for it, Laura."

"But…"

"Laura, I know you need da money. You still stripping down at the club on Morningside?"

"Yeah."

"So hook me up with some information about your girl, Tara, and I'll come by and see you tonight with the money. Promise, baby girl."

Laura smiled, thinking about the five grand. She really needed the cash right now because niggas been acting cheap down at the club. Plus, she really wanted to see Handsome Pete. Anyway, her and Tara don't talk like that anymore so why should she care, she thought.

"Ahight, Petey, Carlos got her a place over in Inwood. Nice too." And with that, Laura began informing Handsome Pete about her somewhat home girl.

"Good looking out, Laura. You know I got mad love for you. So I'm gonna see you tonight, right?"

"Of course, baby. You still know where I'm at?"

"Off of Lenox on 135th street."

"I'm glad you remember. You better come through."

"I am…around midnight."

Handsome Pete hung up and looked over at Squeeze and smiled. "Got it for you, son. Her apartment number and everything."

Squeeze let out a dim smile and gave Pete a pound. "You definitely on point, my nigga."

"Nigga, I said I got you."

With that information, Squeeze called up Nappy Head Don and his partner and put everything in motion for tonight. This was his payback and he loved every minute of it. Him and Handsome Pete jumped into his Escalade and drove off. Tonight, Carlos was gonna feel his wrath.

10:55 pm: da Heights

A black Denali pulled up to the address on Indian Road. The truck was filled wit' niggas. Both dreads, Nappy Head Don and Rude Bwoy Rex, were there along with Handsome Pete and Squeeze.

Squeeze sat up front with Nappy Head Don and Handsome Pete sat in the back with Rude Bwoy. Squeeze gripped a Glock and Nappy Head Don had two fully loaded Uzi's. He was ready for anything.

"She up in here, Pete?" Squeeze asked.

"She should be. Carlos keeps her locked up in her apartment most of the time."

"Ahight. What apartment she in?"

"Top floor. Apartment number 12B."

"Mi ready," Nappy Head Don uttered.

"Pete, you stay here and keep the truck running," Squeeze said.

"Yeah, whatever."

The other three men stepped out of the truck and walked into the lobby. They rode the elevator to the twelfth floor and stepped out one by one. Squeeze thought about how they were gonna do this. He knew shortie wasn't going to open the door for three strangers but Nappy Head Don had other methods of getting at Tara. They came to apartment 12B and Squeeze knocked.

"Who is it?" Tara called out, confirming that she was home.

"Tara?" Squeeze spoke.

"Yeah? What you want?" Tara said with attitude.

"It's about your girl, Laura," Squeeze mentioned.

Tara cracked open the door but kept the chain on which was the mistake Nappy Head Don was waiting for—like that little security chain was real protection.

When he saw the side of her face, Nappy Head Don brutally kicked the door in, violently pushing Tara down on the floor. Everyone rushed inside the apartment with their guns drawn as Tara tried to crawl to her bedroom, knocking items down and screaming madly. She tried to go for the .22 she had stashed in her dresser drawer but she didn't make it that far. Rude Bwoy Rex quickly caught up with her and yanked her by her long black hair and dropped her to the floor.

"Bitch, where you going?" Squeeze shouted then punched her across her eye.

Tara screamed out frantically, trying to fight them off. They all stood over her and Nappy Head Don had his gun pointed at her precious head.

"Bitch, shut up, yuh hear? Yuh wanna die tonight?" Nappy Head Don threatened.

Tara continued to be loud and resistant so Rude Bwoy Rex made her shut up and be still the easy way. He just beat the bitch in the head with his pistol until she was unconscious.

"That'll work," Squeeze stated.

They quickly carried the knocked out Tara downstairs to the truck where a few residents noticed but they knew to mind their own business. Handsome Pete smiled when they loaded Tara in the back.

"Damn, y'all actually kidnapped the bitch," Handsome Pete said. "Shit."

No one said a word as Nappy Head Don jumped into the drivers' seat and pulled off hastily.

Handsome Pete's phone began to ring and it was Laura calling him about tonight. He answered and told her he'd be at her place in a few minutes then hung up. He looked down at the unconscious Tara and stared lustfully at her in her short jean skirt, brown halter top and bare feet.

"Damn, shortie got nice toes," Handsome Pete proclaimed. He so badly wanted to fuck her but he knew tonight wasn't the night. He had another agenda on his mind.

They dropped Handsome Pete off at Laura's then proceeded to Brooklyn. Squeeze had a very important phone call to make.

Next Day 5:15 p.m.

Tara was tied to a bed and stripped butt naked. Rude Bwoy Rex and Nappy Head Don raped and beat on her something serious, not even using a condom as they came in her over and over again. Squeeze damn near had to choke the bitch to give up her boyfriend's number.

She finally disclosed the information to Squeeze. He was about to make that call but he had to admit that Tara was a feisty and stunning looking bitch. If it wasn't for the fucked up situation with her man, Carlos, he'd probably would have got with her on the real and treated her better than Carlos.

Tara remained bound to the bed, crying. She had finally stopped trying to free herself. The two men had already had their way with her and her face was battered as if Mike Tyson had whooped on her.

Squeeze dialed Carlos's number. It rang three times before someone picked up.

"Who da fuck is this?" Carlos asked.

"Carlos?" Squeeze inquired.

"Who dis?"

"Wake up, nigga. I got your bitch!" Squeeze announced. He had always wanted to say that to a nigga ever since he saw *State Property* with Beanie Sigel.

"Who da fuck is you, puta!" Carlos shouted.

"Da wrong nigga you fuckin' with! You think you can strike on a nigga and I'm gonna let this shit be. You know a nigga gotta come hard," Squeeze stated.

"Nigga, get da fuck off my phone."

But before Carlos uttered another word, Squeeze put the phone over Tara's mouth and she shouted out, "Carlos... Carlos... please"

Squeeze quickly removed the phone from Tara's pleading and beaten lips and said, "That's you, right? Her name is Tara. Fine bitch you got, Carlos."

"Nigga let her fuckin' go. She ain't got shit to do with you and me."

"Yeah, whatever, nigga. You gun down my nigga in da hospital and wanna plead for your bitch's life? Fuck you! You think I couldn't get to you? Nigga, you don't know who you're fuckin' with."

"Puta, fo' real, when I see you..."

"Come see me then, nigga. I rest out in Brooklyn. You know where I be," Squeeze shouted. "I got niggas in here raping your bitch as we speak. Pussy good too, nigga," Squeeze laughed.

Carlos' face tightened when he heard about his shortie getting raped like that. His heart raced and his eyes began to turn red. He felt like tearing up but his face was too tense and angry. He never admitted it to her but he loved Tara and now this.

"Puta, on da real, I'm gonna see you and I'm gonna fuckin' gun down you and your entire fuckin' family. You have my word on dat."

"Nigga, whatever. Come get your bitch in Prospect Park tonight after we done fuckin' her!" Squeeze said then hung up.

Carlos roughly threw the house phone against the wall, smashing it into pieces. He gripped his head and wondered how niggas knew where Tara rested her head at. He knew he had a snitch somewhere. That was the only way niggas were able to get at his bitch like that.

He called Miguel and Manny on his cell and put them on to the situation. They both came to his aid right away. Both met Carlos down by Inwood Park where Carlos waited fuming. Miguel and Manny rolled up in a blue Hummer and were strapped.

"Carlos, what da fuck happened? Who kidnapped Tara?" Miguel asked.

"Dat fuckin' puta, Squeeze. He's gonna die, homes. I'm gonna bury him and his fuckin' mami."

"Carlos...." Manny began to speak but paused as he looked away.

"What's up Manny? What the fuck you gotta say?"

"I think I know who gave up Tara," he admitted.

"Fuck you talkin' about, Manny?" Carlos shouted, stepping up to Manny.

"I was talkin' to that nigga, Handsome Pete..."

"Fuck you doing' talkin' to that clown ass nigga?" Miguel chimed in.

"I saw that nigga up on Dyckman last week and you know we did business together so I wanted to see if he still wanted to do business... and...."

"You think Handsome Pete gave up Tara?" Carlos asked.

Manny looked at Carlos and said, "I know he did. He used to hang with niggas from Bed-Stuy and do business up here all the time."

"Manny, that's my word, you tell me where dat nigga rest at!" Carlos demanded.

"He fucks wit' that bitch, Laura and you know Laura and Tara used to be tight like dat. I know Handsome Pete got that bitch to give up Laura's address. Dat nigga can talk a bitch into eating out her mama's pussy," Manny assured him.

"Where dat bitch live at? I wanna see dat muthafucka," Carlos stipulated.

"She lives on 135th street off of Lenox," Manny informed him.

Without anything else being said, Carlos jumped into the H2 with Manny and Miguel and headed down to Harlem to pay some folks a visit.

Handsome Pete enjoyed every minute of tearing that pussy up and Laura had some good fuckin' pussy. It was so good that Pete ended up staying the night at her place after Squeeze and 'em dropped him off. He had fucked Laura damn near all night.

"You gonna be my next baby mama," Pete joked while he stroked his erection into her.

Laura moaned out, "Hmm, cum in me, baby…I wanna have your fuckin' baby…cum for me…cum for me." Laura panted.

And no doubt, Handsome Pete came up in Laura like that—so fuckin' easy, raw dog and everything. He ain't give a fuck. That was how he did him and that was how he got down. Laura didn't care. She was a gullible stupid bitch.

After Pete done came up in her for the umpteenth time within the past twelve hours, he spread apart her thighs and began to eat her out on the soiled, wrinkled and stained sheets. He licked off her cum with his tongue—he was a nasty nigga, too.

Handsome Pete and Laura were so enthralled with their sexual activity that neither one of 'em noticed Carlos and his crew standing off in the dark corner watching.

"Pussy good, Handsome Pete?" Manny uttered. He shocked

Pete with his sudden presence. "I ain't expect you to be here too. Fuckin' A!"

Handsome Pete jumped up and quickly turned around wide-eyed and stared at Carlos, Miguel, Manny, and another stranger.

"Wha' da fuck...? Manny, Carlos...!" Handsome Pete shouted.

Laura tried to cover herself up but Miguel rushed over and snatched the sheets off, exposing her raw naked body. Manny quickly went up to Handsome Pete with a .45 in his hand and pressed it to Pete's temple. Laura cried out as she stared at the men who were suddenly in her bedroom. She threw her arms across her breasts and she remained folded across the bed.

"Please, Carlos, you know me. You know me and Tara are cool. Carlos, I ain't do nuthin'," Laura tried to plead.

"Bitch, shut da fuck up!" Miguel shouted, slapping her across her face and knocking her down to the floor.

"Manny, what's good? You know we do business together. Why you doing this to me?" Handsome Pete asked as he peered into Manny's terrifying eyes.

"You a bitch ass nigga, Pete. We did business together. I fuckin' hooked you up wit' my peeps and this is how you do me?" Manny shouted.

"Fuck you talkin' about, Manny?" Handsome Pete replied back.

But Manny didn't reply. He just beat Handsome Pete over the head with his gun as Laura cried out.

Carlos finally stepped in and spoke after his niggas handled theirs. He looked fiercely over at Laura and asked, "Bitch, who gave up Tara's address?"

"I don't know, Carlos," Laura lied.

Carlos didn't say a word. He went over to where Laura was, sat down next to her, and just as casually pulled out a long, thick knife while stroking his goatee.

"Laura, I'm gonna ask you again. Who gave up my girl's

address? You know, bitch. Just tell me the truth and I won't torture your ass," Carlos said offhandedly.

Laura was in full tears as she stared frightfully over at Carlos. She trembled, naked breasts exposed. She looked over at Handsome Pete who Manny had beaten down to the floor. He was naked and bloody but still conscious of his surroundings. He knew he was in a fucked up predicament. Laura broke down in tears then admitted, "He made me do it, Carlos."

"This bitch-ass-nigga here?"

"He made me...Handsome Pete..."

"Carlos, da fuckin' bitch is lying!" Pete yelled out.

"Shudda fuckin' nigga up!" Carlos demanded.

Manny kicked Pete in the mouth with his Timberlands, knocking out a few of Pete's teeth. Pete clutched his jaw, screaming out in agony.

"He forced me to," Laura cried out.

"Ahight. Y'all niggas take his ass up to the roof. I got shortie down here," Carlos said.

They followed Carlos's directions and hauled Handsome Pete's naked ass up to the roof leaving Carlos behind with Laura. Carlos remained quiet until his soldiers left the room. Laura was still crying and trembling, fearing Carlos to the fullest.

"I'm sorry, Carlos. You know Tara's my girl...we cool. I didn't mean no harm to come to her," Laura begged.

Carlos stood up and noticed a white envelope filled with cash on the dresser. He went up to it, picked up the money and asked, "This you?"

Laura stared at the money. "It's Petey's money. He brought it with him," she explained, lying through her teeth.

"And you fuckin' him."

"He was paying me," she said.

Carlos still had the knife gripped in his hand while he casually stood and talked to Laura. He paced back and forth, seemingly keeping his cool with Laura about the situation.

"Carlos, I'm sorry. I didn't know what was up wit' him. He just called me up out of the blue and wanted some information. He lied and said Tara was in trouble."

Carlos looked over at her and knew she was lying. "Laura, you always been a stupid fuckin' bitch," he scolded.

"I know, Carlos. I'm sorry." She looked up at Carlos, wiped the tears from her face and said, "Carlos, please do me right. It's my fault, I know but I'll suck your fuckin' dick right now and I won't say shit about Handsome Pete."

Carlos looked over at her and a faint smile appeared on his face. Laura smiled too as if everything was cool between them. He walked up to Laura with the knife still in his hand and Laura pulled at his shirt, letting off strong sexual vibes as she parted her thighs. Suddenly, Carlos lunged at her with the knife, plunging it deeply into her chest. Laura clutched onto him tightly and gasped. Carlos pulled out the knife and thrust it into her again and again and again. He stabbed her twenty-one fuckin' times and left her for dead, sprawled on the blood drenched mattress.

"Fuckin' bitch! You always been a hating ass bitch on Tara. Fuck you!" he cursed. He went into the bathroom, cleaned off the knife and himself a little then joined his soldiers up on the roof. On the rooftop, his men had Handsome Pete by his ankles as they dangled him from four-stories up.

"Carlos, please, don't do this man. I ain't do shit. Whatever dat bitch said, she's fuckin' lying!!" Pete pleaded and begged.

"Talk to me, Pete. Tell me about your boy, Squeeze. Where can I find him?" Carlos quietly demanded as he peered down at him.

"I don't know, man," Pete replied.

"Drop him."

"No, no! Chill, chill, yo. I got you...I'll let you know what's up," Pete shouted.

"You better make it quick."

"All I know is that he stays out in Canarsie. He got family out there."

"You better come up wit' sump'n better."

"He don't say much to me."

"Then what good are you?"

"Ahight...Carlos, yo...I heard from a reliable source that he stays out in Coney Island wit' some young bitch. I think her name is Lindsay. I used to run with her brother, Pooh. I know she lives on the fourth floor of building 6, I think."

Carlos smiled. "You sure?"

"Nigga, I'm positive. He beefing wit' y'all cause y'all killed his man Pooh a year back."

"Pooh? Nigga don't ring bells in my head," Carlos stated.

"Everything I told you is legit, Carlos. Please pull me up."

"Carlos, dis nigga is getting heavy," Manny complained.

Carlos looked down at Handsome Pete one more time and said, "Then let him go."

They didn't hesitate. Both men simultaneously let go of his ankles and dropped him down four-stories into the alley. Handsome Pete landed on his head, breaking his neck and splitting open his fuckin' head. It was a gruesome sight to see.

"Let's go see this nigga," Carlos said.

Carlos made a few phone calls then him and his henchmen made their way to Harlem to meet up wit' an old friend. They met over by the Hudson Parkway late in the night. The Hummer pulled up next to a white Cadillac where two men were seated. Carlos gave the men sitting inside the immaculate Cadillac much respect. They both were from the Ol' Skool and were true O.G.'s from Harlem. Carlos knew their names because in Harlem, Washington Heights, and even Brooklyn and Yonkers, these men's names and reputations definitely rang bells. He also knew you didn't fuck wit' niggas like them.

Carlos stepped out of the H2 and approached the Cadillac. He peered inside and gave 'em dap, saying, "Johnny, Tooks, what's going on? Long time."

"Carlos, get in the car," Tooks softly ordered.

Carlos didn't argue. He did what Tooks told him. He hopped into the backseat while Miguel, Manny and the third man remained seated in the Hummer.

"I'm hearing about your beef with some cats out in Brooklyn. How you handling that?" Tooks asked him.

"I'm gonna handle it, Tooks. In fact, I had to drop a nigga off the roof to find out where da fucker rest his head at," Carlos explained.

"And the club thing?" Tooks inquired.

"Man, you know how dat goes. Wrong place, wrong time. There's a little message I need to send out but I need that from y'all," Carlos said. "I'm bout' ready to fuckin' go to war wit' this puta. He disrespected, Tooks. He took away my family. Now he kidnapped and raped my woman. Tooks; you know this puta gotta get handled. I'm ready to kill him and his fuckin' family!" he shouted.

"Calm yourself, youngin'," Johnny said.

"I don't mean to get loud in your ride, Johnny, but I'm ready to wild out."

"Listen...this man, Squeeze, you beefin' with...fall back on him," Tooks said.

"What?" Carlos shouted, looking at Tooks in shock.

"What I mean is don't kill him yet."

"Why not, Tooks? This puta gotta get handled. He disrespected me."

"Yeah, I know that, Carlos, but when you come at him, save him for me. I need to ask this Squeeze a few questions about his homeboy that's on the run right now," Tooks explained.

"Fuck that!" Carlos shouted.

"Youngin...calm down 'for I have to step out this car and deal with you," Johnny said.

Carlos sighed.

"We got your back on this, Carlos," Tooks explained. "But after I'm done speaking to the man, you do with him what you please. But until then, I want Squeeze alive. If you gotta go after his men then so be it."

"Ahight, whatever but this some bullshit."

"Ahight, youngin, be gone," Johnny told Carlos.

"Before I leave, let me get that," Carlos said.

Tooks looked over at Johnny and said, "Pop the trunk, Johnny."

"For this knucklehead? He a hothead, Tooks."

"But it's owed to him."

"Yeah," Carlos uttered.

All three men stepped out of the car and approached the trunk where Johnny lifted the hood to reveal the contents inside. Carlos smiled, reached down and pulled out the deadly Mp5K sub, and the Heckler and Koch, a fully automatic 9mm that can riddle a man like Swiss cheese in less than 3 seconds.

"This is what da fuck I'm talking about," Carlos said, admiring the weaponry in his hands.

Soon Miguel and the rest exited the H2 and grabbed a weapon for themselves. They were like hyped little children on Christmas day.

"Y'all boys play nice now," Johnny uttered as he shut his trunk and got back in the car with Tooks.

"It's on. It's definitely on," Carlos assured.

This was what Carlos lived for, gunning down the men who disrespected and tested his gangsta on the streets of New York. He was crazy and Carlos didn't hesitate to let you know how crazy he was. Deadly, fearless and ruthless, he wasn't gonna let nobody stop him from rising to the top and keeping a strong grip over his region.

Carlos is gonna do Carlos until someone puts a bullet in his head and ends it…but while Carlos was busy plotting so were others.

Friday night 9:15 p.m.

Squeeze was positioned on the couch with Lindsay not even thinking about his beef with Carlos or the kidnapping of his bitch, Tara. He knew that Nappy Head and Rude Bwoy were going to kill the bitch after they got done beating and raping her. They'd probably leave her battered and naked body on a park bench somewhere.

He was feeling good because Squeeze knew he'd hit Carlos hard with that one and he was going to continue to strike at Carlos until the muthafucka stopped breathing.

Squeeze peered at the television as Lindsay rested in his arms. His phone went off, breaking his attention away from the TV. He reached for it shouting out, "Who dis?" Squeeze was shocked by who answered.

"Promise, nigga."

"What da fuck? How you get dis number, nigga?" he asked baffled and shit.

"I got my ways, Squeeze. You know dat."

"Fuck you doing calling me, tho'?" Squeeze asked.

"I heard what happened to Show. I'm sorry, man. You know he was like a brother to all of us," Promise said, giving his condolences.

"You know...shit like dat happens in da game. He will be missed."

"How you holding up?" Promise asked.

Squeeze sighed. "I'm good, yo. I'm doing me. You know how dat go."

"Yeah."

"So what's good wit' you? I see you doing your thang avoiding the feds and shit."

"You know I ain't built to be behind bars."

"You know dey gonna keep coming for your ass. Dey ain't gonna stop," Squeeze let it be known.

"Yeah, I know and I'll be ready when they come," Promise said.

Squeeze chuckled. "You a cowboy now, nigga?"

"Doing me, sun," Promise stated.

There was a brief silence over the phone. It was awkward for a minute but then Promise spoke up. "Squeeze, why you let me be dat day?"

"Fuck you talking about?" Squeeze returned.

"Candy's bathroom in Rochdale when you and Show came bombarding up in her crib looking for me. I knew you knew I was up in the shower hiding. You crept in with the gun, stopped and then walked back out. What went down wit' dat?"

Squeeze sighed, "Nigga, what made you think I let you be?"

"Cause I know you. When you after someone, you leave no stone unturned. You hunt dat man till you find that man," Promise answered.

"I don't know..." Squeeze started. "It just ain't seem right, you hiding behind the shower like some scared dog. Nigga, just be happy I let you be."

"Thanks, man, and if it means anything, I'm sorry about jooksing you and Show at y'all club. I was angry. I felt that y'all disrespected me...you know what I'm sayin'. I felt y'all turned y'all backs on a nigga when I needed y'all the most."

Squeeze sucked his teeth then uttered, "Man, go ahead wit' dat. I still owe you for dat. We ain't cool like dat no more, Promise, but because you my dog, I gave you dat pass...understand? Second time around, it ain't gonna be so fuckin' easy with the peace between you and me."

"Yeah, ahight. When we see each other, so be it but for now... I still got love for you, nigga. We da only ones left."

"We can't live forever, right."

"Some of us try to."

"Nigga, stop tying up my phone. You hot right now. You do what you gotta do and I'm gonna continue to do me," Squeeze stated.

"One, my nigga," Promise said.

Squeeze hesitated then replied, "One." He paused then added,

"And yo, watch your back out there. I definitely wanna run into you again," Squeeze said half jokingly.

"I will. You watch your back, Squeeze."

"Eyes in da back of my head, my nigga," Squeeze said and there the conversation ended.

For Squeeze, no matter what the situation, it was good to hear a familiar voice from back in the day and around the way. Nevertheless, he knew a war waged on between himself and the men that wanted to see him fall.

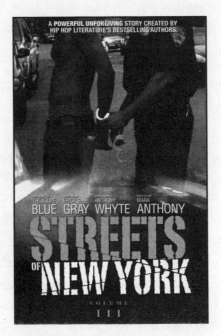

Street of New York
Volume III

ANTHONY WHYTE

He's the master of this literary domain, holding the book game down like it was his kingdom. Author of the classic, Ghetto Girls Series, editor and CEO of Augustus Publishing, the hottest on the book scene. A true pioneer and leader, Whyte's style has been copied never duplicated. He's way ahead of his time. In grand steeze, he continues to reign. Since '96 when he coined the phrase, Hip Hop Literature, Whyte has been forever bringing reading back to real life.

Hit up Anthony Whyte at www.streetlitreview.com

ERICK S GRAY

Known as Mr. Prolifick, this young and very talented storyteller is honing his skills as a legend in the book game. He's written classics such as the exciting erotica, Booty Call *69 and the best fiction and award winning, gangster saga, Crave All... Lose All. Hailing from South Side. Jamaica, Queens, Mr. Prolifick goes hard for his on the STREETS OF NEW YORK.

Hit up Erick S Gray at www.streetlitreview.com

MARK ANTHONY

The author and publisher is a talented veteran of the book game. Reppin' Q-Boro, the publishing house he started and the area he's from. Mark Anthony has conquered the publishing world while writing several stories of grit and grime... from Paper Chasers to Ladies' Nite, his style definitely appeals to readers of all sex, especially to the ladies.

Hit up Mark Anthony at www.streetlitreview.com

WHERE
HIP-HOP
LITERATURE
BEGINS...

AUGUSTUS
PUBLISHING

Augustus Publishing was created to unify minds with entertaining, hard-hitting tales from a hood near you. Hip Hop literature interprets contemporary times and connects to readers through shared language, culture and artistic expression. From street tales and erotica to coming-of age sagas, our stories are endearing, filled with drama, imagination and laced with a Hip Hop steez.

GHETTO GIRLS IV
Young Luv
ESSENCE BESTSELLING AUTHOR
ANTHONY WHYTE

hetto Girls IV Young Luv
4.95 // 9780979281662

Ghetto Girls
$14.95 // 0975945319

Ghetto Girls Too
$14.95 // 0975945300

Ghetto Girls 3 Soo Hood
$14.95 // 0975945351

THE BEST OF THE STREET CHRONICLES TODAY, THE **GHETTO GIRLS SERIES** IS A WONDERFULLY HYPNOTIC ADVENTURE THAT DELVES INTO THE CONVOLUTED MINDS OF CRIMINALS AND THE DARK WORLD OF POLICE CORRUPTION. YET, THERE IS SOMETHING THRILLING AND SURPRISINGLY TENDER ABOUT THIS ONGOING YOUNG-ADULT SAGA FILLED WITH MAD FLAVA.

Love and a Gangsta
author // ERICK S GRAY

This explosive sequel to **Crave All Lose All**. Soul and America were together ten years 'til Soul's incarceration for drugs. Faithfully, she waited four years for his return. Once home they find life ain't so easy anymore. America believes in holding her man down and expects Soul to be as committed. His lust for fast money rears its ugly head at the same time America's music career takes off. From shootouts, to hustling and thugging life, Soul and his man, Omega, have done it. Omega is on the come-up in the drug-game of South Jamaica, Queens. Using ties to a Mexican drug cartel, Omega has Queens in his grip. His older brother, Rahmel, was Soul's cellmate in an upstate prison. Rahmel, a man of God, tries to counsel Soul. Omega introduces New York to crystal meth. Misery loves company and on the road to the riches and spoils of the game, Omega wants the only man he can trust, Soul, with him. Love between Soul and America is tested by an unforgivable greed that leads quickly to deception and murder.

$14.95 // 9780979281648

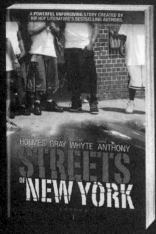  

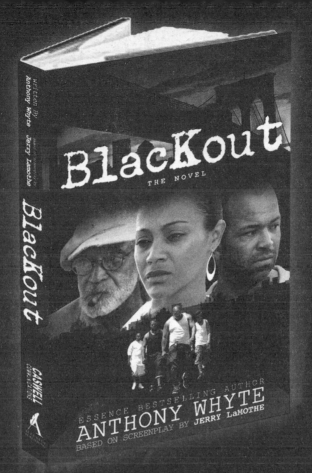

The lights went out
and the
mayhem began.

It's gritty in the city but hotter in Brooklyn where a small community in east Flatbush must come to grips with its greatest threat, self-destruction. August 14 and 15, 2003, the eastern section of the United States is crippled by a major shortage of electrical power, the worst in US history. Blackout, the spellbinding novel is based on the epic motion picture, directed by Jerry Lamothe. A thoroughly riveting story with delectable details of families caught in a harsh 48 hours of random violent acts, exploding in deadly conflict. There's a message in everything… even the bullet. The author vividly places characters on the stage of life and like pieces on a chessboard, expertly moves them to a tumultuous end. Voila! Checkmate, a literary triumph. Blackout is a masterpiece. This heart-stopping, page-turning drama is moving fast. Blackout is destined to become an American classic.

BASED ON SCREENPLAY BY JERRY LaMOTHE
Inspired by true events

US $14.95 CAN $20.95
ISBN 978-0-9820653-0-3

CASWELL
COMMUNICATIONS